Siani

Tydfil Thomas

Siani

British Library Cataloguing in Publication Data

A catalogue record for this book is available from the British Library

ISBN 09539553-0-3

Published by:

Tydfil Thomas

First Edition 2000

Printed by: Rainbow Print (Wales) Ltd, Merthyr Tydfil
Tel: (01443) 691114

Chapter 1
1873

"Get back to your place, Lewsyn Jones," Siani hissed, her eyes ablaze, as she glared at the sandy-haired youth who was pushing forward in the pawnshop queue. She clutched desperately at the mirror she was taking to Mr Cohen's pawnshop, knowing full well that it was her only hope of getting money for food for her family.

Lewsyn gave her a defiant look, and said, "You're the one pushing in front of me, Siani Davies, and if you're not careful, that mirror will end up in splinters on the floor."

"Just try it boyo. You'll see stars you've never seen before," she snapped, glaring at him fiercely.

Sian, usually known as Siani, was a tip-girl, sixteen years old, who worked on the monstrous, desert-wasteland of hideous cinder tips that loomed in all directions around Dowlais, Merthyr Tydfil. She worked in all weathers, emptying the heavy iron trams of rough ironstone clinker, and skin-scorching cinders, which came in endless snake-like processions from the vast ironworks, and created something akin to a lunar landscape.

She and her younger sister, Alys, earned four shillings a week for this brutal, back-breaking work, which they endured only because there were eight mouths to feed at home. Their father, Joshua Davies, and Benjamin their brother earned insufficient wages at Dowlais Colliery to feed the family, and now that the colliers were on strike, money was hard to come by and food was scarce.

"If I don't get something from the old Jew for this mirror, there'll be no dinner for us today or tomorrow," Siani thought, biting her nails and trembling at the prospect, as she stood in the queue.

Lewsyn could see tension in every line of Siani's body and he turned to her saying, "Don't look so worried, let's have a smile." She tried to ignore him until he added, "My Mam says that your mother hasn't been to chapel lately. Another baby on the way is there?"

"Tell your nosey-parker of a mother to mind her own business," she retorted. She swallowed hard, knowing that her mother was too sick to have any more babies. She'd had ten in the last fifteen years, but only six had survived. That was enough to exhaust any woman, and she blamed it all on her ram of a father. Her Mam was now a shadow of her former self and was going into a decline.

At last, Siani reached the counter in the dark, dingy pawnshop. She looked around in amazement and saw rows of sombre, black Sunday suits hanging on a long rail below the grimy ceiling. The smell of mothballs and stale sweat assailed her nostrils and made her feel sick. Then she noticed shelves stacked with boots, shoes, cast-iron kettles, brass candlesticks and all manner of things, set out in rows.

She stared intently at Mr Cohen who stood behind the counter dressed in a shiny, black suit, with a small black skull cap perched on the back of his bald head. He reminded her of a big, black crow; his nose was like a prominent beak, and his preying hands were like greedy claws. At last her turn came, and in a tremulous voice she asked, "Can you give something for this?" as she placed her precious mirror before him.

He moved his thick, pebbled spectacles to the end of his long, hooked nose and examined the mirror carefully before saying, "Two shillings, not a penny more." Almost reluctantly, he put the coins and receipt on the counter, and Siani grabbed them quickly, before he could change his mind. Oblivious to the smirking of Lewsyn ~~Davies,~~ she stalked out of the shop.

His eyes followed her and he thought to himself, "She's not a bad-looking girl when she's out of that dirty, canvas dress and battered straw hat she wears on the tips, and she's developing quite a nice figure now that she's growing up."

Siani was tall and slender, and had the same clear skin, large green eyes and dark, wavy hair as her mother. Lewsyn and his father often passed her and Alys on the tips, when they themselves were going to Trecatti Pit, and his father always insisted that it wasn't fit work for young girls. "It makes them as rough as badgers," was his usual comment. Lewsyn was inclined to agree, though he had to admit that there was something different about Siani.

*　　*　　*

Llewelyn Jones, Lewsyn's father, was a respectable, God-fearing man and it had gone against his grain to let his eldest son go to the pawnshop that morning with his oak-cased wall clock. Only the threat of their being sent to the workhouse to do stone breaking, had made him give in.

"If you can get a few shillings on this clock, it will keep us off the parish, and out of the stoneyards for the time being," he had said.

Lewsyn inched his way towards the counter and felt his heart miss a beat as he handed the clock to Mr Cohen who looked at it quizzically and held it to his ear to listen to its deep, resonant tick. He examined its clean, round face with its clear Roman figures, replaced the glass cover carefully and finally announced, "Four shillings." Lewsyn's spirits soared; he picked up the coins and the ticket, and walked up the road, whistling.

He had promised to go with his father to the union meeting that night, to find out about the possibility of strike pay from the A.A.M. "By God, we need it," he said to himself. He was still angry about the humiliation he and his father had experienced at the hands of the Parish Officers, and when he passed their office on the way home, he thumbed his nose at the bastards.

Mari Jones a frugal, sharp-tongued woman, heaved a sigh of relief when he handed over the money. "Good boy! This will help to keep us going for a week or two," she said. "If only your father weren't such a proud man, I'd send our Tim and Gwen down to the soup kitchens."

"I agree with Dad. We don't want charity, we're better off fending for ourselves," said Lewsyn. "I'll go with him to ask for a permit to pick cokes on the tips, then perhaps between us, we can make a shilling or two."

Mari was worried about him, because at seventeen years of age, he seemed to be outgrowing his strength. His lean young face with its prominent cheek-bones, bore the unmistakable signs of hunger, and not even his cheeky grin and over-bright eyes could disguise the fact that he was undernourished. "I'll make sure he'll have food in his belly, even if I have to go without it myself," she resolved.

* * *

Siani climbed up the rutted, rocky road leading to Nant Row and found her mother sitting on the settle by the fire in the kitchen. Proudly, she handed the two shillings to her saying, "We'll be all right now, Mam, we'll have food for dinner."

"Thank you, bach, you've saved us yet again," Lizzie Davies croaked before collapsing into a paroxysm of coughing which left her in a clammy sweat. Siani mopped her brow, gave her a cup of water, and when she was calmer, asked her, "Shall I send our Mag to Mr Morris's shop for a loaf of bread and two penn'orth of dripping?"

"Yes, that will do for our dinner, then later you and I can make some 'cawl' which will last us for a couple of days."

While she waited for Mag, Siani looked around the kitchen which she and Alys, her twelve-year-old sister, had cleaned the day before, while they had the place to themselves. They had black-leaded the brick grate and the oven, had polished the brass fender so that you could see your reflection in it, and had cleaned the brass candlesticks on the mantlepiece. While Alys was busy polishing the oak chest of drawers, Siani had scrubbed the tabletop beneath the window until it was bone-white and the grain of the wood stood out. She had allowed Alys to polish their six plain wooden chairs before they were put back around the table, after Siani had scrubbed the flag-stoned floor and sanded it. Both girls had been glad to do this for their mother because she was so ill, and they knew that she liked their home kept clean.

One quick look at the grandfather clock in the corner of the kitchen told her that it was time to bring the kettle to the boil and to put the dishes on the table. Her mother was nursing Will, her youngest child, now barely two years old, and she noticed how listless and careworn she looked.

Soon, Siani was busy slicing the crusty, white loaf Mag had brought back and she scraped on the dripping. She brewed a pot of tea and poured out a cup for her mother who remained on the settle, keeping an eye on Will who was biting at a crust. Just then, David, her middle brother, aged ten, came back with Alys and handed five pennies to his mother saying proudly, "We've been selling small coal, Mam."

"Da iawn, Dave," she said ruffling his dark curly hair. "You're a real little man, bringing home your earnings."

They all gathered around the table and ate the bread and dripping voraciously, then supped the hot, sweet, fragrant tea which Siani poured out. Lizzie Davies ate little and listened to Alys and David talking about the foraging that was going on for cinders and coal.

"Our Dad's got a permit because he works for the Company," said Alys. "He and Ben should be able to bring home enough to keep our fire going and sell a bit on the side. They did well today."

"Where is he now?" asked Lizzie.

"He and Ben are taking their barrow around the streets, on their way home, and they'll be calling at The Colliers' Arms to find out about the time of the union meeting tonight," she added.

"Enough said. I don't suppose I'll have a brass farthing from him," Lizzie moaned. "It will all go on beer."

She put her hand into her apron pocket, and when the meal had finished, she turned to Siani saying, "Take this shilling and go to the market for a piece of scrag-end of mutton, and some vegetables so that I can start making some broth. If there's any money left, then buy some more bread."

Later in the afternoon, when the dishes had been cleared, and the broth was simmering quietly, Siani and Alys persuaded their mother to have a rest.

"You look exhausted, Mam, go and lie down. I'll keep an eye on the broth," said Siani. "Go before Dad comes home because you never know what mood he'll be in."

"That's true, if he's had a skinful, as likely as not he'll give me a black eye," said Lizzie dolefully. She dragged herself into the downstairs bedroom, bent down to take off her shoes, and as she did so, she was overtaken by another severe bout of coughing. Siani rushed to her side and was shocked to see her bringing up bright red, frothy blood.

"Mam fach, what's happening?" she asked, panic-stricken. "Bring a bowl and some water, quickly," she called to Alys, who blanched when she saw the state of her mother and retreated quickly from the room.

Siani held her in her arms until the coughing subsided, and wiped away the blood from her trembling lips before laying her carefully on the bed.

"Oh, that was a bad pull," said Lizzie, still gasping. Her colour was like chalk, but her eyes were unnaturally bright, and she began to tremble violently.

"Let me wrap you in this blanket," Siani said, noticing that her mother had come out in another sweat and that she was suffering a bad reaction. "I'll stay with you, Mam, never fear," she said, squeezing her hand gently as she helped her into bed.

Lizzie Davies closed her dark, sunken eyes and looked exactly like a corpse; it was then that Siani began to realise how ill her mother was. Eventually, when her breathing was calmer, and she was resting, Siani decided to tip-toe to the door, but her mother caught her arm saying, "Close the door, I have something I must say to you…" She gasped, tried to sit up and then murmured, "If anything happens to me, I want you to promise that you'll look after your brothers and sisters."

"Oh Mam, don't talk like that!" Siani said, terrified at the prospect of losing her.

But Lizzie persisted. "Promise me, Siani," she repeated, gripping her hand.

The haunted look in her mother's eyes frightened her, and in a voice, little more than a whisper, she said, "Yes I promise, but you must get better, Mam, for all our sakes."

Chapter 2

Siani's home was a small, three-roomed, stone cottage with a slate roof, and it stood at the lower end of a row of similar cottages, straggling along the hillside overlooking Dowlais. It was the property of the Dowlais Iron Company, which had built hundreds of cottages to house their workers who rented them. Nearby was a fast-flowing brook which, in the winter, tumbled down the hillside into a pond below, but in the summer became a turgid trickle of polluted water.

Her house overlooked the vast Dowlais Ironworks, where huge stacks and furnaces belched out clouds of sulphurous smoke and tongues of fierce flames, which at night, lit up the sky for miles around. Day and night, the lives of the inhabitants were dominated by the noise, clangour, smoke, glare and filth, which spewed out from this huge cauldron. Dowlais was a place where dirt was coined into gold for ironmasters, and where families like Siani's fought for survival.

Joshua Davies had come from the quarries of North Wales some twenty years before, to seek a living as a miner in the Dowlais coal pits which fed the voracious furnaces and produced excellent house coal.

Grim-faced, pugnacious and feckless, he barged into the kitchen that January afternoon in 1873, having just left The Colliers' Arms. He was a big, brawny man with a fine head of auburn hair, and in his younger days he had stood out from the smaller, dark-haired, dark-skinned Welshmen of the south. It was his fearless spirit of adventure which had brought him to Merthyr Tydfil as a youth of eighteen, and he had soon learnt to defend himself against the ruffians whom he had encountered.

He stood before the fire warming himself, his powerful arms akimbo, and announced, "I've brought home a few bags of riddlings to keep the fire going, and now I'm ready for food. There's a good smell coming from that saucepan, so be quick Siani, put some food on the table for me and Ben."

"It's bread and dripping for you. Mam said that the cawl will come later when it's cooked." Siani pushed the food before him and watched him wolfing it down. He belched noisily, and from where she was standing, she could smell the beer on his breath. She began to feel sick, not only because of his piggish behaviour, but also because of worry about her mother. She looked warily at Ben, her eldest brother, who now sat at the table, and hoped for some indication of her father's mood, but after a morning combing the tips, he was too pre-occupied to do anything but swallow his food and sup his tea.

"Where's your mother?" Josh growled at Siani.

"Having a lie down, she's not well," she murmured.

Leaning back in his chair, and patting his stomach, he said, "I think I'll join her."

"No you won't! Mam needs rest, she's ill," Siani protested, barring his way to the bedroom door.

"Get away!" he shouted, clouting her across her head before he lumbered into the bedroom and slammed the door. Siani heard a low moan coming from her mother and dared not think of what was happening.

"I'll get even with him one day, however long it takes," she vowed, as tears of misery and despair rolled down her cheeks.

Josh had a thick head when he got up, and he barked at Ben, "Get moving, or we'll be late for the meeting."

She looked at her brother, now fourteen years of age, and asked, "What time will you be home tonight?"

"Wait and see," Josh snapped.

"If you want a bowl of cawl before you go to bed you'd better come back early," she said to Ben, who winked at her and whispered,

"I'll be back as soon as I can."

The inducement worked and he brought home the good news that there would be some strike pay from union funds in the form of food dockets. "Diolch i Dduw," said Lizzie Davies, when Ben told her, and she took comfort from the love and support she had from her children.

* * *

The month of January was often the most cruel one of the year, so Siani thought, but it seemed harsher than ever this year, with snow, gales and frozen rain, lashing the outside of the cottage. Due to the strike, an eerie silence seemed to pervade the whole of Dowlais, and the customary glow of the furnaces had been replaced by the icy glaze and barren bleakness of a white, winter wasteland, which was unnaturally clean and silent.

"Give me the smoke, noise and dirt of the works in full blast, rather than this menacing chill that enshrouds us all. It smells of death," Siani thought as she watched the frozen spectres searching desperately on the tips for fuel to keep the fires burning at home.

Lizzie Davies was huddled in the corner of the kitchen, getting paler and weaker by the day. Siani was almost afraid to be left alone with her, and had nightmares of big blotches of blood splashed on pristine snow, leading from their cottage to Pant Cemetery. "Dad should call a doctor before it's too late. I'll corner him and make him face up to it," she decided.

Early in February, Lizzie had another massive haemorrhage, and Josh began to realise that Siani's warning was coming true. Lizzie was just skin and bone and had a look of gossamer transparency about her. In desperation, he asked the parish doctor to call, and was thoroughly shaken when Dr Wharton said, "Your wife is in the final stages of TB, Mr Davies. She won't last long, best keep the children out of the bedroom."

Paralysed with fear, he thought, "Oh my God! What am I going to do with six children?" Unable to face Siani, or any of the neighbours, he went to talk to his mates in The Colliers' Arms.

"Stay at home with her," Abraham Jenkins warned. "If the men hear that you've deserted Lizzie and the children at a time like this, they'll give you a bloody good hiding."

Siani's reaction on learning of the doctor's words was one of numb acceptance. "I thought so. Mam has been dying for some time, but has kept it to herself to protect us," she said bitterly.

* * *

Some days later, Josh and Siani heard the death rattle in Lizzie's throat and looked at each other in alarm. "What is it Dad? Shall I prop her up?" she asked, wringing her hands in despair.

"No, leave her be, girl. She's on her way out, let her go peacefully," he mumbled.

Eventually it stopped and Lizzie's head fell back on the pillow, her unseeing eyes staring fixedly at Siani, who screamed and ran out of the room. She stood in the kitchen sobbing helplessly, and looked for the comfort which her father was incapable of providing. He leaned over the mantlepiece, staring into the fire like a deaf mute, and kept his feelings locked inside himself.

"Why is he so uncannily cold towards me?" she asked herself as waves of grief and terror swept over her.

At first light, Siani went to call Bessie Bowen who lived two doors up, and asked her to come to see to her Mam, as she had promised. Seeing Siani's ghost-like face and red eyes, Bessie threw her arms around her and rocked her gently to ease her grief. Warm-hearted Mrs Bowen was like a second mother and had been a loyal friend to Lizzie Davies throughout her short life.

While she and Josh saw to the grisly task of laying out Lizzie's emaciated body, Siani crept upstairs to break the news to the younger children, who seemed to have sensed the presence of death, and lay huddled together on the big bed. She took Will into her arms, and she faltered as she said, "Mam's gone into a long, deep sleep and we must not disturb her. She's with the angels now, we must all try to be brave."

She took them downstairs where Mrs Bowen took Will on her knee and mothered little Mag. Siani set about making a pot of tea for them all while Ben sat by his father who still seemed to be stupified.

"Make it strong and put plenty of sugar in the cups, we can do with it," said Bessie, trying to ease the strain which surrounded them all.

Josh's voice sounded hard and cracked when later he said to her, "I'll have to see to a few things, will you stay here while I'm out?"

The parish doctor called and certified that Lizzie had died from Tuberculosis. "Try to keep the children out of the bedroom Mrs Bowen," he said, yet again.

It was a subdued and worried Josh Davies who later returned with an undertaker, who had agreed that he would provide a cheap coffin, on the understanding that he would be paid by the Ivorites Friendly Society when they were back in funds.

Elijah James by name, he took a quick look at the pathetic family and briefly acknowledged the presence of Mrs Bowen. Dressed in his crow-black suit, his hooked nose and lantern jaw made him look more like a Welsh Jew than ever, so Bessie Bowen thought. She watched him disappear into the side room where Lizzie Davies was laid out, and she heard him discuss with Josh the plain, bare essentials of the coffin and the funeral.

When they re-emerged, he turned to Josh saying, "I don't suppose you've got a drop of anything in the house…"

"No, but I'll soon put that right, if you'll come with me," Josh assured him. "I won't be long," he called to Mrs Bowen over his shoulder, and left her with Siani so that he could complete the arrangements.

They repaired to The Colliers' Arms, where Mr James explained that as soon as the death was registered, he would arrange for the grave at Pant Cemetery to be opened.

"I know where it is, our children are buried there," Josh said. The thought of it made his flesh creep, and he downed his whisky in one gulp before calling for another to be put on the slate.

He returned home some time later, considerably fortified, so Bessie Bowen thought, and he acquainted her with what was being done.

"I'm glad that Lizzie won't have a pauper's funeral. She was a good wife and mother and deserves the best," Bessie said pointedly.

"I've also been to see the Rev. Theo Evans and asked him to officiate. He's promised to call here this afternoon," he said, confident that he had now fully discharged his duties.

"Lizzie would have liked that, because she was a faithful member at Bethania Chapel until she became too weak to walk there," Bessie said. Her mind went back to the days when Lizzie had been one of the prettiest and jolliest young women in Bethania, and she reminded herself that was before she met this hard, cruel North Walian.

By the time the Rev. Theo Evans arrived, Siani and Mrs Bowen had tidied the place, and they were all sat ready and waiting for him.

"So good of you to come Mr Evans," Bessie Bowen said, speaking for them all. She looked in awe at the tall, dignified preacher, whose fine features, penetrating eyes and mane of black hair, gave him an aura of authority of which even Josh Davies was aware.

"I had to come, Lizzie was a loyal member of my flock. My wife and I were very fond of her, and you will recall that she was in service with us before she got married," he said, looking straight at Josh, who averted his gaze.

Sensing the tension around them, Bessie asked, "Would you like to see Lizzie, Mr Evans? She looks very peaceful now."

"Yes, indeed I would, and perhaps it would be appropriate if you come in with me," he said to the family. "I'll say a little prayer for her, and one for you all at this sad time."

They entered the bleak, bare bedroom where Lizzie lay, covered by a large white sheet. Mrs Bowen turned it back to reveal her pallid, waxen face. The children hung their heads and seemed frozen to the ground, but Will, sensing the anguish of the scene, let out a strangled cry, and buried his face on Siani's shoulder. He sobbed throughout the Welsh prayer which Mr Evans offered for the repose of Lizzie's soul.

One by one, they left the room and Josh closed the door firmly saying, "Nobody is to go in there again until the undertaker has been."

Siani sensed that her father was ill-at-ease with Mr Evans, and she herself scarcely knew what to do or say. It was Mrs Bowen who came to the rescue, yet again, when she asked about the readings and the hymns for the service.

"I'll leave it to you, Mr Evans," Josh said harshly. "You'll know what she'd like, and you'll see she's given a proper farewell."

"Yes, I'll do my best for her," he said quietly, and shook hands with them on leaving.

* * *

Josh Davies and family, in their shabby, threadbare clothes sat huddled together in the front pew of the large, imposing chapel, with its high panelled roof. He stared fixedly at the coffin, which rested in stark isolation in front of the big seat, beneath the elaborate, oak pulpit.

Long-lost memories raced through his mind and he squirmed slightly as he looked up at the balcony and remembered Lizzie as she had been seventeen years ago. He had been so taken with her that he had joined the chapel choir in order to get to know her. She had been healthy, fit and buxom when he started walking out with her, and her rippling laughter and sparkling green eyes had captivated him.

Before he knew it, he had fallen completely under her spell. He had been a lithe young buck in those days, and she had teased him about his curly chestnut hair and massive shoulders, which she had said made him stand out from other men. Strong and silent was how she described him, and they couldn't have been more different from each other. It was after that blissful walk to Pontsarn to see the Blue Pool that trouble had reared its head, and six months later, she had told him she was pregnant.

His thoughts were interrupted by the sonorous voice of the Rev. Theo Evans, who intoned from the Scriptures: "All we like sheep have gone astray…"

"Too true," Josh thought, "and I paid the price." He secretly believed that Lizzie had only married him because she could not face the disgrace of giving birth to a bastard, and of being hounded out of this very chapel. Lizzie's father had demanded that he should marry her, and then had treated him like a leper. He was glad when he and his family had decided to emigrate to Bethlehem, in Pennsylvania, and then he had shown Lizzie who was boss.

Siani also heard these words and knew who Mr Evans was referring to. Ten babies in fifteen years! That's what had killed her Mam, who was loving, kind and good, but had been cruelly ill-used by her father. The service continued and she felt her throat tighten as the dolorous singing reached a crescendo in the final hymn:

"O fryniau Caersalem ceir gweled,
Holl daith yr anialwch i gyd."
(The hills of Jerusalem could be seen
Throughout the journey in the wilderness)

She tightened her hold on Mag and Will and felt as though her heart was breaking, yet by the end of the hymn a strange calmness came over her and a sense of peace. She thanked God that her mother was safe at last: safe from lust, violence, misery and starvation, and once more she pledged herself to keep the promise she had made to her on her deathbed.

* * *

Lewsyn Jones, seated on the balcony, watched Siani out of the corner of his eye. "No wonder she was so fierce in that pawnshop queue and gave me such a look," he said to himself reproachfully. "She's got her hands full now, poor girl, looking after that brood. I hope she can stay at home to see to them, instead of slaving on the tips, but knowing her father, I wouldn't be too sure," he thought.

Siani, oblivious to the concentrated gaze of those near her, gathered her black woollen shawl around her thin shoulders, and shepherded the youngsters behind her father as the coffin was carried out by the bearers. Outside the chapel, she waited with Alys, Mag and Will as the cortege assembled on that freezing February day. She watched it wending its way up the steep, uneven road to Pant Cemetery, the coffin carried shoulder high, her father, Ben and David following immediately behind. She turned, unable to bear the anguish of yet another Welsh hymn, whose melancholy strains drifted down the valley, and carrying Will in her arms, she led the way back to Nant Row. There, Bessie Bowen and her eldest daughter,

Blodwen, who was Siani's best friend, were waiting for them.

"Come to the fireside, all of you" she said, putting her arms around them. "Blod and I have brought a bit of food from home for you."

It was an hour later when Ben and David returned from Pant Cemetery, chilled to the marrow. David brushed fine snow from his thin tweed jacket and Ben slowly undid his muffler after his hands had thawed out.

"Where's Dad? Why didn't he come home with you?" Siani asked immediately.

"Some of his mates have taken him to Pant Tavern to revive him. He was badly affected at the graveside," said Ben.

Her heart sank. "Was he indeed? And how does he think we feel?" she asked, her voice quivering with emotion.

Mrs Bowen listened to this conversation then said quietly, "Come to the table all of you. I've cut up a freshly baked loaf and brought some homemade blackcurrant jam and Welsh cakes. Eat what you can, while I bring you a cup of hot tea to warm you up."

Flushed with anger and a sense of betrayal, Siani found it impossible to eat, but saw to Will, who was biting on a buttered crust spread with jam. As the others munched away, Siani surveyed the scene, and realised that her troubles were starting up in the same old way.

"Are you sure you'll be all right, Siani?" Blod Bowen asked, seeing the look of dismay on her face as they prepared to leave.

"Yes, I've got to get on with things. I'll see the boys in bed, then Alys and I will wait up for Dad. You've been very kind to us, both of you," she said unsteadily, as they gave her a parting kiss.

"See you tomorrow, bach," said Bessie, who was exhausted by the day's events.

Alys was soon nodding off and went to lie on the bed while Siani sat alone in the silent, desolate kitchen. She dozed fitfully, and much later was awakened by a noise, when two men came through the door supporting Josh who was legless and helpless.

"Lay him on the floor. When he comes round, he can see to himself," she said, with loathing and disgust.

She slammed the downstairs bedroom door and lay on the palliasse alongside Alys. She pulled the 'cartheni' over them both, and listened to her father's crescendo of snores, which seemed to shake the whole house. "He can stay there forever as far as I care," she thought, and drifted off into the sleep of exhaustion.

Chapter 3

Union funds ran out and strike pay stopped at the end of February. "What are we to do, Ben?" Siani asked, her voice trembling with fear and despair. "There's hardly a crust left in the house and very little coal. Thank God Mam can't see what's happening."

Ben looked glum and scratched his head. His large brown eyes had an anxious look and his pale face was pinched with hunger. Though he was fourteen, he was small for his age, due partly to the fact that he had been working underground with his father in low coal levels since the age of ten. He now admitted that the Company was stopping people going on the tips because they were selling much of what they foraged. "Our Dad's in a devil of a mood because he relied on selling coal and cokes to provide him with beer money," he said.

"More shame on him. It was never intended for that, but to give people a chance to pick fuel to keep them from freezing to death in the winter," she said bitterly.

"There's only one thing for it, Siani, I'll have to persuade him to go to see Roger Williams, the Relieving Officer, to get some money from the parish to keep us going."

The dreaded word 'parish' frightened Siani, who instantly feared the workhouse. "I'll try Mr Morris once more to see if he'll give me some food on tick, but I doubt it, because of the hefty bill we owe him."

After a cold, miserable and hungry weekend, Josh Davies finally gave way on Monday morning and joined the queue outside the parish office in Dowlais. It was a long queue of gaunt, shabby, desperate men, prepared to do almost anything to get food for their starving families, except capitulate.

Muffled against the biting north-easterly wind, they stamped their frozen feet, and braced their ill-clad bodies in a vain attempt to keep warm. They moved slowly, because within the poky office, Roger Williams and his assistant demanded full details from each applicant. Once inside the door, Josh listened intently to these interrogations, and got ready to do battle when his turn came.

"Name, address and family circumstances," Roger Williams barked, without even looking up. A big, burly man, he was renowned for his parsimonious, inflexible attitude and was generally regarded as a heartless brute by the applicants. Staring at his bald head, Josh gave him the facts in an equally surly tone.

"What is your application?" Williams asked.

"For stone-breaking on Brecon Road and for parish relief," Josh retorted.

"The stone-yard is full. It will have to be the workhouse for you." Roger Williams rasped. He raised his bull-dog face, and narrowed his bleary eyes before announcing, "Josh Davies, you can have 7/6d a week for yourself and your children, on condition you break stones in the workhouse yard and take your eldest son with you. That's the new rule."

Josh exploded. "Go to hell, keep your charity. Ben and I won't go to any bloody workhouse! For two pins I'd give you a taste of this," he snarled, brandishing his fist before Roger's fleshy, bulbous nose.

At a signal, a police officer rushed in from a nearby room, pinioned Josh Davies's arms behind him, and dragged him backwards before flinging him out on to the road. "Don't you come back here or I'll arrest you for threatening behaviour," he shouted after him.

Ben rushed forward to see to his father. "What happened, Dad?" he asked. Why did they throw you out?"

"That bastard Relieving Officer wanted to put you and me in the workhouse yard to break stones for 7/6d a week, and I told him what he could do with it," he said, dusting himself down, and spitting in contempt at the door of the office.

"What are we going to do now?" Ben asked, sick with fright at the thought of what Siani would say.

"You can do what you like, but I'm going to The Colliers' Arms for something to steady me up after that ordeal," said Josh, who walked up the road, his face distorted with rage and hatred.

Ben hung about the market square in Dowlais, afraid to go home to tell Siani what had happened, and unwilling to add to her misery. He himself was so hungry that he felt as though his stomach was caving in. He knew that as a striker, he had to stand foursquare with all the others who were suffering, but life was becoming almost unbearable.

He worried about Will and Mag, who were too young to understand all that was happening, but who knew only too well what hunger was. He walked up and down wondering what to do, and he looked for some way in which he could earn a few pennies. He offered to hold the reins of the ponies of carriers who were quenching their thirsts in 'The Vulcan and Providence,' but was warned off by the regulars for invading their pitch. He looked with envy at the Dowlais stables where the pit ponies were being kept while the strike was on, and wished that like them, he too could be so fortunate as to have one good meal a day.

He was deep in thought when David appeared, having been sent by Siani to look for him, with strict instructions that he should come home at once. "She's in a temper, Ben, and she wants to know what's happened to Dad. The fire's nearly out and she's threatening to go down to the Works' Office herself to apply for a note to pick shindles on the tips."

"She's wasting her time, because there are no more permits and very little coal left, certainly not enough to sell," Ben added. "She'll have to wait until we've both earned something to take home with us," he said, looking David up and down with circumspection.

"What do you mean, Ben, why are you looking at me like that?"

"I mean that you and I are going to stand outside the market, begging."

"Oh no, Siani wouldn't be willing for that," he said, starting to cry. At eleven years of age, David was timid and insecure. His patched jacket, worn-out boots and dark, tousled hair gave him a waif-like appearance.

"Come on, there's no time to waste. I'll shout 'Please spare a penny for the strikers', and you hold out your cap," he said, dragging David behind him.

They stood outside the main entrance to Dowlais market, but had little success until Ben noticed that some people were wearing leeks and daffodils, and he whispered to David, "It's Dydd Gwyl Dewi (St. David's Day). What about giving them a song?"

Together they struck up, 'Dafydd y garreg wen' and gradually David's delightful treble voice brought in a few ha'pennies, which Ben collected. He worked his way through a few more Welsh airs, such as 'Llwyn On' (Ashgrove) and 'Ar hyd y nos' (All through the night), and by the end of the afternoon, they had tuppence ha'penny. Their red noses, chilblained hands and frozen feet finally forced them to give in, and Ben decided that they should go inside to spend their earnings. "Let's see if we can cadge something from the stall-owners before they close," he said warily.

They stuck their heads inside the market house and were immediately aware of the unbearably delicious scent of fresh apples, pears and oranges on the first stall near the door. David's mouth watered at the sight of the rich, colourful display, which Mr Rowlands had arranged on his stall in polished perfection. Ben could feel the yearning and hunger of his little brother, and sensed his desperation, so he took a ha'penny from their earnings and said, "Here Dave, go and ask Mr Rowlands for a bag of damaged apples. I'll go further on to see what I can scrounge."

Mr Rowlands looked askance at his late customer making such a request, but when he saw the look of anticipation on the little boy's face, he relented. He poked about in a box behind the counter, found four yellow, mottled apples and put them in a brown paper bag, then handed them to the boy who gave him his ha'penny with a radiant smile on his face.

"Can I help you clean up?" he asked, having noticed that Mr Rowlands was very stiff and moved with great difficulty. He scrutinised David's face before answering. "Do I know you, boy? What's your name?"

"David Davies, sir, I'm Siani's brother."

"Young Siani, who works on the tips and looks after the family? Yes, of course I know you, and I knew your mother, poor thing. I remember her as a girl in Bethania Chapel. Sorry I was to hear that she died so young. Here, take this sweeping brush and sweep around the front of the stall, then you can bring in the boxes of vegetables and the potatoes from outside, and stack them for me behind the counter. Can you manage that while I'm counting my takings?"

"Oh yes, sir," said David, putting his precious bag of apples near the scales. He worked with a will, carrying boxes of carrots, swedes and onions carefully inside, but even so, a few rolled on the floor. The sack of potatoes was too heavy for him to move, so he decided to wait for Ben, who was talking to Mr Price, the butcher.

"Have you got any left-overs for broth?" Ben asked, eyeing some scraps of beef and neck of lamb on the chopping board, which Mr Price was beginning to clear.

"No, they all go to make these sausages," he said, pointing to long strings of them hanging from metal rods at the back of his stall.

Ben was so hungry, he felt like snatching a few of them and running off. "Got anything for a penny?" he pleaded.

Mr Price looked around and came across a marrowbone with a bit of meat on it. "You can have this, if you like, I was keeping it for my dog." He wrapped it in newspaper, and Ben grabbed it eagerly, before putting his penny on the counter.

He went across to see what David was up to, and watched him struggling with a heavy sack. "What are you trying to do, Dave?" he asked.

"I'm sweeping up for Mr Rowlands and I've got to clean behind this sack."

"Here, let me help you," he said, pulling it forward. Between them they managed to drag it inside the stall so that David could finish his sweeping.

"What about these vegetables on the floor, Mr Rowlands? Am I to throw them away because they're damaged?"

"No laddie, if they're any good, you can take them home to Siani. Sweep any rubbish into a sack."

The two boys scrabbled around on the floor, gathering as much as they could lay their hands on, and put the vegetables into a paper bag.

Mr Rowlands came out to inspect the front and turned to the boys saying, "Da iawn, bechgyn". They watched in amazement as he took three glossy, red apples from the front of the stall, put them in a brown paper bag, and handed them to David, with the words, "Give these to Siani from me."

The boys smiled broadly. "Thank you Mr Rowlands," they chorused, and raced off to the top end of the market. We've still got a penny left, so we'll spend it on some stale bread from the stall by the back door," Ben said eagerly.

They trooped home, guarding their possessions jealously. "Wait 'til Siani sees these, she'll wonder how we got them," David said.

"Whatever you do, don't tell her that we've been begging," Ben warned, "Tell her we worked for them."

Tired of waiting, Siani had chopped up a broken chair to put on the fire, and had made 'pelau' out of small coal and clay to keep it going. The kitchen was clean and warm and the boys were relieved to see a fire glowing in the grate.

She could see by their red noses and rosy cheeks that they were cold, and she watched them blow on their fingers after they had put their paper bags on the table.

"A fine pair your are! Where have you been?" she asked as they came to the fire to thaw out.

"Down in the market with Mr Rowlands, helping out," said David immediately.

"Yes, we've been giving him a hand," Ben reaffirmed, "and he gave us a few things in return."

"Oh yes, but where is Dad? I thought you were going with him to the Relieving Officer, Ben."

"Well, everything went wrong and Dad got thrown out of the office," Ben explained, and gradually unfolded the whole story.

"So, while you've been working, Dad has been on the barrel again." Siani groaned at the thought of it, and tears of frustration rolled down her cheeks.

"Cheer up, Siani," said David, "Wait 'til you see what we've got." He went to the table and showed her the vegetables, and Ben unwrapped the big marrowbone, which seemed to smile at Siani through her tears.

"You **are** good boys," she gulped, putting her hands on their shoulders.

"And there's something else," said David, handing her a brown paper bag.

She peeped into it cautiously, and took out three polished red apples, one by one. There were cries of ecstatic delight from Will and Mag, when they saw them gleaming on the table.

"Can we have some?" was their immediate response.

"Mr Rowlands seems to like you, and he said that he remembered Mam coming to Bethania Chapel," said David quietly.

Siani smiled at the thought of him. "He's always been a kind man, I only wish I could afford to buy regularly with him." She cut the sweet red apples in half, and shared them out, and they all agreed that he was indeed a very kind man.

Without delay, she set about preparing the cawl and soon the kitchen was filled with the delicious aroma of onions, parsnips, carrots, swedes, potatoes and the marrowbone, simmering on the hob. Their mouths watered at the prospect of the first square meal for days. Siani cut half a loaf into thick chunks, ready for them to eat with the cawl when she had ladled it into their basins.

They waited impatiently for her to give the signal that it was cooked, and Ben, who was ravenous, meanwhile picked up the crumbs she had left on the table.

At last, she called out, "You can come to the table, Alys will bring the basins to you as I fill them. She put the plateful of bread on the table for them to help themselves, and finally, she sat down herself with Will on her lap.

They ate avidly, and were silent until David said; "This is good. Siani is as good a cook as Mam was."

"Not quite, but she taught me all I know." Siani fed Will from her own basin and watched him savour each mouthful. She looked around the table at their contented faces, and could almost feel her mother's presence at that moment.

Josh came in later, still in a churlish mood after his bruising encounter with the Relieving Officer. He sniffed, "There's a good smell here, what's for supper?" He stood before the fire, his arms akimbo, and he waited.

"I've kept you a bowl of cawl, and it's thanks to the boys that you can have that much. They worked for Mr Rowlands in the market and he repaid them."

Josh winked at Ben saying, "Good boy, I always knew you had it in you. You're like me, not afraid of work."

"And me," said David, "I was the one who got a start for us."

Ben's tufted, sandy hair almost stood up on end, and he wondered what his father would say if he knew the whole truth.

Siani emptied the remainder of the broth into a large basin and served it to her father with a thick chunk of bread. She watched him gulping the food greedily and felt bitter resentment at his total lack of concern for them.

"Dad, I've used up all the small coal today to make 'pelau', otherwise there would have been no fire in the grate and no cawl either. So how are we going to manage?"

He pushed the empty basin away and said gruffly, "We'll have to beg, borrow and steal. I expect Ben has told you what happened to me this morning in the parish office. They wanted to put both of us in the workhouse yard to cut stones! I told Roger Williams to go to hell. I'm not going to any bloody workhouse and neither is Ben."

Siani looked away miserably, and realised that it was pointless trying to argue with him, so she prepared Will and Mag for bed, and took them into the downstairs bedroom where she could have peace and quiet to think about the desperate situation facing them.

Chapter 4
February 1873

George Williams, under-manager in the Accounts Office at Dowlais Works, was confronted by his uncle, William Williams, financial manager of the huge concern. "I tell you we'll have to do something about our Achilles' heel," Uncle William complained. "People go scavenging for coal, then sell much of it and make a nice bit of money on our backs. It's got to stop, otherwise the strike will go on forever."

George stared at his highly-polished leather boots and felt decidedly uncomfortable in face of his uncle's reprimand. His usual duties in the Accounts Office were concerned with aligning wages with the market price of iron and coal, but while the strike was on, he had been given special responsibility for controlling permits to strikers and their families, who foraged on the Company's tips. He stroked his auburn whiskers nervously and wondered what to say in reply. "What do you want me to do, Uncle? You know it's difficult, if not impossible, to keep people off the tips. The most I can promise is that I'll make sure the permit system is tightened still further."

"Do so, or we'll become laughing-stocks," Uncle William said grimly. He was a gruff, hard-working manager with a sound reputation for firm, effective, financial control. He had risen to the top through sheer ability and dogged determination, and he hoped he could train his nephew to follow in his footsteps. As a widower, without children, he had taken George under his wing after the boy's father was killed in a mining explosion. For a time, he and his mother had lived with him and he had grown fond of him. He had even paid to send him to an expensive school at Cheltenham, in the hope that it would give the lad a good grounding.

In fact, Uncle William looked upon George as the son he had never had. With this in mind, when he came of age, he arranged a wealthy marriage for him with the only child of coalmine owners at Abercanaid. Lucy was in line to inherit a fortune built up by her ancestors, and Uncle William fervently believed that once he had trained George in financial management, he too could set about making another fortune in the steel industry, now being developed at Dowlais. But sometimes, he had secret doubts about whether his nephew had the sterner qualities of ruthlessness and determination necessary to take him to the top in the tough industrial world.

George was glad when the interview ended. He knew that he could not risk incurring his uncle's displeasure, and he also realised he would have to tighten the permit system. At the same time, he understood only too well that Dowlais employees would demand the right to pick 'shingles' as they called them, because they had to have a fire in their grates in this bitter weather. To try to stop them would be to produce riots, because the men were in a militant mood, yet Uncle William was quite right when he said that his fuel should not be sold. "I'll have to look at the scheme and work something out," he decided.

In the meantime, he took comfort from the thought that before long, his beloved wife would be in his arms. His spirits rose at the prospect of the dinner party she had arranged that evening at their large, detached, gabled house in Caeharris, which was a wedding present from Uncle William.

With that in mind, he settled down once more to examine the list of permits, granted since January when the strike began, and searched for evidence of duplication and abuse. Dispirited, he pushed the record book away from him, and concluded that unless he had intricate knowledge of all the families in Dowlais, and the employees at the works, it would be impossible to prove such abuse. "That's why we employ clerks, they should know," he told himself. He looked once more at the long list of names for permits, hoping to see a pattern emerging, but in vain. "Damn the strike and all its added responsibilities!" he said under his breath. He slammed the record book shut and decided that he would be better prepared to tackle 'the Achilles' heel' next day, after he had savoured the delights which Lucy had promised.

When he arrived home that evening, he was immediately aware that intensive preparations were in full swing for the dinner party. The dining room, with its rich mahogany furniture and pale green walls had never looked better. The silver had been polished to perfection and the decanter and accompanying glasses sparkled in the soft glow of the gaslight. Lucy had arranged a display of ferns and plants in the drawing room, which toned in with the elegant, green plush furniture and Italian gilt mirrors.

He took her in his arms and complimented her on her good taste. "You do me proud, my darling. I'm sure you'll be the most attentive and charming hostess in Dowlais tonight."

She revelled in his praise and assured him that the preparations were well in hand. Nothing had been spared by her and her staff on this occasion, for she knew that dear George delighted in good living. The menu she had chosen consisted of crimped cod in a cream, savoury sauce, followed by pigs' feet and rabbit; the main course included two boiled fowls and roast loin of pork stuffed with herbs and apples, and a choice of half-a-dozen vegetables. The wines had been selected by George, who prided himself on his good judgement in such matters.

Their guests included a banker, an engineer, the Company's Medical Officer and their wives. George thought that Lucy, in her pink brocade gown, outshone all the ladies, and he noticed that his guests admired her slim figure and pretty hairstyle. She was at her best on such occasions and sparkled in the presence of company like this.

The meal was served to perfection, the conversation flowed effortlessly, and under George's beneficent influence, his guests soon relaxed completely. The ladies complimented Lucy on her hospitality and marvelled at the beautiful concoctions which her cook had produced as desserts – meringues a la crème, vol-au-vent of pears, and artistically decorated cream trifles. George could almost feel Lucy preening herself.

The ladies withdrew to the drawing room, while the gentlemen lingered over the port-wine and cigars. It was then that the serious talk took place about the strike, its effect on trade and the recent epidemic of sickness in the area. These were problems which George's guests thought they knew a great deal about, and on which he valued their judgements. He reassured himself that it was important to have influential friends in high places at times like this.

When the last of their guests had left after midnight, George took his wife into his arms and kissed her. "I'm proud of you, you have mastered the art of entertainment to perfection, my darling," he said, as he led her upstairs to bed.

Next morning, he rode down to his office resolute and reinvigorated. He summoned his officials to his office and in the manner of his uncle, he laid down the law. He stood behind his desk with his back to the fire and looked them up and down before attacking. "As I rode down here this morning, the tips were crawling with men, women and children, scavenging and burrowing like moles. I even saw a horse and cart on top of one tip into which panniers of coal were being emptied. "This must stop!" he bellowed. "When I issue permits to pick coals, they're intended for immediate family needs, not for selling. From now on, you must see that only one basket per permit is taken home each day, you must inspect the permits and warn the holders that any abuse will result in immediate confiscation. See to it at once!"

A deathly hush fell upon his frightened staff, some of whom knew how desperate the strikers were, and who were reluctant to be so heavy-handed with them. George himself sensed trouble ahead, but knew he would have his uncle's support if the going became rough. After another morning's work on the permit system, he felt he was making progress at last. He decided that he would declare a moratorium on new permits, except in cases of extreme hardship, and entered a note in the register of permits to that effect. Then he added a further condition, that henceforth all permits were to be reviewed weekly. "This will add to my work-load, but I'm determined to be in control," he told himself. He heaved a sigh of relief when this was done and decided it was time to go home for luncheon.

Lucy was in fine spirits and declared that she had complimented the cook on last night's dinner and had decided that she would be giving dinner parties every week in future. "Mama told me that it's the best way of gaining a large circle of friends. I'd like to be known as the best hostess in Dowlais," she said excitedly, her eyes lighting up at the prospect.

George gave her his blessing, but added the important proviso that Uncle William should be invited on a regular basis as a special guest at their home, because they owed him so much.

"Of course, dearest," she said sweetly.

After an ample luncheon, he felt very much on his mettle as he mounted his horse and rode back to his office. His eyes searched the tips, and this time he noticed the absence of carts; he discerned officials checking long lines of men and women carrying baskets of coal, coke or cinders on their shoulders, on their backs, and even, in some instances of young women, balancing small tubs of fuel on their heads.

He was pleased that his stern instructions were being carried out with such speed. "That was the answer – more discipline," he thought, and he complimented himself on his effective action. "I'll call to see Uncle William tonight to tell him of the dramatic improvement," he decided.

Over a glass of port, Uncle William expressed his satisfaction. "Keep up the pressure, we're hoping the strike will collapse before long. I know you have an unpopular job, but if you do it well, I'll see that you'll reap your reward," he assured him. "Nothing would give me greater pleasure than to see you step into my shoes when I retire, and to see you produce a son to follow on in due course."

George coughed awkwardly when, with a twinkle in his eye, Uncle William asked, "Any signs yet?"

"No sir," he stammered, "but I'm hoping."

Uncle William fixed his eagle eye on George saying, "When this strike is over, you and Lucy should go to Llandrindod Wells to take the waters. That will put new life into her," he chuckled to himself, as he recalled his earlier days at the resort when the young ladies had been very frisky and full of fun.

George got to his feet, ready to leave. "I'll keep you informed about the situation with regard to the coke-pickers on the tips," he said. He had begun to feel slightly uncomfortable and sensed the power Uncle William wielded over him. He was a formidable character, and one word from him, or one look from those sharp, beady eyes was enough to frighten anyone. But if he were honest with himself, George would have had to admit that he was beginning to feel slightly anxious about not having a child. He and Lucy had been married for almost two years and she showed no signs yet of conceiving.

She was now twenty-three and he himself was twenty-five, so it was time to start a family. She was the sweetest girl, and was so accomplished, but she seemed satisfied with life as it was – a round of pleasure, fashion and entertainment. He decided he would have to talk to her now that Uncle William had raised the issue so bluntly.

Chapter 5

Siani could only come to one conclusion, which was that she must plead for a permit to pick coals and cokes on the tips. Now that the Workhouse Test was being applied to her father and Ben, it was hopeless for them to think that they could escape it by begging for a permit from George Williams. The bosses were hand in glove with the Board of Guardians, and everyone in Dowlais knew it. But she herself, as a former tip girl, might stand a better chance, so she got up at dawn, put on her working togs and slid down the icy roads to join the queue that was forming outside the Works' Office.

It was extremely cold, so she pulled her scarf tightly around her head and knotted it at her throat. She gathered her shawl over her thin shoulders, clutched it around her body, and stamped her feet on the ground in a vain attempt to keep them warm. Her clumsy boots were worn through, but she had stuffed a wad of paper inside them to fill up the holes.

The wait seemed endless and she began to wonder whether she would ever see the inside of the office before David came down with his wicker basket. She had told him to come by nine o'clock on the assumption that she might be lucky enough to get a permit of some sort. "Please God, make it come true," she said to herself, as she stamped her feet in unison with other women in a similar plight. They all agreed that times were hard and that Siani had had more than her fair share of trouble.

"Your father is his own worst enemy," said one of the older women, "it's time he put his family before drink and whoreing."

Siani felt her cheeks burn with shame and was more than relieved when the grill in front of the office was raised and a clerk called out, "When I open the door, remember that you come in one at a time, and you leave by the back door. Any squabbling and you remain outside, is that clear?"

Siani was the seventh to be admitted and her hopes had plummeted to the bottom of her boots because those before her had shouted angry protestations on being rejected. When she entered the ante-room to the main office, she sensed its warmth and noticed the glow of oil lamps. She took off her scarf, and as she did so, her long black wavy hair tumbled down on to her shoulders. She waited nervously to be summoned into the inner sanctum feeling very uneasy about the outcome.

As she entered the large room, she was confronted by three men seated behind a table with their backs to the fire, which crackled in a highly-polished grate. The handsome one with the reddish whiskers seemed to be the most important, because he gave orders to the others seated on either side of him. He raised his head and scrutinised her from head to foot before saying, "What's your name, and what work do you usually do for the Company?"

The ring of authority in his rich, deep, cultured voice almost unnerved her, but she found her courage and directed her sharp, green eyes towards him, saying quietly, "I'm Siani Davies, sir, and I'm a tip girl."

He held her gaze until one of his assistants broke his trance. "That's right sir, she lives in 2 Nant Row and has been out of work since 1st January."

He fumbled for words. "Who else in your family is employed by us?"

"My father and brother, sir, but they've had to apply for stone-breaking."

He narrowed his dark brown eyes and peered at her more closely. "So you would be the only one picking cokes for your family needs?"

"Yes, sir, unless you allow my eleven-year-old brother to help me carry them home."

He looked at her again and secretly marvelled at the beauty of her eyes, the daintiness of her features and the lustre of her black, wavy hair, which made the shabbiness of her clothes seem insignificant. She had a strange, unsettling effect upon him; he fingered his moustache, brushed the front of his check waistcoat and leaned forward, pursing his hands. "You haven't been before, have you?" he asked, puzzled.

"No sir, I've been looking after my mother who died recently, and seeing to my brothers and sisters."

She felt uncomfortable being stared at by this toff, with his smart clothes, auburn side-burns and mysterious dark eyes, so she lowered her head and stared at her boots, while his assistants checked their lists.

He turned to one of the clerks, who said quietly, "Genuine hardship, sir, father and brother out of work and so is the applicant and her sister."

George looked uneasy and perplexed; he ran his finger around the inside of his stiff, winged collar and drummed his fingers on the table. He felt unsure of himself, and hesitated as he said, "If I give you a permit for a week, will you promise that you won't abuse it?"

"Oh yes, sir" she said, and her whole face lit up at the prospect. Yet again she felt his eyes upon her and this time her heart missed a beat.

He paused, "Very well, a permit is granted for one week only." A clerk entered her name and address in the ledger while his colleague made out the permit for George to sign. He leaned across the table, handed it to her and said, "Remember your promise to me. Your young brother can help you carry your pickings home."

She smiled and thanked him; he was entranced by those green eyes with their dark, curled lashes and said to himself, "You find beauty in the most unexpected places in Dowlais."

Siani was very pleased with herself as she left the building. She had heard that George Williams was vain and arrogant, but he had been very kind to her that morning. Whatever people said about him, she could tell by him that he was a gent; she had heard that he had married an heiress and that he and his young wife lived in a large villa in Caeharris. "I expect she has everything she could wish for, unlike the rest of us who don't know where the next meal is coming from," she thought ruefully.

She spotted David waiting for her with his basket at his side and bending over him she murmured, "I've got a permit for a week." She produced it for the official on duty to check before they started their long, steep climb up the towering tips, and then hid it safely inside her bodice.

They worked like beavers, gleaning every piece of coal or coke they could lay their hands on, and by the end of the day, their basket was almost full. They grabbed it by its handles and dragged it along the rough pathways. Young David, unused to the work, found it hard going, and almost over-balanced more than once. "Steady now, Dave, or you'll have spilt more on the ground than we'll have left in the basket," she warned.

After grubbing on the tips all day, Siani's face was black with coal dust, her hands and knees were rubbed raw, and her back was so stiff she could barely straighten it. Her one consolation was that if she and David could keep up the effort, she could be sure of a fire in the grate at home. They were almost there when they met Lewsyn Jones near Ivor Lane.

"Here, let me give you a hand," he said, seeing them struggling with such a heavy basket.

"Thank you Lew," said David, "I'm almost too tired to put one foot in front of the other," and Siani admitted she too was exhausted.

He took hold of both handles and hoisted the basket on to his shoulder, and as he did so, he said to Siani, "So you've managed to get a permit out of George Williams, you must have a way with you. Be careful, because he's difficult to deal with."

She looked at him quizzically. "What do you mean by telling me to be careful? I hope you don't think I've been scraping, least of all him, as one of the bosses."

"I wouldn't dream of such a thing," he said with a broad smile. He set the basket down on the road outside 2 Nant Row, and then with a jaunty farewell, he went up the road smiling.

"He's a real nosey-parker," Siani said.

"He likes to tease you, that's all," said David wearily.

She thought again and wondered if she was too hard on Lewsyn, who, after all, was kind enough to give them a helping hand.

Proudly, they dragged the basket into the kitchen and then flopped down wearily on a chair. Ben rushed to look at their precious pickings and immediately set about building up the fire so that he could heat the boiler.

"By the look of you, you'll be glad of a bath," he said, giving David a slap on the back.

"Yes, Ben, we're both frozen to the marrow," he admitted.

"Cheer up! I'll make you a cup of tea while you thaw out," Alys said, bustling about the kitchen.

Mag and Will were meanwhile sitting by the table drawing on some coloured sugar paper Mr Morris had given them, and Siani was pleased to see them looking happy. She glanced around the room while she sipped her tea, and asked quietly, "Where's Dad?"

"Gone to a union meeting, there's something brewing with regard to the strike," Ben said.

"Do you think there could be a settlement?"

"It's hard to say. By now, most people are feeling the pinch and the men are getting restless." Then he added gloomily, "The trouble is, that even if they gave in at once, it would take time to arrange terms."

Josh and Ben attended an urgent meeting in the long room upstairs in The Colliers' Arms. News had come through about an important meeting between the ironmasters, coalmine-owners and the workmen's representatives at a large hotel in Cardiff. Josh was quite agitated and warned Ben that they should not give in without a fair settlement. "They're not going to do us down after all the sacrifices we've made," he said grimly.

The shabby room was packed and the atmosphere crackled with tension, as the men waited for the meeting to start. Joe Griffiths, Chairman of the Dowlais lodge, took a deep breath, got to his feet and started a long preamble about the negotiations that had been taking place.

"Come to the point," shouted Josh from the back of the room. "What's the offer?"

"Yes, what's the offer?" chorused a number of others around the room.

"After a great deal of hard bargaining," Joe emphasised, "The offer on the table is that we return to the wage rates of December 1872." Immediately, there was uproar in the room and he lost control of the meeting.

Dai Dando, one of the militants, jumped up on his chair, stabbed his finger at Joe and shouted, "That's no damned good, we'll still be 5% down on our 1871 wages."

The pandemonium continued until Joe got back on his feet and shouted, "Either you shut up and listen to me, or else I'll close the meeting. If you accept this offer, we'll have staved off a 10% cut and the bosses will not have had a walk-over. The alternative, which is continuing with the strike, doesn't bear thinking about in many families."

Llew Jones got to his feet at that point and agreed with him, saying, "We've got to face it that we never will get back to the 1871 level, the markets are against us."

"What do you know about markets?" shouted Josh, "This offer is a bloody insult after all that we've been through."

"But you haven't gone short of beer, have you?" shouted Llew angrily.

"I'm going to put this offer to a vote," Joe said, banging the table, trying to call the meeting to order.

The secretary and treasurer got to their feet at once, ready to count the hands. After two recounts, the offer was accepted, by a majority of ten votes, and Josh Davies demanded that "under protest" should be inserted in the minutes.

"Under protest, be damned," said Llew Jones to Lewsyn, "It's a pity he didn't protest against his motherless children begging outside the market, and young Siani out scavenging for coal on the tips."

Chapter 6

Josh and Ben avoided Llew Jones like the plague when the meeting finished. On arriving home, Ben, bursting with excitement, said to Siani, "We'll be back at work soon, the bosses have climbed down after all."

"Is that right, Dad?" she asked, noticing his sullen expression.

"Yes, but don't think we've won a victory, because our wages are back to where they were in 1872, which means that we've lost 5%," he said bitterly, and spat into the fire to show his disgust.

Siani heaved a sigh of relief, "I suppose we must be grateful it's only that much," she said wearily, "At least we'll have money coming in, and I won't have to worry about where the next mouthful of food is coming from."

"You and Alys can prepare to go back on the tips," Josh said gruffly, "I've got a lot of debt to clear, as you well know."

"Oh yes, and who's going to run the home and see to Will and Mag?" Siani snapped.

"You are, and Alys. I can't afford to keep you two at home, I've got to pay for your mother's funeral."

Siani exploded. "You won't be paying for Mam's funeral, the Ivorites will do that. The biggest debt you'll have to clear is in The Colliers' Arms and I'll see you in hell before I'll give you a penny ....."

She was suddenly stopped by a sharp smack across her mouth. "See if that will teach you to bite your tongue, you hussy," Josh shouted and went out, slamming the door behind him.

"Now you've done it," said Ben, who watched her wipe the blood from her swollen lip, and cursed his father inwardly for his violence.

There was an awkward silence in the kitchen as she stood by the tap, bathing her mouth. Then Alys spoke, "Why can't I go to the tips by myself? I'm twelve now and I can manage."

"No, you'll never be able to push those heavy iron trams, or clear them all on your own. And besides, the other girls would take advantage of you; you know how ready some of them are to lash at us with their tongues and fists when they feel like it.

"But I could go with her," David protested, "I'm eleven and I'm strong enough to push the trams and shovel out the slag and clinker."

"I was hoping you'd stay in school to make up for the rest of us," Siani cried, still dabbing her lip and looking a picture of misery.

She slept little that night for thinking of her father and his cruel ways. "There's Alys, so delicate that a puff of wind would blow her over, and David, a bright, sensitive boy, who would do well if he could stay in school. Little Mag is only five and Will just two years old, and they're missing Mam more than they can say. How can I look after them and go out to work all day? I'll have to get through to Dad somehow," she decided.

The kitchen was deserted when Josh came downstairs next morning. The fire burnt low in the grate, there was a smell of soda coming from pans of washing which stood on the table, and Siani was out of the room.

"Gossiping with Blod Bowen, I expect," Josh thought, as he rummaged around in the pantry looking for something to eat. He found nothing, not even a crust, and he turned away in disgust at the thought that Siani had not kept anything for him.

She came in from the back yard, carrying an empty clothes basket, and saying, "That's one line of washing done, now I'll get on with the rest."

"Where's my breakfast?" he growled, like a disgruntled bear.

"Siani was ready for him and gave him a withering look of cold contempt. "There's no food in the house, so Ben has taken Will and Mag down to the soup kitchen before he and Dave go begging outside the market." Then, turning to face him, she cried, "Why can't you see what you're doing to us? You've never looked after us as a father should, and unless you want Alys to join Mam in an early grave, she must stay off the tips."

Much to her surprise, her father, who was standing by the fire, began to blubber, and she knew that she had touched a raw nerve. But still she continued, "You expect us to hand over our wages, but let me warn you, I need at least twenty-five shillings a week to feed and clothe us when you and Ben go back to work."

Josh swore under his breath, "Don't start again. I've told you I've got debts to clear, and anyway, who says that you're going to handle the money?"

"I'm the eldest. I'm sixteen. Who's been running the home since Mam died? Certainly not you!" She pulled herself up to her full height. "If we had relied on you, there'd have been little or no food in the house, hardly any fire in the grate, and we would all have ended up in the workhouse."

"Oh, go to hell," he shouted, "I'm in charge here," and he stormed out, unshaven, half-dressed, and bent on only one destination – The Colliers' Arms.

*　　*　　*

By the end of March 1873, the workmen had returned to work and the furnaces had been re-lit. Josh and Ben were told to report at Trecatti Drift Mine where coal had to be turned out quickly for the hungry furnaces. Siani pleaded with Mr Morris, yet again, to let her have some food on tick for them to take to work in their tommy boxes. "I'll clear every penny we owe once their wages start coming in," she promised. Reluctantly, he gave way.

Josh remained adamant that she and Alys had to go back to work. "In that case, I'll go with them," David said. "Alys is too weak to shove those trams, and Siani can't manage on her own." Josh didn't argue, but warned them to bring their wages home direct to him, as he needed every penny.

The day they restarted was exceptionally wet; water streamed off the girls' battered hats and knotted scarves, and ran down their necks, soaking their scanty underclothes. Their badly-worn boots quickly filled with slimy water. A mixture of coal-dust and a thick reddish-brown deposit from the iron-stone clinker, caked on their sodden clothing, which clung to them like hideous shrouds. David's patched coat and trousers seemed to shrink visibly and almost fell apart. He and Siani battled on, but Alys wilted under the elements, her teeth chattered and her body shivered so that she could barely stand up.

When the hooter sounded at mid-morning for a short meal break, Alys went towards the tall stack by the brick-works seeking warmth, and soon fell asleep in her sodden clothing. Jemima Jones, a big brawny tip girl, noted for her caustic tongue, was standing nearby having a puff on her clay pipe. "You'd better leave her dry off, she won't be much good this afternoon," she said pointing to Alys.

49

"Mind your own business, Jem Jones. I've brought my little brother to help me today, in case you haven't noticed."

"Pity you didn't bring your old man as well, to keep him out of the pubs," she scoffed.

Siani picked up a lump of coke and flung it straight at Jemima, hitting her smack in the mouth. "That's for you, and there's more to come if you say another word," she shrieked, her patience exhausted.

At the end of the shift, they trekked home, bone-weary and soaked through, their hands bleeding as a result of handling the rough trams and iron-stone clinker. When they got to the corner of Nant Row, they saw Mag and Will waiting for them.

"I've put coal on the fire, and I've put the kettle to boil," said Mag proudly.

Siani bent to give her a kiss. "You're a good little girl, but you know that I've warned you and Will not to go near the fire while I'm out, in case you burn," she reminded her.

Hardly had she got in and removed some of the grime from her hands and face, when her father and Ben walked in, black from head to foot. They took off their heavy, hob-nailed boots, undid the cords around the legs of their trousers, threw their caps behind the settle and went to the tap to slake their thirsts.

"Fill the boiler and put it on the fire," Josh barked at Ben and Siani, who between them, hoisted it into position on the fire, while their father was bent over the sink removing some of the coal-dust from himself.

She went to the pantry and brought out a loaf of bread, some cheese and a bottle of pickles, which she put on the table. Her father was left to dole it out while she and Ben went outside to drag in the long zinc bath and put it before the fire. Alys, meanwhile, had rolled up the rag mat and put it in the corner of the room.

Ben joined his father and the others at the table, while Siani went to get soap, flannels and towels ready for bathing.

"Where's the tea?" called Josh. "Have you forgotten it?"

"No, it's brewing on the hob," she said, and with both hands, she carried the big, brown china teapot to the table for her father to pour out the strong, dark tea he liked so much.

Alys was slumped on the settle, overcome by exhaustion, and Siani murmured to her, "I can't see us keeping this up for long, can you?"

She shook her head and tears ran down her face. Siani grimaced, filled the bath with hot water and finally called out, "Come on Dad, everything is ready for you and Ben, Alys and I want our food now."

While the bathing ritual was in progress, the two girls sat at the table. Alys was indifferent to her food and watched listlessly as Ben washed his father's back, then rinsed off the soap- suds with jugs of hot water. His turn came next, and last of all came young David.

Once the kitchen had been cleared, the girls took a bowl of hot water into the bedroom and had a good wash down in the candlelight. Sensing her sister's exhaustion, Siani persuaded her to get into bed. "Have a good night's rest, then you'll feel better tomorrow," she said, trying to comfort her.

She took their smelly wet clothes into the kitchen and put them on the guard in front of the fire to dry off. By then, Josh had gone to his usual rendezvous, and the atmosphere was more relaxed. Ben talked excitedly about pay-day coming up on Friday. "It's such a long time since people have had money in their pockets, that they'll go mad," he said.

"I want you to watch Dad, to make sure that he'll give you the twenty-five shillings I've asked for *__before__* he goes inside the Colliers' Arms to start paying off his debts." Siani warned. "I must have the money Ben, if I'm to feed us all and keep my word to Mr Morris."

"I'll try, Siani, but you know what he's like," Ben said, with a note of despair in his voice.

"I'll come up there and I'll wait outside," she warned. "You must see to it."

On Friday afternoon, Siani stood outside The Colliers' Arms. There was a bustling, excited and jolly atmosphere in Market Street, Dowlais, and she watched women carrying home heavy baskets full of provisions and envied the warm, happy smiles on their faces. How she wished she was in their privileged position, instead of having to wait impatiently outside this detestable public house. Eventually, Ben came out saying, "Dad's having a devil of an argument with the landlord, but he's given me this." He put fifteen shillings in her hand.

She stared at it incredulously, and then her temper flashed. "For two pins, I'd go in there and expose him to his cronies and the molls he associates with," she said stamping her foot.

Ben looked weary and down-hearted. "Let's go home, Siani, I've had enough," he said. "Perhaps we can call in Mr Morris's shop to get some food on our way."

"I'll have to pay something off the bill before he'll give me anything," she said angrily, her voice quivering with emotion.

"Come on, let's try him, I'm starving and the little ones will be waiting for us, expecting some sort of a treat."

"You're quite right Ben, they've been asking for days for bread, butter and jam, like Blod's mother gave them. From now on, I'll keep whatever money David and I earn, and Dad can whistle for it. He'll pay dearly for what he's done to us today."

Siani's mind went back to the suffering endured by her mother and to the unfairness of life. If she had been properly treated, she would have been as plump and jovial as Mrs Bowen, and she herself would be as bonny and buxom as Blod. Instead, her mother was in her grave at the age of thirty-five, and she was becoming a miserable, half-starved creature. She knew that she would have to put up a fight for the sake of them all and was determined to do it now.

Chapter 7

In the balmy month of June 1873, George Williams was becoming restless. The Works were now back on target, output was rising, so were profits, and he felt it was time to get away from his ledgers and worries to a sweeter and more relaxing way of life. "What Lucy and I need is a complete change," he decided.

Lud White had recommended Brighton, but on reflection, George thought that Llandrindod Wells, with its pure air and healing springs would be a better proposition. Besides, trains went from Dowlais up through Mid-Wales and the scenery was breathtakingly beautiful. It would be less fatiguing for Lucy to travel there than to make the tiresome, tedious journey to Brighton.

When he mentioned it to her, her face lit up. "George, that's a wonderful idea. Dirty Dowlais in the summer is such a hot, smelly place, that I would welcome a change. But you know, dearest, that I'll have to have some new gowns to go on holiday. I'm told that important people like cabinet ministers and their wives travel there from London to take the waters," she added, wide-eyed with excitement at the prospect of meeting them.

George kissed her saying, "Have whatever you like, my dear, I want you to be at your best. I'll reserve a suite at the Pump House Hotel for the month of July."

Lucy was in her element being fitted by her dressmaker for her fine lawn dresses with pretty, flouncy skirts for wear in the daytime, and when it came to evening-wear she chose rich brocades, which set off her fair colouring to perfection. She had two new capes just in case she needed protection when they went walking in the park and when they went to take the waters at the pumphouse. Her milliner made her some of the smartest and most eye-catching hats imaginable and she even ordered a parasol in the hope that they would have fine, hot weather. George himself was measured for four lightweight summer suits and bought two grey top-hats to go with them.

When their large portmanteaus were packed, he put his arm on Lucy's shoulder and said, "I think we'll withstand scrutiny, dearest, no matter who we'll encounter. Uncle William has promised to send his carriage to take us to the station, then all we'll have to do is sit back and enjoy the scenic run through the mountains to Llandrindod Wells."

The day of their departure dawned bright and fair and Lucy was as pretty as a picture in a blue taffeta dress, matching cloak and pretty cream hat decked with cornflowers and poppies. They soon left behind the filth and grime of Dowlais with its stark landscape, and they found themselves enjoying the unspoilt beauty of Mid-Wales, where the sight of sheep and cattle grazing peacefully in green fields surrounded by neat, well-trimmed hedges gave them a sense of peace and well-being. The gentle, rolling hills and clean, sparkling rivers tumbling over rocks and spilling over weirs filled Lucy with delight. The time flew by and she was not in the least bit fatigued by the time they reached the elegant spa of Llandrindod Wells.

The hotel proprietor had arranged for a carriage to meet them at the railway station and their portmanteaus and hat-boxes were taken care of by the coachmen and Lucy's personal maid. Lucy was entranced by the tall, impressive hotels they passed en route to their hotel which was near the lake and pumphouse. On arrival, she was also impressed by the elaborate, palm-filled vestibule, where they were given a lavish welcome and were taken to a fine, airy suite of rooms overlooking the lake.

George was so delighted that he swept Lucy into his arms in a frenzy of delight. He led her to the big bay-window and pointed out an imposing, distinctive building alongside and said, "That's the famous pumphouse where we'll take the medicinal waters. I'll take you there each morning, dearest, then afterwards, we'll listen to the orchestra in the assembly room, saunter around the lake, watch the swans with their families of little cygnets, and we'll admire the colourful floral displays in the park. After all that exercise and fresh air, and the liberal dosage of spa waters, we'll be as hungry as hunters and we'll come back here for luncheon."

Lucy's eyes sparkled with delight as he continued, "In the afternoon, we can recline on the verandah, or play croquet, and in the evening we'll dress for dinner and I'll take you to dances where you can show off your beautiful, new dresses. I want the whole world to know that I'm proud of my charming wife," he said, kissing her fondly on her lips.

Lucy giggled at the prospect of so much pleasure and exclaimed, "George, dearest, it will be like a second honeymoon!"

He kissed her again and said, "This time it will be even better."

They settled down to enjoy themselves and dined in style every evening on five or six courses of fresh, locally produced food of amazing variety, and they sampled the extensive wine list which met with George's hearty approval. Lucy soon had a bloom about her; her rosy cheeks, gleaming, blonde tresses and bright, blue eyes proved to George how much she was benefiting from the holiday.

"My dear, I've never seen you look so radiant," he said one evening as they were dressing to go down to dinner. "I believe you are putting on a little weight."

"I hope not, George dearest," she said, as he put his arm around her slender waist.

Moving closer, he kissed her and whispered into her ear, "Nothing would please me more than to see you having to loosen your corsets because you're in the family way. I'm hoping that before long you'll be telling me some good news, my sweetheart."

The handsome, well-dressed ironmaster and his dainty, fashionable wife certainly caused heads to turn wherever they appeared. They made a great impression in the Asssembly Room dances where Lucy showed off her smart brocade dresses and George displayed his considerable prowess as an accomplished dancer of great style. In the local gazette, their names appeared regularly alongside those of Members of Parliament and rich industrialists from the Midlands who attended a variety of functions held in the Assembly Room. George and Lucy preened themselves that this was the social recognition that they merited.

The holiday passed all too quickly, and by the end of the month, reluctantly they prepared for their return to Dowlais. They both felt thoroughly invigorated; their blood had been purged of impurities by the spa waters and their lungs had been cleansed by the pure country air. Lucy especially had lost her pallor and was brimming with good health.

After returning home, she invited Uncle William and her Mama and Papa to dinner, so that she could tell them all about their delightful holiday. She also wanted to give each of them a pair of fine, leather, hand-made gloves, which she had ordered at the Central Wales Emporium as presents.

In the animated conversation, George went on at length about the spring waters, the beauty of the lake and gardens, while Lucy was far more concerned about the social scene and the fact that she had been introduced to a Cabinet Minister and his wife. George had to remind her about their romantic episode at the Lover's Leap and the Shakey Bridge, and she giggled as he recounted how he had only just saved her from falling over the slender bridge.

"My dear, I've rarely heard you enthuse so much about a holiday," said her mother, while her father agreed that Llandrindod Wells would take some beating.

Uncle William smiled at them and said, "Now let me tell you my good news. I'm going on a voyage out to Spain with Mr. Clark to look at some iron ore, which is mined in the Somorrostro Mountains. We need better quality ores for the new techniques we are introducing for making steel, and this is probably the best source that we'll find. But there'll be some delicate financial deals to be made, so I might be away for several weeks. In the meantime, I'm relying on you, George, to keep an eye on the wages front and keep your ear close to the ground for any rumbling from trade unions."

They were all very impressed by the importance of this piece of news and George was particularly pleased that he chose this occasion to announce it before his in-laws. With great deliberation he said, "You can depend on me, uncle, I'll scrutinise the wage sheets and I'll balance the books weekly, and as for trade unions, you know that I have ways and means of finding out what decisions are taken at their meetings."

Lucy's father smiled knowingly and agreed that there were always a few ready to spill the beans in return for small favours.

*   *   *

It was late September, just before Uncle William left for Spain, that Lucy made an appointment so see Dr. Ludford White. She complained of nausea and vomiting in the mornings and confided in him her hope that she might be pregnant. After examining her carefully, he agreed that she was in the early stages, and that her pallor was not due to anaemia, but to the nausea which plagued her.

"Take it easy until you are past the three months stage, and don't hesitate to call me if you need to," he said reassuringly.

George was overjoyed when she gave him the good news. "It's the spa waters that did it. We'll have to go to Llandrindod Wells every year in future," he said, with a gleam in his eye.

"We'll keep it as a secret for the time being," Lucy said, with a coy look.

"Can't I tell Uncle William before he goes away? It will please him no end," George said excitedly.

She looked pensive and then with a little giggle she said, "We'll just tell him and my Mama and Papa, no one else."

George threw his arms around her and kissed her saying, "I'm so pleased, my darling. It's the best piece of news we could possible give them."

Lucy decided to continue her social round for as long as possible. "I have so many lovely dresses to wear before

I lose my figure," she reminded George. So the dinner parties and soirees continued and Lucy added to her reputation as being the prettiest and most sought-after hostess in Dowlais.

Chapter 8
Summer 1873

No matter how hard she tried, Siani could not do much to clear her debt at Mr. Morris's shop. He had almost bankrupted himself by giving so much credit during the strike. She tried to pay a shilling or two each week off the bill, but she still owed him more than ten pounds and she felt guilty about it.

"The trouble is that Dad squanders money in the pubs and beer shops, and until he gives me enough to pay for our food, I'll never be out of debt," she complained to Alys.

She dreaded the weekends, when, with seven hungry mouths to feed, food disappeared fast. Mr. Morris had refused point-blank to let any more items go down on the bill.

"I'll have to teach Dad a lesson, that's all there is for it," she resolved, after the last piece of cheese was disposed of by Ben and David one Sunday evening. Next morning, when she filled her father's tommy box and jack, she did so without comment.

Josh opened it in the course of the morning expecting to find some moist, creamy Caerphilly cheese, but instead had only dry bread. He pushed it aside for Ben. When he decided to have a swig of tea from his jack, he found it contained cold water. His ugly temper flared, and he vowed revenge.

"I'll teach that bloody girl of mine a lesson when I get home. I'd have better food than this in the workhouse," he shouted. Ben ate some of the bread and gave the rest to the rats, which scurried around the pit stall whenever they smelt food.

Siani and David went to work that same day with no food for their mid-day break. She confided in David about the hopelessness of her position and added, "I've decided to go down to the office to ask for a 'sub'. I'll make an excuse that I want it for food for my sister who is sick. They'll check up to see how much we've done, so let's start."

"All right, Siani, we'll try to clear ten trams before then, to stand us in good stead," he said sympathetically.

They raced for the Works Office when the hooter sounded for dinner break and Siani knocked loudly on the outer door. There was the sound of the grille being released, and a clerk appeared who viewed them superciliously through his pince-nez and asked in a curt manner, "What's your business?"

"I want a sub, and I need it urgently for food, my sister is ill," Siani pleaded as she leaned forward towards the grille.

"I'll have to take particulars from you, give me your name and works number," he said, flourishing his pen and making quite a performance of it.

They waited impatiently while he checked his returns. "How many trams have you cleared today?" he asked sharply when he came back.

"Ten, mister, honest now, you can ask the gaffer," David said instantly.

That seemed to satisfy him, and he flourished a piece of paper which he passed through the grille and said to Siani, "Put your mark here," pointing to a receipt.

"How much are you giving me?" she asked warily.

"Two shillings."

Proudly, she signed her name, 'Siani Davies' and then snatched the money eagerly. She and David ran off quickly and made for a small shop behind Odessa Street, where they bought a crusty loaf, some dripping and a penny twist of tea and sugar mixed.

Alys thought she was dreaming when she saw them come home early bringing food with them, and managed to give them a faint smile.

"Put the kettle on and go and call Mag and Will, then we'll all sit down and have food together," Siani said to David as she bustled about the kitchen.

They were not the only ones to finish early, Josh had also decided to slake his thirst on something stronger than water, and had come up from the pit early. Just as Siani was biting into a thick slice of bread and dripping, the door flew open and in stormed her father. He took one look and shouted, "So, it's bread and dripping and a cup of tea for you, is it?" With one sweep of his hand, the dishes were flung off the table and the children ran to the corner of the room screaming.

Siani tried to explain what had happened, but he landed her such a blow across her face that he sent her reeling across the kitchen. She screamed as she saw him unbuckling his leather belt and raced towards the door, followed by Alys. Terrified, they ran down the road towards the brick-works and eventually reached a low wall where they sat down, panting. "I'm not going back there," Siani cried, nursing her bruised face and swollen eye, "I've had enough." Large tears rolled down her face and she was convulsed with loud sobbing.

"And I'm staying with you, because I'm afraid of him," Alys whimpered as she buried her face in her hands.

They hid in a nearby lane until they saw Josh leave the house and walk in the direction of Dowlais Top, then they plucked up courage to creep back to get their clothes and a blanket for the night.

Consternation broke out when they reappeared; both Mag and Will threw their arms around Siani, beseeching her, "Don't leave us." She almost gave in to their frantic pleas, until she saw lying on the kitchen floor, the leather belt and steel buckle which Josh had thrown there in his temper. She gathered up their few belongings and gulped back her tears saying, "Come on Alys, there's no time to waste, he may come back."

"Are you going for good?" Ben asked, his face creased with anxiety.

"Not for good, but just long enough to bring Dad to his senses. Look after Mag and Will, see that they have food ----," she said, choking on her words, then left quickly, unable to hold back her scalding tears any longer.

That night, they both slept in a hollow down by the ovens at the brick-works, and despite the coolness of the autumn, they awoke feeling refreshed next morning.

"You've got a beautiful black eye and your cheek is quite swollen," Alys said, looking at Siani as she prepared for work.

"It's nothing to what I would have had, if I'd stayed at home. Dad seems to have it in for me more than ever since Mam died."

"I'm coming back to work with you on the tips, Siani, I can't hang about all day with nowhere to go, and it's only fair that I should help," Alys said, pushing back her long brown hair.

"All right, just do what you can without exhausting yourself. I've got a few coppers left, so you can go to the nearest shop to get some bread and cheese for our dinner. I don't know about you, but I'm starving."

When David joined them at work, he looked downcast and miserable. "What's wrong, Dave? Is Dad as mad as ever?" she asked.

"He was so drunk when he came home last night, he didn't even miss you and Alys, but this morning, when he found that his box and jack weren't filled, he blamed Ben for not seeing to it. I don't know what's going to happen to us, Siani, because without you, there's no one to see to things. Dad doesn't realise how much we rely on you, and have done since before Mam died."

"And this is what I get for it," she sobbed, pointing to her black eye.

Jem Jones listened to all this as she puffed on her clay pipe, and curled her lip while saying, "So you're old man's had another go at you, has he? He's given you a real shiner."

Siani ignored her taunts and concentrated on emptying her next tram with David and Alys, who were doing their bit. At noon, when they had their dinner, Blod Bowen wanted a full account of what had happened and was full of sympathy. "I don't blame you for leaving the cruel devil, you've put up with him for too long. I'll ask my Mam to find you some lodgings as soon as possible. You'll be better off."

After the girls had spent two nights under the stars, Ben came looking for them and pleaded with them to return home. "Dad says that he'll beat the living daylights out of you if you don't come back soon," he warned.

Siani ignored the threat and did not waver. "Tell him I'll come back as soon as he promises to give me enough money to buy food for us all and to put that strap away.

What about Will and Mag? Are you looking after them and making sure they have enough to eat?"

Ben tried again to persuade her to return and even promised to protect her if necessary, but she was adamant, so he gave up.

*   *   *

Later in the week, Blod Bowen rushed up to Siani saying, "My mother's found you a room in the back of a house in Sand Street. Come and see it after work."

The girls were pleased at the thought of having a bed to lie on and swore David to secrecy. "Don't mention it to anyone, not even to Ben," Siani warned.

They met Mrs Bowen on the corner of Sand Street and were taken to the basement of a tenement lodging-house. As they crossed the muddy, cobbled yard leading to it, they noticed the rubbish and ashes which littered the place. And what was worse, they saw that the privy in the corner of the yard was adjoining the room being offered to them. "That's not a very good sign," Siani thought.

Mrs Bailey, a fat, slovenly, grim-faced landlady came out to meet them, looked them up and down, and explained that the last occupant left without warning and had not given her enough time to clean the room. She rattled the heavy steel latch on the rough, wooden door and eventually managed to open it, but left it hanging askew on one iron hinge. She stood back and said to the girls, "Go in and have a look."

They stepped inside and were confronted by a rough, brick grate which Siani decided had not been black-leaded for many a long day. The only window in the room had a broken pane, which had been stuffed with rags and below it was a rickety table and a few wooden chairs. They went to the end of the room where they saw a mattress on the floor next to the wall, and as they approached it they became aware of a foul, offensive smell. They backed off quickly and looked at each other in horror before they made for the door.

"How much are you asking for this room?" Siani asked fiercely.

"A shilling a week." Mrs Bailey saw the look on their faces and added, "Not many landladies would take you in as young as you are and looking as you do."

"And not many lodgers would want to live in a place that smells like a sewer," Siani retorted. "Go inside and see for yourselves," she urged Mrs Bowen and Blod.

They soon retreated and Bessie Bowen turned to Mrs Bailey saying, "Burn that mattress and fumigate the place or you'll have the health inspector after you."

They walked away silent and dismayed, and eventually Siani said, "We're not going there, Mrs Bowen, we'll be better off sleeping rough for the time being."

"Perhaps you'll feel better about it once it's been cleaned up. Remember, it's hard to find lodgings for young girls who can't afford to pay much."

"Apart from the stench, I don't like the place, there's something evil about it," Siani said with a shudder.

"I'll warn Mrs Bailey again that if she wants to let it, she'll have to clean and repair it. She's keen on the money, so she'll see to it."

The girls made their disconsolate way back to their brick-works hide-out where they bedded down for the night, after they had nibbled the remainder of their bread and cheese. When darkness fell, Alys snuggled up to Siani for warmth and comfort and fell asleep quickly. It was a bright, starry night and the orange glow from the works gave Siani reassurance. She lay on her back deep in thought and decided, "I can't give in to Dad yet, he has to learn his lesson. Once he sees sense, only then will Alys and I go back home."

Chapter 9
Autumn 1873

Young David looked a picture of misery on Saturday morning when he arrived at work without any food. His face was pinched and he was unusually silent, so Siani concluded that something had upset him at home.

"What's the matter, Dave? Has Dad been causing more trouble?" she asked.

He shook his head and stared at the ground. Worried and concerned, she went to him and put her arm around his shoulders to comfort him saying, "You know you can tell me about it, Dave, whatever it is."

He began to cry and then admitted the awful truth. "Dad came home late last night with a woman and they slept in your bed. They made a lot of noise, laughing and joking with each other, and when I left this morning, they were still there."

Siani gasped, and she felt her stomach turn over. "The old devil! I ought to have realised that something like this would happen. Mam must be turning in her grave!"

Alys, standing nearby, heard it all and began to tremble. "Does this mean we can't go back home, Siani?" she whimpered.

"It means that we'll have to return as quickly as possible to get rid of her," Siani said fiercely. Turning to David she added, "When you go home today, tell Dad that Alys and I are coming home at once and that we want our bedroom back."

As Saturday was a half-day, the girls went to the Wages Office to collect their pay, and sent David ahead of them with a further message warning Ben to keep the youngsters out of the way when they arrived. Alys was shaking with fright at the prospect before them, but Siani was ready for the fight.

They had almost reached Nant Row, when David came down to meet them. He hung his head, and with a guilty look said, "Dad is willing for you to come back, but says that Biddy is staying there."

Siani's eyes flashed with temper and indignation as she said, "We'll see about that. You and Alys had better stay outside while I handle this."

She marched boldly into the kitchen where her father was sitting in his armchair by the fire, alone. He turned quickly on hearing her footsteps and looked her up and down before saying, "So the wanderer has returned!"

"Yes, I've come back and you know my terms. I want that woman removed and the house-keeping money you promised me."

His lip curled as he called to Biddy in the bedroom, "Come and see this bitch of a daughter I've been telling you about."

Siani froze when she saw her. Biddy was tall, slim and dark-haired like her mother, but her face had been powdered and rouged and her lips were a vivid scarlet, the hallmark of a harlot, so Siani thought. As soon as she opened her mouth, Siani felt a wave of revulsion sweeping over her.

"What is it, Josh, me love? Is it trouble she's bringing yer?" she asked, putting her hand on his shoulder, and drooling over him.

The two women eyed each other, and Siani, ready to spring, yelled at her, "This is my home, you hussy, and that's my bedroom, so you can get out."

Josh stood up and shouted, "Biddy is here to stay, and if you don't like it, you can get out. I make the rules in this house."

She rounded on him like an animal at bay and shrieked, "If you have that creature in Mam's bed, I hope she'll come back to haunt you. You starved her to death and I hope that you'll rot in hell!" In a blind fury, she turned and spat at Biddy, full in the face.

Josh's temper exploded. He grabbed Siani and pitched her out, head-first on to the road, slammed the door after her and turned the key. Totally unafraid, she picked herself up and banged on the window shouting, "I've not finished with you yet," then she turned to Alys who was cowering against the wall and said, "Let's go and tell Mrs Bowen what's happened."

Bessie Bowen knew as soon as she saw them that they were in trouble. "Dewch mewn," she said, leading them into her clean, warm kitchen. "What is it? Has your father beaten you again?"

By then a reaction had set in. "Worse than that," Siani bawled, "he's thrown us out and brought an Irish woman into the house. She's there as brazen as brass, and we're not wanted."

"That's true," Alys sobbed, "and he took no notice of me at all. We've got nowhere to go, Mrs Bowen, and I'm frightened out there on the tips at night. There are tramps sleeping down there."

Bessie Bowen felt her heart go out to them but realised that she needed time to think. "Here, sit by the table while we talk things over," she said, pouring them a cup of tea from the teapot on the hob.

"What if I go to see your father? Perhaps I can persuade him to take you back," she said, eventually.

"It's a waste of time, Mrs Bowen. We won't stand a chance with that woman in our house," Siani said bitterly.

"Well, then, there's only one place left for you. Before long, you'll be facing the winter, and the weather will become fierce up here in the hills. You can't face months of sleeping rough, so I'm afraid it will have to be the workhouse for you."

Siani was aghast. Such a thought had not entered her head. "Oh no! Not the workhouse, anything but that," she said, appalled at the prospect.

Alys agreed saying, "I'd rather live in a basement than go to the workhouse." But Siani shook her head and buried her face in her hands in despair.

Mrs Bowen put her arm around Siani's heaving shoulders and said, "You owe it to yourselves and to me to look at that basement just once more. The blocked drain has now been cleared, and the room has been whitewashed inside and out. It looks and smells much cleaner. So what about it? I'll help you all I can."

They stared at each other hard, and fear drove them to nod in agreement. Mrs Bowen went immediately to get the key and once more they set out. When she saw it, Siani had to admit that there was a marked improvement now that the blocked privy had been dealt with, the yard had been cleared, and the mattress had been burnt. She looked uneasily at the door which still hung awkwardly, causing the big steel latch to protrude, and she also noticed that the broken windowpane was still stuffed with rags.

"What about it?" Bessie asked anxiously. "I've had to threaten Mrs Bailey with the health inspectors to get her to do this much."

Siani hesitated and gave her a look of desperation before saying eventually, "I suppose we ought to give it a try. What do you think Alys?"

She nodded agreement.

"Now stay here both of you while I talk to Mrs Bailey about the rent and things, then I'll go back to my house to get a scrubbing brush and a bucket. We can make a start right away so you can have a roof over your heads."

While she was gone, the girls had another look around, even venturing into the privy. "Yes, it's much better than I expected," Siani admitted, "that awful stench has gone and it's cleaner."

"Let's stay," Alys pleaded. "If Mrs Bowen helps us to make up a straw mattress, and gives us some coal and sticks to get a fire in the grate, we could manage for the time being. Please Siani, let's try it, for my sake," she begged.

"Don't rush things, Alys, there's still a lot to think about."

"I can't stick another night out in the open after all we've been through today. I want shelter and I want food in my belly," she said, collapsing into floods of tears.

Mrs Bowen returned with Blod who was carrying a bucket of coal and a bundle of sticks. "What's this I hear about your father? Up to his old tricks again, is he?" Blod said angrily. "He deserves to be horse-whipped."

"Oh Blod! I don't know what to do," she sobbed, "I'm at the end of my tether! Alys wants to stay here tonight, but how can we?"

Mrs Bowen decided to take over. "Now you two, dry your eyes and wash your dirty faces in this bowl I've brought for you. Blod and I will soon scrub this place out and get a fire going in the grate. You go and buy some food for yourselves, then you'll feel much better. By the time you come back, this place will look more like home."

"But we won't have a bed to lie on, and I'm bone-weary through sleeping out on the tips," Alys moaned.

"One thing at a time, merchi," said Bessie Bowen. "After we've black-leaded the grate and wiped down the furniture, we'll go back home for some sacks and I'll get fresh straw to make a palliasse for you."

"Thank you, Mrs Bowen, you are like a mother to us," Alys said plaintively, and Bessie turned away to hide the tears which ran down her cheeks.

The girls went to Dowlais market and made straight for the stall where the women from up-country were selling Welsh butter and cheese. Their colourful check flannel skirts and shawls had caught Siani's eye and she felt in need of the reassurance of some good food. Noticing her keen interest, one of them said in a soft, lilting, Welsh accent, "You can have a pound of Caerphilly cheese for threepence, and half a pound of salt butter for tuppence ha'penny."

Siani felt irresistable pangs of hunger overtaking her and said, "I'll have both, and four of your home-made faggots." Then they went further on and bought a loaf, two pieces of bread pudding, a packet of tea and a bag of sugar. They left the market to go back to the basement in the notorious Sand Street, guarding their purchases carefully.

The prospect of food revived Siani's fighting spirit. "We'll show Dad we can manage on our own. He'll rue the day he turned us out," she said to Alys.

To their delight, there was a fire crackling in the grate and a clean, wholesome smell of carbolic soap in the room when they re-entered it. "It looks much better Mrs Bowen," said Siani, putting her goods on the table.

"Yes, it's surprising what hard work and a bit of elbow grease can do to a place like this. I've sent Blod ahead of me to start on the palliasse, and I'm going now to see how she's getting on. The kettle's on the boil, so you can make yourselves a cup of tea and have something to eat."

They wasted no time and were soon enjoying bread and butter and Caerphilly cheese.

* * *

Blod and her mother arrived later, puffing and blowing, and laid the palliasse in the corner on the floor, well away from the fire. Alys smiled approval at the prospect of a good night's rest and thanked them profusely.

Siani herself was satisfied that with food and shelter, they would now survive. "Thank you Blod, you've been a good friend to me in my hour of need," she said, her eyes brimming with tears.

"One final word before we leave," said Bessie Bowen, "see that you bolt this door every night and don't open it to anyone. Remember there's a lodging-house at the end of the street, and you never know whether there are tramps roaming about looking for things to steal and getting up to all kinds of trouble. I've left some candles for you, and you can pull the blind down to cover the window. See that you look after yourselves," she added.

Siani threw her arms around Mrs Bowen and buried her head on her shoulder. "I can never thank you enough for all you've done for us," she said, sobbing quietly.

Bessie hugged her and kissed her saying, "You know where I am if you need me, cariad."

The girls locked up as instructed and looked around at their new surroundings in a state of bewilderment. In the dim candlelight, they looked forlorn, weary and ill-at-ease. It was Siani who broke the silence by saying, "Come on let's go to bed. I'm nearly dropping," and they lay down as they were on the clean palliasse, and slept all night.

Chapter 10

Sunday dawned crisp and clear, with a nip of Autumn in the air. It was well past day-break before the girls bestirred themselves and Alys admitted that she'd had the best night's sleep since leaving home.

Siani busied herself re-kindling the fire and then took their small iron kettle off the hob to fill it ready for breakfast. She saw Mrs Bailey hobble across the yard to the privy and watched her go to the standpipe with a bucket and a jug. "I've a good mind to ask her to lend us a bath and a boiler so that we can have a good soak," she said.

"Go on, Siani, I'd love one, and this is our only free day," Alys said.

Siani slipped out quickly and caught up with Mrs Bailey who readily agreed saying, "Of course you can borrow them. Sunday is a quiet day, my other lodgers won't want them today, they're not working."

The girls ate their breakfast of toast and tea quickly and went to gather more cokes on the nearby tips in order to build up the fire to heat the water. By the time they came back and collected the long, zinc bath and the oval boiler, the fire was glowing. When the water had been heated, they locked the door, pulled down the blind, then started on the bathing ritual.

Alys went in first, attended by Siani who knelt down at her side and washed her all over with a piece of flannel and some soft white soap left by Mrs Bowen. She took a jug of warm water, rinsed her light brown hair, and towelled her all over after she had stepped out in front of the fire. Alys, now aged twelve, was beginning to show the first signs of puberty. "Before long, you'll be a woman like me," Siani said, giving her a knowing smile.

Her turn came next and she added more hot water so that she could lie back and relax while Alys waited on her. At last, she began to feel as though her cares were slipping away. "It's a long time since I enjoyed a bath so much," she sighed. Then she dried herself before the fire. Looking at her, Alys hoped she would grow like her, for despite all the hard work and the lack of nourishment, her body remained shapely and well-proportioned.

They groomed each other's hair, getting rid of the knots and tangles which had built up, and soon Siani's long, black, wavy hair shone like jet and her fair skin glowed with health. She tied back Alys's fine brown hair with a piece of white tape, which accentuated her enormous grey eyes and delicate colouring. Looking at her she said, "A few hearty meals is what you need, merchi, and now that we're on our own, I'll see that you have them."

Blod called later and was amazed to see them looking spanking clean in their Sunday dresses. "Well, girls, you seem to have settled in here, in spite of it being such a dump," she said.

"It was this or the workhouse, and it's thanks to your mother that we're here at all. Have you seen anything of my father and his fancy woman?" Siani asked, eager for news.

"Not a glimpse of them, and I don't want to after what's happened to you. Don't let's talk about them, because I have a nice surprise for you." Blod took out of a basket a large plate covered with a cloth and put it on the table. "See what's in there," she said proudly.

They uncovered a large, oval plate of meat, vegetables and gravy, which Bessie Bowen had cooked that morning. "Dad has killed a pig ready for the winter, and we have plenty of spare-rib, so he told my Mam to see that you two had a share."

Their faces lit up and Alys was even tempted to pinch a piece of the rind. "Fingers off!" said Siani, "I'll put it in the oven to warm up and we'll enjoy our dinner later."

They went over the events of the previous day and the time soon flew by. "Tell your Mam I'll always be grateful to her for helping us out," Siani said.

"It's time for me to go, girls. I can smell that sage and onion stuffing, the food is now hot, so I'll leave you to enjoy it. We'll talk again in work tomorrow," Blod said, getting to her feet.

The juicy, succulent pork disappeared mouthful by mouthful as the girls munched their way steadily through it with the stuffing, swedes, carrots and potatoes. They eventually finished off with the crisp crackling which Mrs Bowen had included for them, and were replete.

"I think Blod's mother must be the best cook in Dowlais," Alys sighed happily, still savouring the meal.

"You're not far wrong, but I could cook like that if I could afford to buy the food. I'd soon make you strong and healthy. Don't forget that Mr Bowen keeps his pigs in a sty at the bottom of his garden. Nothing goes waste in that house, and his vegetables are home-grown. If Dad followed his example, we wouldn't be where we are today.

They washed their plates and cutlery, banked up the fire and got ready to go for a walk. "I'm dying to see Will and Mag," said Siani. "Let's hope that they'll be playing outside, otherwise we'll have to lie in wait for them,"

By a stroke of luck, they met them on the rocky road, coming back from a walk with Ben. They shrieked with delight and made a bee-line for the girls. The hugging and kissing went on for several minutes and Will begged Siani to come home with them.

Ben looked hard at his sisters and admitted, "I've been worried about you, but you look much better than I expected. Has someone taken you in?"

Siani gave him a furtive look. "Let's just say that we've managed to have a roof over our heads, but I'm not saying where, because I don't want Dad to know. Is that Irishwoman still there?"

"Yes, I'm afraid so. Dad is handling the money and she makes the food, what there is of it. She's a real slut and stays in bed until mid-day."

"I'm not surprised. I hope she gives Dad the pox and you can tell him from me," Siani said bitterly.

He sensed it was time to move on, so he lifted Will on to his shoulders and took Mag by the hand. "Let's go home now and have something to eat," he said, trying to humour them.

"Why can't Siani and Alys come with us?" Mag asked, resisting him.

"We'll come once the Irishwoman has gone," said Siani, giving them a kiss.

The parting was painful and tore her apart emotionally. "I can't go through that again. We'll have to work out something with David when we see him next," she said to Alys on their way back to their basement.

A sense of guilt grew inside her, and she began to feel a constant anxiety about the fact that she was breaking her promise to her mother. David too was becoming more and more withdrawn and she sensed his deep unhappiness.

Unable to bear it any longer, she said to him, "Dave, if I tell you where Alys and I are living, will you promise that you won't tell Dad?"

"You can trust me, you know whose side I'm on," he said miserably.

"In that case you can bring Mag and Will to 13 Sand Street on Saturday. I've got to see for myself that they're all right.

"I'll be there. They keep asking for you all the time," he admitted.

They arrived with David in the afternoon and nearly went wild with delight when they saw the girls. Will clambered on to Siani's lap for her to nurse him, while little Mag sat between her and Alys, and looked around the basement with interest.

Siani thought both of them looked shabby and unkempt, but was appalled when she discovered that they had nits in their hair. "Where have you been to pick these up?" she gasped.

"Dunno. Biddy I'spect," said Mag innocently.

"Alys, heat some water, I'm going to wash their hair with carbolic soap. And get the tooth-comb from the back of the drawer," she added.

When all the commotion was over, they sat at the table while their hair was drying and ate the bread and butter and jam that Siani had saved for them. Mag began to complain that she did not like Biddy because she shouted at her. "Can Will and I come here to live?" she begged.

"Dad wouldn't be willing and there's not enough room," Siani explained, putting a protective arm around her.

"We could sleep between you and Alys," she protested, pointing to the bed in the corner.

"No, it's out of the question, there'd be no one to look after you while we're in work," Siani said.

They left reluctantly, and on their way home Mag confided in David, "If Biddy threatens me with the strap again, I'll tell Siani about her."

*   *   *

Life in 2 Nant Row went from bad to worse, with Josh and Ben missing work through sleeping late. Biddy wasn't worried because she could then spend more time in the taverns, but when pay-day came, Josh soon realised the price he had to pay for the pleasure of her company. He had started to slide deeper into debt and Mr Morris once more cut off his credit and refused to serve him unless he paid his debt in full.

It was a week to the day after the children's first visit that Siani and Alys heard frantic sobbing and loud knocking outside their basement door at mid-day. They had come home early from work and were having a wash and changing their clothes. Siani rushed to the window and, to her amazement, she saw Mag standing outside with Will clinging to her skirts. Sensing trouble, she opened the door immediately.

"Nefoedd mawr! What's happened to you?" she gasped as she stared at the angry red weals across Mag's face, arms and legs. She picked her up and took her inside and tried to pacify her so that she could say what had taken place.

"Biddy beat me for taking money from her purse," she cried, still shaking uncontrollably. "She put me across a chair and leathered me with Dad's belt from the back of the door."

Siani screamed and tears flowed down her cheeks. "Where was Dad when this happened?"

"He and Ben had gone to work and Biddy was late getting up."

"So, did you take the money?" Siani asked, trying to keep calm.

"Yes, I was going to get something for me and Will for dinner, and had to go down to Odessa Street because Dad has stopped buying with Mr Morris."

Eventually, after Mag had calmed down, Siani turned to Alys who was nursing Will and said, "Give them a crust while I get dressed. I'm going up to Nant Row to give that Irish hussy a taste of what she's done to Mag."

"Don't, please, for our sakes, don't do it, Dad will kill you," Alys pleaded.

In the general pandemonium which ensued, they hardly noticed the arrival of David who said, "Dad has come home and has sent me to take Mag and Will back with me."

Siani gave him a withering look. "Can't you see the state of her? She's not going anywhere, I'm going to bathe those awful stripes to ease the pain. I've a good mind to go to the police to report that bitch for what she's done to our little sister. You can tell Dad from me that these two won't go back home until Biddy Donovan leaves our house, and that's final."

David's face registered a mixture of shock and horror, and he left dreading the inevitable reaction from his father when he delivered the ultimatum.

Chapter 11
October 1873

All was peaceful and quiet in the Sand Street basement, where Siani, Mag, Will and Alys slept, huddled together on the straw palliasse on the floor. Since they had only one blanket, which barely covered them, they remained fully-dressed as a protection against the cold of the frosty October night. The dying embers of the fire gave out little heat or light, but they were so tired they were past caring.

Suddenly, they were awakened out of their sleep by a loud hammering on the basement door, and Siani's heart nearly stopped when she heard her father shout, "This is the bloody place where my kids are hiding. Will! Mag! Come out here!"

Having no response, he gave the door a hefty kick and hurled himself against it with such force that it nearly fell apart. The latch and the bolt gave way under his frenzied attack, and in a drunken rage he staggered into the room. In the dim glow of the firelight, he spotted the youngsters lying between Siani and Alys. Instinctively, Siani jumped up and grabbed a heavy iron poker, ready to defend herself.

Will and Mag cowered on the bed, alongside Alys, as their father advanced on them, and they heard him shout, "Get ready to hold on to these two brats for me, Biddy, while I deal with this girl of mine who is trying to steal them from me."

"Don't come near me or you'll feel the weight of this," Siani shrieked, brandishing the poker.

She saw him bend down to grab hold of Will who cried out, "No, Dad no!" Without a second thought, she came from behind and kicked him so hard between his legs that he dropped the frightened child. Howling with pain and cursing Siani, he turned to hit her, but lost his balance and fell with great force against the sharp steel latch protruding from the damaged door. With a loud groan, he fell to the floor, senseless.

Biddy, who had been standing the other side of the door, let out a scream when she saw Josh stretched out. "Call the polis! Call the polis!" she screeched, hoping someone would hear her.

"Go away, you bitch!" shouted Siani, still brandishing the poker, "if you come near me, I'll knock your block off."

Neighbours from adjoining houses appeared as from nowhere on hearing the hammering, shouting and screaming. Mrs Bailey, still in her nightdress, sensed danger, and she and some of her lodgers dragged Josh into the yard to try to revive him. They saw vaguely in the glow from the furnaces, that blood was pumping from a deep, jagged wound on the top of his head. They splashed his face with water and tried to staunch the bleeding, but failed to revive him. Eventually, they decided to carry him home on some planks from the shattered door, and were led by Biddy, who moaned all the way, "She's murdered him!" And when they reached Nant Row, they laid him on the bed, limp and helpless.

"What's happened?" Ben asked, terrified by the sight of so much blood all over his father's face and shirt.

"There's been an accident. Better call a doctor," said one of the lodgers, emphasising that he had nothing to do with it.

"Siani did it, she hit him with a poker. I heard her threaten him," Biddy wailed, "and she threatened me too. We'd better call the polis."

Dr. Cresswell, the Works' doctor, came sometime later, and looked alarmed when he saw the deep wound on Josh's head. Turning to Ben, he said, "Your father has a fractured skull and his brain may be damaged. Don't move him."

Josh died next day from 'contusions of the brain', so the doctor called it, and Biddy, weeping hysterically, bawled out, "I'm going straight to the polis to tell them who did it."

On hearing from David of her father's death, Siani started to shake uncontrollably. "I never intended anything like this to happen," she sobbed, "I didn't do it, he was so drunk he overbalanced,"

"You must come home, all of you, at once, Ben wants to talk to you," said David, his face like chalk.

With dread in their hearts, the two girls with Will and Mag, went back to Nant Row immediately. When they got there, they found Mrs Jenkins, the 'layer out', performing her gruesome duties. She emerged from the downstairs bedroom with Ben, and looked at Siani saying "I've sent word to Mrs Bowen and the Rev. Theophilus Evans to come at once, you'll need help." Then, after some hesitation, she added, "You can come in with me now, to see your father, but be prepared for a shock."

They entered the bare room where Josh's body lay covered with a sheet and Siani gasped when Mrs Jenkins exposed his face. "He's gone black!" she exclaimed, and Alys, at her side, almost fainted at the sight.

"Better keep this door shut for the time being, because of the little ones," said Mrs Jenkins, looking at Will and Mag who were huddled near David on the settle.

Siani's sense of guilt was so overwhelming, that at times she felt unable to breathe. Twice she fainted and had to be revived by Ben who gave her sips of cold water. The awful truth that her father was now dead, and that she had a part in it, would not leave her.

There was no trace of Biddy Donovan who, so David said, had run away in a state of hysteria. "She's gone to the police, Siani. She said you hit Dad on the head with a poker."

"I did not. She's telling lies," she cried, and called on Alys to support her.

"Well, then, what _**did**_ happen? He must have had a terrible blow to do so much damage," said Ben.

Taking a deep breath, Siani said, "He came down to Sand Street looking for Mag and Will to take them home. Biddy was with him and he broke down the door in order to get in. He was drunk, and in trying to get hold of Will, he fell against the door and hit his head on the steel latch which was sticking out."

"That's right," said Alys, nodding her head, "that's what happened."

"Dr Cresswell says that there'll have to be an inquest so that all the facts can come out, so you'd better stick to what you've just said," Ben warned.

Siani started to tremble at the mere thought of it and later, when Mrs Bowen arrived with the Rev. Theo Evans, she was almost too afraid to look at them.

Bessie Bowen was her usual kind, warm-hearted self and put her arm around Siani saying, "Come now, Siani fach, have a talk with Mr Evans, he wants to help you.

She gave David a signal to take Mag and Will out so that they could talk more freely.

The Rev. Theo Evans looked at the abject figure before him and felt a deep sense of compassion. He took her tear-stained face between his hands and looked into her frightened eyes. "Mrs Bowen and I have been talking. We believe that your father was the author of his own misfortune. If he hadn't been dominated by the demon drink, he would be alive today."

"Quite right," said Alys, "it was his own fault."

Mr Evans continued, "Mrs Bowen and I feel that you are too young to assume all this responsibility on your own, so will you let us help you?"

"Thank you Mr Evans and Mrs Bowen. I'll be more than glad of your help," she gulped, as tears streamed down her face.

"Your father can't be buried unless an inquest or inquiry has been held, so he will have to be taken to the mortuary in Merthyr Tydfil. If you are to be questioned by anyone, no matter who it is, I want to be with you, Siani," he emphasised. "I'll get an undertaker, and I'll go to the coroner's office, and I'll arrange for your father to be taken away."

Siani could feel her head spinning and slumped forward in her chair. Bessie Bowen gave her a sip of water and a whiff of smelling salts before saying, "Try to keep calm, I'll stay with you until this crisis is over."

News travelled fast in Dowlais and next morning, Lewsyn Jones appeared at the door. "Come in and sit down, Lewsyn, it's kind of you to call," said Mrs Bowen.

"I wondered if I could help in some way, he stammered.

"You've helped by just calling to show your concern," said Mrs Bowen.

He could tell by the look on Siani's grief-stricken face that she was in deep shock, so he said to her quietly, "Try not to be too hard on yourself, we all know what he was like and what you've had to put up with."

She glanced up at him and saw at once his deep concern about her. Her mind went back to the pawnshop queue and to her mother's funeral, and tears coursed down her face. He took his red spotted handkerchief from his pocket and gave it to her. He felt he could have wept with her, and before leaving he murmured to her, "Remember, Siani, you can count on me whatever happens." Their eyes met and she realised that deep down, there was a bond between them. He swallowed hard and felt a powerful urge to protect and comfort her.

After he left, Ben turned to Siani and said, "You've got a good friend in him and he's unafraid."

* * *

There was a loud knock on the door of 2 Nant Row later that week, and when Siani answered it she blanched at the sight of a tall, stout constable holding a document in his hand. "Siani Davies, you're to come with me to be examined by a magistrate," he said, "I've had a complaint from a woman called Biddy Donovan that you assaulted your father, Joshua Davies, inflicting a head wound upon him from which he has died."

Siani was struck dumb and started to tremble. Immediately, Alys rushed to her side and said, "She didn't hit Dad, I was there. He fell against the door latch and cut his head open. He was drunk!"

"I'll want a statement from you, young miss," said the officer, "in the meantime, Siani Davies, you're under arrest." He grabbed her wrists and fastened handcuffs over them as she screamed in terror.

Ben pushed forward protesting, "You can't do that, we haven't even had the inquest yet, and the Rev. Theo Evans has said that nobody can question her unless he is present."

"My orders are to arrest her and that's what I'm doing," the officer snarled, dragging Siani away.

Pandemonium broke out with Will and Mag crying at the sight of Siani being led away, and Alys pleading, "Don't take her, she's innocent."

Neighbours rushed out to see what the commotion was and watched with horror as the policeman shouted, "Get in there!" and bundled Siani into the Black Maria.

"Now she's for the gallows," yelled Biddy Donovan who suddenly appeared, having followed the horse-drawn prisoners' van from Merthyr police station. "She's murdered her Da," she shouted to the crowd of curious onlookers, and instantly she ran after the van conveying Siani to a prisoner's cell in Merthyr town.

Chapter 12
December 1873

Mari Jones, Lewsyn's mother, walked home from Bethania Chapel with Bessie Bowen, her long tongue wagging nineteen to the dozen. Her sharp eyes and ears missed nothing and she was generally regarded as one of the busiest gossips in Dowlais.

"What's all this talk about Siani Davies? Did she really kill her father?" she asked.

"I don't know, I wasn't there," Bessie said, "But I'm sure of one thing, he was a blackguard and a bully. He went down to Sand Street that night looking for trouble and he found it."

"Biddy Donovan swears she heard Siani Davies threatening to beat his brains out with a poker."

"Knowing Siani, I doubt whether she would have made such a threat before the little ones, and least of all before that Irish hussy. You'd better wait for the trial, when the truth will come out," Bessie said, her heart going out to Siani who was now locked up in gaol in Cardiff.

"Llew says that the Rev. Theo Evans is going to organise a collection to pay a lawyer to defend her. I don't think it has anything to do with the chapel members," Mari Jones continued, "it's hard enough for us to make ends meet as it is."

"If her mother's own chapel doesn't help her, what chance does she stand, Mari? Tell Llew to dig deep into his pocket," Bessie said, looking her straight in the eye.

That evening, Lewsyn listened to his mother relaying this conversation to his father. "Scum off the tips, that's all she is," Mari added, her sharp, pointed features distorted with spite and venom.

His temper erupted. "Mam, you should be ashamed of yourself to say such a thing. She can't help being a tip girl. Dad has often said that she and Alys work like slaves. Whatever she is, she's entitled to a fair trial and that is why the Rev. Theo Evans is asking all of us to contribute. I'm going to give as much as I can afford and I don't give a damn what you do."

Llew Jones was taken aback. "You've got a lot to say for yourself, calm down. I know her father was a drunken brute but he didn't deserve to die like that."

"He had it coming to him and I'll be at the trial to support her," Lewsyn retorted angrily.

"That's enough!" said Mari Jones, "Your father and I will make up our own minds and I don't want you to have anything more to do with that girl."

*   *   *

The large, impressive courtroom buzzed with activity as lawyers in their wigs and gowns, their assistants in sombre black suits, and grim-faced court officials, moved to and fro prior to the start of the trial. Every seat on the public benches was occupied, and prominently placed near the front, were Ben, Alys, Lewsyn and the Rev. Theo Evans. They looked around in amazement at all the activity and stared in awe at the oak benches, tables and fixtures, and the heavy, high-backed chair for the judge. Mr Evans pointed out the narrow dock with a rail around it and said, "That's where Siani will stand." Overlooking it, were the benches on which the jury were to sit, and he explained, "They are the men who will decide her fate."

They sat quietly, waiting for her to appear. There was a sudden flurry of activity and a gasp of dismay from the public benches when Siani, handcuffed to a warder, was dragged up the stone steps into the dock. Clad in dark grey prison clothing, her face as white as alabaster, her hair bedraggled and unkempt, she looked a pathetic, half-starved figure. Alys started to cry at the mere sight of her and Ben put his arm around her to console her.

Siani stood motionless, with her head bowed as though terrified of the prospect before her. Ben tried to attract her attention and Lewsyn murmured, "I'm here, Siani, don't be afraid." She raised her head slightly, as though searching for them, and they tried to wave to her.

The court usher then barked out, "All rise," and the be-wigged, red-robed judge swept in and occupied his chair. The general hubbub subsided and the clerk of the court got to his feet to read out the charge, ending with the words, "Manslaughter. How do you plead?"

"Not guilty," she whispered, almost collapsing under the strain.

The atmosphere in the courtroom crackled with tension as the prosecution outlined the case and placed on display the cast-iron poker, with its long, sharp tip and the bent steel latch. Their chief witness, Miss Biddy Donovan, dressed in sombre black and looking every inch like a bereaved widow, was put in the witness box to give evidence. She gave a dramatic account of Josh Davies's inconsolable grief when his two youngest children, Mag and Will, went missing. Sobbing at intervals, she explained how she had accompanied him to Sand Street to a basement, where Siani Davies and her sister lived, and where they were hiding Mag and Will.

"The poor man was knocking on the door, begging for his children, pleading for them to come home with him, but they took no notice and would not answer," she cried, dabbing her eyes with her handkerchief.

"What did he do then?" asked the lawyer, gently encouraging her.

"He put his hand through the window, released the bolt and gave the door a good shove," she explained. "When it fell open, he was confronted by Siani Davies, brandishing a poker. He tried to rescue his little ones, but was set upon by that vixen," she said, pointing to Siani, "and the poor man fell to the ground, his brains beaten to a pulp."

There were gasps of horror and cries of "Shame!" from the public benches. The distraught Biddy collapsed into floods of tears, had to be revived with a glass of water, and was given a chair to sit on.

"Stay there while my friend asks you a few questions," said the lawyer.

Biddy was very upset by the relentless questioning of Mr Lloyd Williams, the defence lawyer, who seemed to doubt every word she said. He made her so confused that in the end she did not know what she was saying. Overcome by terror and grief, she had to be assisted from the witness box! "Shame on you for treating a decent woman like a whore," she snarled at him as she went back to her seat. Lewsyn, Ben and Alys hissed at her, and her Irish friends made a grab at them. But for the presence of an usher, a fight would have broken out at that moment.

Dr. Cresswell next gave evidence and stated that he had been called in as the Works' doctor. He had attended to Joshua Davies at his home and had warned his son that his father had a fractured skull and should not be moved. There was a deep, jagged wound on the top of his head and a lot of congealed blood. As he was unconscious, it was impossible to question him, and when he visited the following day, he found that the patient had died. He had attended the post mortem at the Infirmary in Merthyr Tydfil, and he and Dr. Job, the Workhouse surgeon, had concluded that Joshua Davies had died of 'contusions to the brain'.

Under close cross examination by the prosecuting solicitor, Dr. Cresswell would not say whether such a severe head wound was the result of a blow by a poker, nor under further cross-examination by Mr Lloyd Williams, would he confirm that it could have been caused by a steel door latch. Pressed to examine the poker and the latch, and to notice the bend in the cross-bar of the latter, he admitted to Mr Lloyd Williams that it could have been the latch.

Siani's face was ashen grey and she looked as though she had seen a ghost. Only her handcuff to her gaoler's wrist, and the bar, which she clutched at the side of the dock, enabled her to remain upright. Alys had already fainted and had been carried outside by Ben to recover.

As the law stood, Siani was not allowed to give evidence, nor could she be cross-examined. Instead, Mr Lloyd Williams, the eminent barrister engaged for her defence out of funds collected by the Rev. Theo Evans, took her through her unsworn statement in which she denied emphatically hitting her father on the head with an iron poker. She stated that his injury was caused by his stumbling against a sharp, steel door latch in the dark basement when he was drunk and unsteady on his feet. She maintained that she had only picked up the poker to defend herself if need be from attack, and that Biddy

Donovan who was outside could not possibly have seen what happened in the room.

Alys was called into the witness box, and looked as though she was about to collapse again, but somehow she rose to the occasion. She emphasised that she certainly did not see or hear Siani hit her father with the poker. She explained how she saw him stumble across the room towards the mattress where she lay. "He bent over me to grab Will and I smelt the beer on his breath. Somehow, he dropped him, and then I saw him stumble and I heard him hit his head on the latch," she said, weeping bitterly.

"Was the door swinging awkwardly?" Mr Lloyd Williams asked.

"Yes, Dad had kicked it in and the latch was jutting out."

"Thank you, my dear," Mr Lloyd Williams said quietly.

Mrs Bailey took the witness stand next and emphasised that when she came on the scene, the latch was covered with blood, and there were big patches of blood on the flagstones near the body.

"Where was the poker?" asked Lloyd Williams.

She thought hard.

"Near the grate, I think."

"Was there blood on it?"

"Not that I know of, sir, I didn't pick it up."

"But you are certain there was blood on the latch?"

"Yes, it was sticky when I took hold of it."

The judge was busy writing while both Alys and Mrs Bailey withstood searching cross-examinations and remained unshaken in spite of the prosecution's attempts to break them down.

Exercising his right as the defence lawyer to sum up first, Mr Lloyd Williams emphasised that it could not possibly be proved beyond all reasonable doubt that, in the confusion inside the small, overcrowded basement that night, Josh Davies had been wilfully attacked by his daughter. "***She's*** not a murderer, she's a martyr!" he proclaimed, his voice ringing around the courtroom as he pointed to the pathetic figure cringeing in the dock.

There were shouts of "Hear! Hear!" from the back of the courtroom and pandemonium broke out as Lewsyn lunged at one of Biddy's henchmen who had spat at him.

"Order! Order!" shouted the court clerk who threatened to have them removed for misconduct.

The lawyer for the prosecution in his summing up, did his utmost to sow the seeds of doubt in the minds of the jury by saying, "There is something of a mystery about this case. Why did Joshua Davies drop his son and stagger to the door where he fell, covered in blood?"

"He was drunk!" shouted Lewsyn from the public benches.

"One more word from you, and out you go," shouted the court clerk.

The prosecuting lawyer hastened to complete his case. "No mere blow from a door latch would have caused his death." Stabbing his finger at Siani, standing in the dock with her head bowed low, the lawyer shouted, "She killed him! She used the poker on him!"

At that point, Siani fainted and lay helpless on the floor. The courtroom erupted and the judge, glaring fiercely at the rowdy hecklers, gave orders for it to be cleared. Fights broke out, Lewsyn and Ben lashed at Biddy's Irish supporters and the police had to draw their batons before the room could be cleared.

In his summing up, Judge Lionel James warned the jury that they had to be unanimous in their verdict, and reminded them that if there was any element of doubt, the defendant was entitled to the benefit of it. "You must consider all the evidence carefully," he emphasised.

There followed an endless wait during which Ben, Alys, Lewsyn and the Rev. Theo Evans went down to the cold, dank cell where Siani was locked up. When she saw them, she seized Ben's hand and asked about Mag and Will. "Promise me, Ben, that if I go to the gallows, you'll look after them."

"Of course I will," he said choking on his words.

Lewsyn saw the despair and misery engrained on her face and took her hand. "Now Siani, don't talk like that, we're going to take you back to Dowlais with us tonight," he said.

She shook her head. "I don't suppose I'll ever see Nant Row again, or that the people will want to see me. Thank you for coming down here, Lewsyn, I'll always be grateful," she said, looking pathetically into his eyes.

The officer in charge called out that their time was up, so they left Siani clinging to the bars of the cell while Mr Evans said a prayer for her. They could hear her sobbing as they made their way back to the courtroom, heavy-hearted and despondent.

Weak and helpless, Siani was dragged up the stone steps back to the dock. Her head swam when she saw the sea of upturned faces gazing at her, and she thought that many of them were baying for her blood. She gripped the rail around the dock with her free hand, her knuckles white with tension. In the distance, she heard the judge address the jury and ask them a question. There was a long pause and then she heard the words, "Not guilty, my lord." They echoed and re-echoed through her mind and she sank to the floor unaware of the pandemonium which broke out in the courtroom.

When she was eventually brought to her feet, she heard the judge say to her, "Siani Davies you are now free to leave this court." He swept out, her handcuffs were released, and from the public benches she heard Lewsyn shout, "Good girl, Siani."

Cheering broke out as she was led into the well of the court and Mr Lloyd Williams came forward to congratulate her. Almost immediately, Ben, Alys and Lewsyn surged forward, wild with excitement, and the Rev. Theo Evans put his arm around her shoulders saying, "God bless you, Siani, I have prayed for this moment."

A court usher led her to a room where she discarded her prison clothing and put on the clothes Alys had brought for her from home. Then they all left the court buildings for the railway station and Siani felt as though she was walking on air and that she was in a trance.

A smile of utter relief wreathed her face as the train chugged its way up the Taff valley, and in the hubbub of conversation she fell asleep, utterly exhausted. She awoke to see the flames of Dowlais lighting up the midnight blue sky. Alys had wrapped her mother's black and white check flannel shawl around her, and at her side was her friend, Lewsyn Jones who said, "You're almost home now, Siani, and I'm here to look after you."

Chapter 13
1873

George Williams and Ted Martin took their responsibilities seriously and liaised with each other frequently while Mr Clark and Uncle William were in Spain. The purchase of shares by the Dowlais Company in the Orconera Iron Ore Company was in its final stages when Ted Martin invited George and Lucy to dine at his home.

For Lucy it was an opportunity to wear her favourite turquoise blue brocade dress with its smart bustle, and the rope of pearls which George had bought for her. She loved visiting the Martins, not just because she admired their richly furnished home and excellent cuisine, but because she knew that Ted was making a name for himself in the Company as an efficient engineer who was likely to follow in the footsteps of Mr Menelaus. She wanted George to be able to keep pace with him on the financial side where his Uncle William wielded so much power.

After an excellent meal of Michaelmas goose followed by delicious confections and trifles, the ladies retired to the drawing room, leaving Ted and George to talk serious business in the smoking room.

"There are certain things I must tell you in private," Ted warned ominously. "I've picked up rumblings of discontent in the forges, rolling mills, workshops and collieries. As an engineer, I have close contact with the men, and I've noticed that they're becoming hostile to the Company. Not only are they complaining about the wage rates, but they're demanding better working conditions and greater freedom from company control. The old paternalistic approach is breaking down," he warned.

George listened intently and took a grave view of this situation, which Ted saw as a sinister threat to the Company's interests. In the quiet confidentiality of the smoking room, they were able to speak frankly to each other.

"It seems as though the storm clouds are gathering yet again and we're heading for another strike," George admitted. "The best course of action is for me to contact the South Wales Employers' Association to alert them of the situation, and to find out whether this discontent is widespread or peculiar to our area."

"That would be a good move, George, because if there is to be another strike, we need time to build up our coal stocks. We don't want to be taken unawares so that production will come to a sudden stop."

"I don't think there's any danger of that, because the men haven't had time to recover from the last one yet, but if there is another show-down, the more protracted it is the better for us because in that way we can wear them down. We've got to play for time, Ted," George emphasised.

"I agree, and the sooner that your uncle and Mr Clark come back on the scene the better. Compared with us, they are old hands at this trial of strength."

*   *   *

In the ensuing weeks, George was so pre-occupied with Company matters that he failed to notice that all was not well with his beloved Lucy. He thought she was more tired than normal, but attributed it to late nights and all the entertaining that went on. "Stay in bed in the mornings, dearest, and take plenty of rest," he urged her, feeling slightly uneasy about her drawn look and pallor.

She concealed from him the giddiness, and bouts of dragging pain that she experienced, until one morning, early in November she was forced to give way and admit that she was unwell. George dispatched a servant to Dr. White's house with a note saying, "Come quickly, Lucy is bleeding."

After examining her, the doctor ordered immediate bed rest and promised to keep a close watch on her. "This is the danger period. Once she's over the first three months, she should be all right," he said, seeking to assuage George's anxiety.

Lucy rested for a few weeks and seemed vastly improved so that Dr. White gave her permission to return to her normal routine. "Just take life a little easier," he advised, and gave her a tonic for her blood. While she had been fretting in bed, she had made a long list of the expensive presents she wanted to buy, and the provisions she was going to order. George was pleased to see her show such spirit, especially as Uncle Willliam was due home soon.

He arrived during the first week in December, elated by the success of his visit to Spain and the deal which had been arranged. Seated at the fireside in his book-lined study at home, he savoured a glass of sherry as he talked to George about his achievements. "We're all set now for further expansion. Our supplies of ore are secured, and we have a perfect arrangement whereby we export coal to Spain on tramp steamers, and bring them back full of superior iron ore," he said triumphantly. George listened avidly to this good news, twirled his sherry glass between his fingers and then prepared to give Uncle William his perspective on the business.

"I don't want to detract from your stunning success, Uncle, but I feel it my duty to warn you that there are problems brewing here in Dowlais." He outlined his conversation with Ted Martin and told him of his contact with the South Wales Employers' Association.

Uncle William was taken aback but murmured approval of George's action. "Mr Clark and I will be attending their next meeting. We cannot allow a strike to place in jeopardy the progress we have made with our new deal. The men should realise that the Company's prosperity is *their* prosperity. All this talk of hatred and disillusionment is being stirred up by agitators who know nothing about market forces or industrial competition," he said fiercely.

George felt relieved that he had shed the full burden of responsibility, at least for the time being, and turned his attention once more to his beloved Lucy. She had re-joined the social round in which the ironmasters' wives sought to outdo each other in style and affluence.

I'm going to have a soiree before Christmas and then I'll withdraw from socialising until after the baby has come," she said to George.

He smiled at her devotedly. "I'll agree as long as you don't overdo it, darling, and that you promise to rest every afternoon."

Lucy seemed her happy self once more and even went for a jaunt to Cardiff with her mother. When George next looked at his bank statement, he realised that she had spent a great deal of money. A thought suddenly crossed his mind, "Perhaps she has ordered a layette for the baby," he said to himself, smiling at the prospect.

Elaborate preparations went on for the soiree and the house was a hive of activity. The silver candelabras were polished to perfection and the rich mahogany furniture gleamed in the candlelight. Lucy had even engaged a harpist to entertain their guests with folk songs and Christmas music. The prospect of their enjoying the savouries and sweetmeats which the cook and her assistants had prepared, and listening to delightful music in such beautiful surroundings, filled her with pride. She had thought of everything, even to the mulled wine and mince pies which would round off the evening. She was confident that it would go off well.

The night before the big event, George waited impatiently for her to come down to dinner. In the end, he bounded upstairs to see where she was and found her lying on the bed, holding her stomach.

"What is it, darling?" he asked, then noticed a large patch of blood on her petticoat on the bed.

"I became ill when I went to the bathroom," she groaned. "I thought that if I were to lie down, the bleeding would stop, but the pain is awful."

One look was enough to make him realise that the doctor should be called and he sent for Lud White post haste, who was there when Lucy miscarried with an enormous loss of blood. The nurse he had brought with him stayed with her while he went downstairs to George.

"It's bad news, I'm afraid, she's lost the baby and she's very weak. I'm sorry old chap, but I did my level best for her."

George looked a stricken man and buried his face in his hands. "I've had an uneasy feeling for some time, but hoped that she had passed the danger period. I'll go up to see her now. Ask your wife to let our friends know the soiree is cancelled." He stumbled out of the room unable to hold back his tears any longer.

He found Lucy lying prostrate in bed, drained of colour and unable to raise her head. He sat at her side, holding her hand and watched the tears streaming down her face. He got on his knees and kissed her, "Try not to worry, dearest, perhaps it was not to be," he murmured.

She cried herself into the sleep of exhaustion and he remained at the bedside keeping watch over her until the nurse came to release him from his vigil. After a sleepless night, he decided to break the news to Uncle William. Lucy was still asleep when he left, and the nurse assured him that she would keep a close watch on her. He found his uncle tackling a hearty breakfast of ham and eggs, but as soon as he heard George's tragic news and saw his anguished face, he pushed his plate aside.

"How in the name of God did this happen?" he asked. "She has all the love and care in the world showered upon her and this is the result."

George shook his head and struggled to control his emotions as Uncle William continued, "I was looking forward to you producing a son and had high hopes that Lucy would deliver. You'd better ask Lud White to explain why this has happened."

George got to his feet saying, "He'll be calling this morning. He's very concerned about Lucy because she lost so much blood."

Uncle William sensed that George was near breaking-point. "Stay home with her for a few days, my boy, you look exhausted," he said. "You'll have to go down to see her mother and father, so try to reassure them that she'll be all right and don't give up hope."

Lucy remained in bed throughout the Christmas period and slowly regained her strength. Beef tea, chicken broth, liver, iron tonic, were administered under doctor's orders. The social round was forgotten and only her Mama, Papa and Uncle William were allowed to visit her. She was brought downstairs in the New Year and lay on the green velvet chaise longue looking like a Dresden china figurine. George thought he had never seen her look so fragile or so beautiful. It made his heart ache to look at her.

"What would you like to do, dearest, when you get stronger?" he asked, trying to raise her spirits.

A slight twinkle came into her eyes and she said, "I'd like to go to Llandrindod Wells when the daffodils are in bloom and the lambs are in the fields."

His heart leapt and he said, "So you shall, my sweetheart."

Chapter 14

Siani and Ben sat at the fireside in the warm, flag-stoned kitchen in Nant Row, feeling as though they had been caught up in a violent whirlwind, which was only now gradually receding in the distance. She stared into the fire, which burnt low in the brick fireplace, and looked with fondness at the heavy iron kettle, the brass tripet and her mother's prized brass fender. It felt so good to be home and seemed an absolute miracle that she had left Cardiff gaol behind her and had returned to her family just in time for Christmas. She realised that it was all due to the Rev. Theo Evans and the lawyer he had hired to defend her; they were the answer to her prayers during her darkest moments of total despair.

Ben noticed she was deep in thought and turned to her saying, "A penny for them, Siani."

"I was just thinking how good it is to be here, though I don't suppose I'll ever live down the disgrace of being accused of killing Dad. I'll be branded for the rest of my life."

Ben became angry. "You would never have been charged but for that Irish woman, and Dad would have been alive today if he'd listened to you. But let's try to put it all behind us and make the best of things. You are here with us now, and that's all that matters."

Siani sighed, "I suppose you're right, Will and Mag nearly went mad when they saw me, and our Dave cried. When I was in goal, I often thought of my promises to Mam that I would look after you all. It was horrible there, Ben, and it's a part of my life I don't want to talk about."

"I understand how you feel, we'll have a quiet time over Christmas to give you a chance to recover. Dave and I have saved a few shillings and we'll spend them on food. You need good feeding after all the weight you've lost, so cheer up, we'll go to the market together on Christmas Eve."

"Thank you, Ben, you've been a real trump all the time I've been away, seeing to everything here at home and looking after the little 'uns."

"Time for bed now Siani, the rest have all been asleep for some time, and if I'm not careful, I'll be sleeping late in the morning," he said.

"Off you go then, I'll see to your tommy box and jack, and glad to do it. It will help me to get back to normal," she said with a sigh.

Bessie and Blod Bowen were among the few friends awaiting Siani on her return and they cried when they saw her thin, bedraggled appearance. Without any delay, Bessie baked next day and called with two large, crusty loaves. "Now, Siani fach, see that you have enough to eat. I'm going to keep an eye on you after all you've been through," she warned, her pink jovial face full of concern.

Siani soon found that Mag and Will followed her wherever she went, just in case she disappeared again. They were a great help in restoring a sense of purpose to her life and kept her busy. "Can we have something nice for Christmas, just to celebrate having you back home with us?" Mag asked.

Siani smiled. "What would you like, cariad?"

"Some meat and 'taters, and nuts and sweets," she reeled off, at once.

She kissed Mag saying, "You've got to wait until Christmas Day for the answer to such a tall order."

On Christmas Eve, Alys gave the kitchen a good clean, and young David went to work in the market for Mr Rowlands on his fruit stall. Ben came home in good spirits, as it was his last shift until the day after Boxing Day. Immediately, he handed over his pay packet to Siani, and her thoughts raced back to her battles with her father. Her eyes filled with tears as she said, "You're a good boy, Ben, I wish it could always have been like this."

"It's not much, Siani," he said, looking at his docket, which amounted to 15/- after stoppages for the medical fund, his lamp and tools at work.

"We'll manage; as soon as I'm strong enough I'll go back on the tips, and Alys can see to things here. We won't starve and we won't go on the parish," she said firmly.

"After I've bathed and we've had food, what about you and me going down to the market to look for a few things?" he asked, trying to encourage her.

Siani looked slightly uneasy and hesitated.

Ben read her thoughts. "You've got to face people sometime, and it's now or never if we're to have something on the table for tomorrow, so are you coming?"

"Yes, all right," she said, realising he was trying to be kind, but at the same time knowing that she dreaded meeting people.

Well wrapped up in her mother's shawl, in the hope she would not be easily recognised, she set out with Ben as soon as dusk had fallen. They went to the meat stall first, where she haggled with Mr Price about a sirloin of beef. "If you want good meat, you've got to pay for it," he said churlishly, but when he saw that she was about to turn away, he added, "I'll include a dozen of my best beef sausages at that price."

"Done," she said, and handed over a florin.

"He's a tight devil," Ben said, "you did well to get that much out of him. Let's go and see how Dave's getting on with Old Man Rowlands."

"Hello, Siani fach, how are you?" he said, greeting her warmly. "I was asking young David about you and he said you'd be calling later. He's working like a little hero and I don't know how I'd manage without him at the weekends, now that my rheumatics are so bad. What can I get you?"

Once the ice was broken, with encouragement from Ben and David, she bought potatoes, carrots, swedes and cabbage.

"What about some apples? You like nice rosy, red apples don't you?" Mr Rowlands said with a twinkle in his eye.

"Yes, we'll have two pounds, please, and that will be all, we won't be able to carry anymore," she said firmly.

Mr Rowlands put in one extra for good measure, and promised that young David would be home once he had cleaned up and the stall had closed. He squeezed her arm saying, "I'll be thinking of you tomorrow, merchi," and then he handed Ben a small sack with all their purchases so that he could sling it on his back.

On their way out, they passed a sweet stall where the gas jets flared brightly, exposing a mouth-watering display of hard-boiled sweets, trays of toffee and slabs of chocolate. She looked at them longingly.

"Go on Siani, buy a bob's worth, the little 'uns and our Dave have been looking forward to them for months," said Ben.

She hesitated, and then thought of Mag's appealing face, so she bought a pound of mixed boiled sweets, a tray of toffee and half a pound of chocolate pieces with nuts in them.

"That will be 1sh. 2d," said Rosy Jones, the stall keeper, and Siani felt guilty that she had spent so much of Ben's hard-earned money on luxuries.

He beamed with pleasurable anticipation as he hoisted his sack on his back once again. "Wait until Mag and Will see all these goodies, they won't believe their eyes," he said.

"I'm glad you came with me, Ben; now that I've made a start, it won't be so bad next time. Mind you, I had the feeling that some people were staring hard at me."

"Try not to notice them. It will be a seven day wonder and then they'll forget what happened."

She sighed, "I don't think so. Dowlais must be buzzing with gossip and I doubt if I'll ever be given a welcome in Bethania Chapel again."

Later that evening, there was a tap on the door of No. 2 Nant Row and in came the Rev. Theo Evans. Siani's eyes lit up and she quickly made room for him to sit in the oak armchair by the fire. He looked at them all affectionately in turn and said, "I had to come to see how my little family is getting on. Remember you're not orphans as long as you have me." Turning to Siani, he smiled. "Mrs Evans has sent a gift for you to share together tomorrow." On the table he placed a round package with a piece of white muslin peeping from it. "Would you like to open it?"

Carefully, she unwrapped it, and in the soft lamplight, they saw a rich, dark, fruity Christmas pudding smiling at them. There was a gasp of delight, and Siani, remembering what her mother had told her about Mrs Evans's expertise as a cook, immediately thanked him profusely. With tears in her eyes she added, "And it's because of your great kindness that I'm here tonight, Mr Evans."

"Bless you Siani, and bless you all," he said, putting his hand on their heads in turn. His presence seemed to fill the room, and before he left, he turned to Mag and Will saying, "How would you like to come to the New Year's Eve children's tea party in my chapel?"

They looked at Siani expectantly, and she smiled at Mr Evans. "I'm sure they'd love to, and perhaps they can join the Sunday School in the New Year." They clapped their hands with delight.

"Thank you, Siani. Nothing could please me more." His face lit up at such a prospect.

It was almost midnight when David came back from the market, tired out but very happy. "Mr Rowlands was in such a good mood that he sent a few extras for us," he said, placing a large brown paper bag on the table.

Ben peeped inside and saw a box of dates, a bag of nuts and half a dozen oranges. "Good old Rowlands! He's got a heart of gold," he said.

Then they watched intently as David took from his inside coat pocket a carefully wrapped bunch of delicate green mistletoe with its mysterious wax-like berries, which he now held before Siani. "Mr Rowlands sent this specially for you. He says that it's magic and that it goes back to the time of the Druids. You're supposed to hang it on a rafter near the door and wait to see what happens."

She smiled. "He's a real old wag! He's making it all up, but he means well. Perhaps, if I hang it by the door, it will keep out evil spirits." David shook his head but was too tired to argue; he climbed upstairs to bed and dreamt of oranges and mistletoe.

Next morning, Mrs Bowen and Blod called, "Nadolig llawen pawb!" (Happy Christmas to all!) they chorused. "I've brought you a loaf of my best yeast cake," Mrs Bowen said, putting the rich, brown fruitcake on the table.

Siani bent over it, taking in its appetising smell, before she turned to her saying, "How can I ever thank you for all you've done for us?" She gave Mrs Bowen a big hug and tears rolled down her cheeks.

Blod, meanwhile, had spotted the mistletoe. "Aha! And who are you going to catch under the mistletoe?" she asked.

David looked at her, his big brown eyes full of trust and innocence, "Mr Rowlands sent it up for Siani. He says it works like magic."

"Wait 'til I see him, I'll give him magic, I could do with some of that myself," she said with a hearty laugh.

They satisfied themselves that Siani was able to prepare dinner for the family, and then went home to see to their own. Siani put the sirloin of beef in the oven early so that it would cook slowly. It was rare for her to have a joint of this size and she wanted it cooked to perfection. Alys was given the task of cleaning the carrots, potatoes and swede, while Siani cut up the cabbage. Mrs Evans's Christmas pudding was steaming in a saucepan on the hob and all was going well.

To work up their appetite, Ben and David took the youngsters for a walk as far as the ponds. "It will be good for them, otherwise they'll only eat too many sweets," Siani said, but warned them to come back by half-past twelve.

Siani had brought out the plates and dishes and the food was almost ready when there was a knock on the door at mid-day. "Drat it! Who can that be?" she said impatiently. She opened the door and there stood Lewsyn, shifting awkwardly from one foot to the other.

"Hello Siani! I've called to wish you a happy Christmas and I've brought something for Will and Mag," he said.

"Come in, Lewsyn, they've gone for a walk but they should be home at any moment because the dinner is nearly ready."

"It smells good, Siani, and I'm sure you'll enjoy it. I'll leave this bag on the chest and I'll call later to see how they've got on."

She thanked him and followed him to the door where he turned suddenly and bent down to kiss her under the mistletoe. She blushed furiously and as he left she called after him, "Lewsyn Jones, you're the limit!"

He smiled at her mischievously and said to himself, "Our first kiss, and on Christmas Day too."

Ben polished his plate clean and put his knife and fork down with a clatter. "That was fit for the queen," he said.

David said, "I agree. Our Siani is as good a cook as Mam was."

"It's pudding next," Alys said as she helped Siani to clear the plates and dishes.

"You'll have to wait a few minutes while I make some white sauce to go with it," Siani explained.

"Meat, 'taters and Christmas pudding!" said Mag contentedly. "I wish it was Christmas everyday."

Alys brought it to the table and Siani cut it evenly into eight pieces. She shared it out on their plates and poured the sweet white sauce over it before passing it to them.

"This is delicious," said Alys who munched her way through the cherries, nuts, currants and raisins and scraped her plate absolutely clean.

"Would you like some more?" asked Siani, looking at the left-overs.

"Yes please," chorused Mag and Alys.

"Let them have it, girls like sweet things," said Ben jovially.

"I've got something hard in mine," Mag exclaimed, revealing a silver three-penny bit which glinted in the firelight.

"You lucky girl! Make a wish!" said Alys, immediately.

She hesitated, then said, "I wish that Siani can stay with us always."

The expression on Mag's face went straight to Siani's heart and she buried her face in her hands and sobbed. Visions of her mother, father and the hateful gaol flashed through her mind and she shuddered.

"What is it? Have I said something wrong?" Mag asked, utterly bewildered.

"It's not you, Mag fach, it's everything that has happened to us this year," she sobbed, and she looked at the empty seats at the table.

Ben could understand her feelings. "Have a good cry, Siani. It will make you feel better, and let's hope the New Year will bring us good luck all round," he said, putting his arm around her pathetically thin shoulders to comfort her.

"You can have my three-penny bit to bring you luck," said Mag, pressing it into Siani's hand.

"I'll put it in a safe place for you, cariad," Siani sobbed, and she leaned over to give her a kiss.

*   *   *

Will lay fast asleep on Siani's lap, while the boys sat by the table reading and talking quietly. Peace and order prevailed and Siani heaved a sigh of relief that her ordeal was over. "After today, I hope that I'll gradually get better. I must, because I'll have to start work in the New Year on the tips with our David," she reminded herself.

The trial and her unmentionable experiences in Cardiff prison had totally undermined her self-confidence, but she hoped that once she got used to facing people, her fighting spirit would gradually return.

Will stirred in his sleep and opened his eyes. Mag espied him and called out, "What's in the bag on the dresser, Will? Do you want to have a look?"

He slid off Siani's lap and waited for Mag to bring it to the table where Ben and David were seated. "Here, let me help you," said Ben, and took two large, brown hairy coconuts out of the bag. They looked bemused and were uncertain what to do or say. "Shake them and listen," said Ben, and they heard the soft lapping of the liquid inside.

"They're a present from Lewsyn who called this morning while you were out," Siani explained. "There's one each for you."

They were still uncertain what to do with them, and Mag was all for cracking hers open with a poker, until Siani said, "Wait for Lewsyn to come, he'll show you what to do."

Darkness had fallen when he eventually arrived and he was waylaid at once by Will and Mag. "Thank you for the coconuts. Will you show us how to open them?" asked Mag eagerly.

After chatting about the day's events, he gave way to Will's insistent tugging at his sleeve, and seated himself at the table with the youngsters on either side of him. He took out his pocketknife, held one of the nuts in his left hand and said, "Now I'm going to give you all a little surprise." Carefully, he pierced a hole in the top of the shell and scraped it so that there was a neat suction point. He shook it and held it to Will's ear saying, "Can you hear the sweet, creamy milk lapping inside? Would you like to taste it?"

"Please Lewsyn," Will said, his eyes wide with delight at the prospect. He held out his hands, and guided by Lewsyn, he raised the coconut to his lips and sipped the milk ecstatically.

"My turn next," Mag pleaded, and she in turn drained it. "That was lovely," she said, smacking her lips.

Siani watched the scene at the table and noticed how gentle he was with them. They were entranced as they watched him cut the coconut in half and scoop out the luscious flesh, which he cut in pieces on the table. "You can all have a taste now," he said as they gathered around him. Soon they were munching it happily, delighting in its exotic flavour. He smiled, "It's come from across the world, where palm-fringed beaches and miles of golden sand are lapped by deep blue seas, sparkling in golden sunshine," he said. Seeing the look of wonder on Siani's face, he added, "Perhaps you'll see them one day."

She smiled at such an impossible thought and then realised that Lewsyn could make life seem so exciting and full of promise. She watched him working skilfully with his penknife on the shells which he then placed together and threaded with string.

"Have you got a piece of candle?" he asked. When he had lit it, he placed it in the base of the shell, replaced the top and held it by its string; he turned it to face them and they saw the eyes, mouth and features of a man. There were hoots of delight and Will clapped his hands and jumped with joy.

"Let's do the other one," said Mag, eager for a repeat performance.

"I'll put this first one on the mantlepiece in case of accidents," said Ben.

This time, they all had a sip of the delicate milk, and waited for their share of the flesh from the inside. The second shell was given an upward tilt around the eyes and lips, and the thick tuft of hair was bushed out. After another candle stump had been lit and put inside, it took its place alongside the first one on the mantlepiece. They stood back to admire Lewsyn's handiwork with pride, amazed by his ingenuity.

"What are you going to call yours?" he asked Will.

"Lewsyn", he gurgled.

"And what about yours Mag?"

"Siani," she said, pointing to the hair, and they all fell about laughing.

"Oh, it's good to hear laughter in this house again," Ben said.

And David added quietly, "It's the magic at work."

Chapter 15
1874

"It's back to work for us tomorrow," said Siani as she prepared the tommy boxes and jacks. "I'll be coming with you, Dave, and Alys will see to things at home."

"Are you sure you're ready for it? It's perishing cold out there," David warned.

"I've got to make a start sometime, and the sooner the better. If anyone tries to provoke me, or get me into trouble, I'm going to ignore them, and I want you to do the same, Dave."

"I'll stand by you, you know that," he said, secretly pleased with the prospect of having Siani's company.

"Blod has promised to help me, so with luck, I should get by." Siani tried to sound cheerful, but secretly was worried about the hostile reception she might have from some of the tip girls.

Early next morning, she presented herself at the Works Office and asked Johnny Davies, the clerk, if she could start work again. Johnny was a friend of Lewsyn's, and when he saw her, he gave her a special welcome.

"Yes, of course you can re-start. We're in need of tippers now that the Works are going full blast once more. I'll put your name down on the wages list with David."

"Thanks Johnny," she said, giving him a radiant smile before she went off in the direction of the tips.

She and David climbed the precipitous slopes to get to the tipping sites where work was already in full swing. Jem Jones's jaw dropped when she saw Siani approach, she glared at her, leaned on her shovel then called to the others, "Look what we've got here girls, the gaol-bird is back." With her lip curling, she shouted after Siani, "Have you brought your poker with you?"

Siani marched defiantly ahead without saying a word, and turned to Blod who was at the head of the line of trams. "Where can David and I make a start?"

"Right here in front of me and if any one of those creatures tries to raise a finger to you, they'll have to get past me first," she warned, loud enough for all to hear.

"Thank you, Blod, I may be a bit slow today, but I'll soon get back into my stride," she said as she started shovelling.

She and David ate their bread and cheese with relish during the short mid-day break. By three o'clock the light began to fade and Blod called out, "Time to finish now."

"That's ten trams we've emptied today," said David, pleased as punch, "but I bet you'll be stiff tomorrow, Siani, after all this work."

"As long as it brings in the money, I don't care, I never want to be on the starvation line again," she sighed.

With Blod at their side, they plodded their weary way home. "I'm going to choir practice tonight, want to come?" she asked.

"No chance. If I showed my face, the roof of Bethania Chapel would fall in."

"Wait for a while. Once life gets back to normal, it would be good for you," Blod said, trying to reassure her.

That she survived the harshness of the winter, Siani believed was due to the good food she was now able to afford. The heat from the cinders and iron-stone clinker which she and David shovelled from the trams also helped to keep them warm. Gradually, she lost her prison pallor, she became weather-beaten and grew stronger.

Bessie Bowen was pleased with Siani's progress and she also tried to persuade her to join the famous Temperance Choir in their chapel. "My Uncle Abe needs sweet, young sopranos, and I've been telling him that you like music, so why don't you join?"

Siani looked embarrassed and confessed that she was afraid of the reception she might have. "Some of the members would cut me dead, and besides, I have enough to do at home," she said.

"Think about it, and remember that you owe a great deal to Bethania Chapel," Bessie Bowen said.

Siani blushed. "I owe my life to them, or at least to people like you and Mr Evans, but it's the others who worry me."

"Who do you mean?"

"Lewsyn's family for a start."

"Mari Jones has always been a vicious gossip, but I'll soon put her in her place, and so will Mr Evans. Our Blod would look after you, and so would Lewsyn, I'm sure."

"I'll think about it, Mrs Bowen."

A few days later, the Rev. Theo Evans called. He mentioned how pleased he was that Mag and Will now attended Sunday School. "I would be even more pleased to see you coming back to Bethania," he said, looking at Siani.

She lowered her head, stared at her rough hands and her shabby clothes, then gave him an agonised look.

"How can I, Mr Evans? I've thought about it, but everything seems to be against me making an attempt."

"That's what you think, but you won't know until you try. Your case was fought to prove your innocence and to clear your name. I want you to have a better life, Siani, and to set an example to others."

Alys, who had been listening to the conversation, suddenly intervened. "That's right, listen to Mr Evans. I only wish I was well enough, I'd come with you."

Siani was shocked by her outburst and Mr Evans smiled at Alys for giving him such strong support. He got to his feet and putting his hand on Siani's shoulder said, "Come with Blod to the next rehearsal of the Temperance Choir, I'll keep a special look-out for you."

* * *

Siani stared at herself in the murky mirror in the bedroom and then adjusted the collar of her white blouse which Blod had loaned her. She tightened the waistband of her long black skirt and began to feel a little more comfortable. Her newly-washed hair fell around her shoulders but somehow felt untidy. On impulse, she seized some hairpins which had belonged to her mother, and piled her hair on top of her head in a bun. The effect was dramatic: from being a young girl, she suddenly became a young woman. Her graceful, swan-like neck could now be seen to advantage and her features were more sharply focussed. Then she stepped into her best, black, Sunday shoes and slipped out quietly into the kitchen, ready to leave.

Alys gasped when she saw her. "Oh you look beautiful! You've put your hair up and you look grown-up!" she said, full of excitement. "Wait 'til Blod comes, she'll be pleased." Siani carefully wrapped her mother's black woollen shawl around herself and waited for Blod to call.

There was quite a stir in Bethania Chapel when they arrived that Monday evening, and various nods and gestures were exchanged by girls in the choir. Blod immediately took Siani to meet Abraham Bowen, the conductor, who was in the big seat setting out his music scores. "Welcome, my dear, you've come at just the right time, because we're preparing for our Easter Festival. I'm told you have a light, soprano voice, so you can stand by Blodwen near the front of the gallery where I can hear you."

Siani would have preferred to have been hidden at the back, but she went with Blod as directed. Just as they turned to leave the big seat, she became aware of the Rev. Theo Evans looking at her; he smiled and gave her a nod of approval. She blushed furiously, and followed Blod quickly up the stairs onto the gallery. For a while, she sat in silence looking down at the big seat and recalled painfully that the last time she had been there was for her mother's funeral. She felt a sudden urge to run away, and would have done but for Blod's arm firmly linked through hers.

The massive pipe-organ began to play and it soon filled the large, impressive chapel with it glorious sound. "Jack Hughes is warming up. He usually plays the organ for a few minutes before we start our practice," said Blod.

By this time, both galleries were full to capacity with young men and women eager and ready to sing. Siani began to think that her mother would have been pleased to see her in their midst and decided that she would try to follow in her footsteps. These thoughts were interrupted by a sharp tapping by Abraham Bowen who called for their attention by beating his baton on the music stand before him.

Gradually she became mesmerised by his dynamic personality and by his acrobatics as a conductor. She found herself carried along in the tide of enthusiasm he engendered, and in a short time she had learnt the rallying cry of the Temperance cause:

"We are Temperance children,
Dwelling midst the hills,
Working for our Master
Doing all his wills.
To make the people sober
Is our one great aim,
We are always anxious
Drunkards to reclaim."

She felt a chill run down her spine when she came to the last line, and she thought of her father; then she remembered the suffering and agony her family had endured and she sang with greater gusto for the Temperance cause.

The choir continued their practice with some Welsh hymns from 'Telyn Seion' which had been compiled by the famous Merthyr Tydfil musician, Rosser Beynon. It contained a hundred and thirty hymns as well as twenty-two anthems! Siani marvelled at Mr Bowen's ability to get the sopranos, altos, tenors and bass to sing together in rich harmony. He was a perfectionist and would not give up until the rendering was to his complete satisfaction. Her heart was stirred and her soul was uplifted by their singing, which took her far beyond the slings and arrows of misfortune which had blighted her short life.

Lewsyn Jones, seated on the opposite gallery, watched her closely and was certainly impressed. "What a transformation in a girl!" he said to himself, "I must have a word with her afterwards."

Flushed with the effort of singing and excited by this experience, at the end of the practice Siani felt glad she had found the courage to join the choir. Though she would not say so, she was already looking forward to the next practice.

"You've done well," said Blod, linking arms with her again. "I could see Uncle Abe and Mr Evans watching you, and I'm sure they were pleased."

"Thanks, Blod, I enjoyed it, and you've been a great support. I'd never have come without you," she said as they made their way down the steep stairs. They went out through the lobby and after a few cursory remarks with one of the deacons, they joined the throng outside in North Street.

"Hello, Siani," said a resonant baritone voice behind her. She turned, and in the glare from the nearby furnaces, she saw the smiling face of Lewsyn Jones. She felt her heart miss a beat. "Are you going to join the choir and come regular?" he asked.

"I don't know yet," she stammered.

"Of course she is, Uncle Abe and Mr Evans want her to," Blod said protectively.

They turned to go up North Street, and Lewsyn, anxious to know more about her intentions, accompanied them. On their way home, they both talked to her with animation about the Easter Festival, and Siani began to feel that, at last, she was once again part of life in Dowlais.

Lewsyn made an excuse that he wanted to see young Will, and he entered the kitchen of 2 Nant Row with her. He found the youngsters ready for bed, but they soon made a beeline for him. He chatted with them and listened to Siani giving a full, animated account of the choir practice to Alys. "By the sound of her, she's quite taken with the idea," he thought, and immediately decided that not only would it be good for her, but good for him too. "I'll have a better chance to see her more often, and maybe walk her home."

A week before Easter, the Rev. Theo Evans took Siani aside. "I'd like to mention you in my sermon at the Easter Festival. You won't mind, will you, my dear?" She looked slightly uneasy, but he continued, "I think the time is right and I hope you'll trust my judgement."

"Yes Mr Evans," she said, putting her faith and trust in him.

Easter Monday dawned crisp and clear, and in the afternoon, Siani joined the big parade of Temperance supporters and marched behind their banner all the way from Dowlais Top to Bethania Chapel. She was now committed to the cause, and when she saw how the interior of the chapel had been transformed for this special event, she was overjoyed. A large blue and white satin banner edged with gold fringe had been hung behind the impressive pulpit and carried the inscription 'Baner Dirwestol' (Temperance Banner) in gold, with the words 'For Christ, Home and Neighbour' printed below. She thought she had never seen anything so beautiful.

Seated alongside Blod on the balcony, she could see that the chapel was now packed from floor to ceiling.

Stewards were busy giving out leaflets of special hymns chosen by Abraham Bowen for the occasion; deacons in the big seat wore their Temperance regalia and badges of Office; the Temperance Choir sat men and boys on one balcony, women and girls on the other. Siani could feel the excitement and sense of expectation emanating from the congregation who awaited the rallying cry from their leader.

Mr Evans, seated in the pulpit, seemed deep in thought, until he got up to announce the first hymn. The organ boomed out the tune, and Abraham Bowen went into action leading and exhorting the choir and congregation in their singing of 'Mi wn fod fy mhrynwr yn fyw.' (I know that my Saviour lives).

Siani could feel her spine tingling as the singing rose to a mighty crescendo and then died back to the doleful minor key. Tears flowed down her cheeks uncontrollably, and from the opposite balcony Lewsyn could see how moved she was. When they repeated the final verse, he too could feel a lump in his throat, and wished he could be alongside Siani to comfort her.

A hush came over the congregation when the Reverend Theophilus Evans got up to deliver his sermon. He looked around his large congregation, drew himself up to his full height, then slowly and deliberately announced his theme. "Drunkenness produces poverty and promotes sin. In no place is this more evident than in Dowlais, Merthyr Tydfil." His deep, resonant voice rang around the chapel as he announced it yet again.

Siani could feel her heart thumping as he warmed to his subject and he declared, "In spite of all the hardship of recent years, the consumption of alcohol has increased, and the numbers convicted of drunkenness have reached a peak. He pounded the big, black Bible before him and proclaimed, "There are now two hundred and seventy one public houses and 'kiddliwinks' (beer houses) in Dowlais alone!"

She lowered her head as he continued with mounting indignation, "When you pass in the night, you hear the tuning of the harp in preparation for hours of dissipation. And while the drunkards of Dowlais slake their thirsts and wallow in sin, what is happening to their wives and children?" he cried. "They suffer in silence," he murmured, "They suffer in body, mind and spirit!" he thundered. Some of the younger girls in the front row of the choir almost jumped out of their seats with fright, and the sense of revulsion amongst the congregation was almost tangible.

With dramatic suddenness, he turned to Siani, and all eyes followed him. "We have with us today, a young woman who was almost martyred on the altar of drink. I consider it one of the greatest achievements of my life, that I was able, with your help, to rescue her from the jaws of death."

There were audible gasps and responses from the congregation. "Ie'n wir," (Yes indeed) said the senior deacon in the big seat. Siani's head sank lower on to her chest, tears coursed down her cheeks and she could scarcely breathe. "Let Siani Davies's suffering be an example to you all of the consequences of the demon drink."

Siani heard no more after that; her brain ceased to function and she felt faint. Blod put her arm around her to comfort and support her, and the next thing she remembered was the organ booming out the anthem of the Temperance cause.

The choir was singing fervently,
"Come and join our noble army,
Be ye soldiers brave and hardy."

She noticed that a long line of men and women were standing in the aisles downstairs, waiting to go forward to the big seat to sign the pledge. She was lost in wonder, and when at last Mr Evans raised his head and invited her to come forward, she responded with help from Blod, and proudly signed her name. Lewsyn's eyes followed her and glistened with admiration when Mr Evans put his arm around her shoulders and presented her to his congregation. "What courage!" he thought, "What faith!"

Chapter 16

Lewsyn waited anxiously for Siani to emerge from the chapel. When she did so, Blod Bowen was at her side. He noticed how flushed she was, that her eyes shone like stars, and that she was elated.

He waited until they were alongside him then asked, "How are you feeling now, Siani?"

"As though I'm walking on air, I had no idea Mr Evans would make such a fuss of me."

"You've certainly made your mark in Bethania, and no one will dare say a word against you after this," Lewsyn said, looking at her with pride and admiration.

"Let's go and have tea in the vestry, I think we all deserve it," said Blod, leading the way.

The members of the chapel Sisterhood, who were in full charge of refreshments, soon found a place for Siani and Blod. Bessie Bowen hugged and kissed her saying, "Over a hundred people signed the pledge today, thanks to your appearance and Mr Evans's sermon."

"There you are Siani, what did I tell you?" said Lewsyn. At that moment Mari Jones's shrill voice intruded calling him to have food at her table. "I'd better go, I'll see you in choir practice," he murmured, "my mother's on the warpath."

Siani raised her eyes and saw Mari Jones glaring at her. "The Rev. Theo Evans will have to preach more than one sermon to convince that woman of my innocence," she thought.

From the other side of the vestry, Lewsyn watched with longing every move and gesture Siani made and wished he could be close to her, that he could take her home and protect her. Spring was in the air, which made him restless, so he decided that he would have to spruce himself up before the next big event in Bethania Chapel and that he would buy a new suit. Both he and his father were now working in iron and earning good money.

He announced his decision to his mother and father that evening. "Now that there's plenty of work to be had, I've decided to order a suit with Mr Thomas, the tailor, a nice, dark grey one."

"Oh yes, and how are you going to pay for it?" Mari asked.

"I'm going to join his club and I'll pay two shillings a week."

"You'd be better off saving it, I can easily turn your other one and lengthen it for you."

"No Mam, my mind's made up, that one will come for second best."

Llew Jones listened to the argument and turned to his wife. "Let the boy have his way, he works hard and he's grown out of the one he's wearing now. It's time enough for him to save his money when he's our age."

"Thanks Dad, I knew you'd understand. I'll work overtime whenever I can to pay for it, and I'll see you won't go short of money for my keep, Mam," he assured her.

* * *

The anthem, which the Temperance Choir was busy rehearsing for the Whitsun Singing Festival, was 'Gwyn ei fyd,' by Owain Alaw. It taxed them to their limits because of all its high notes, which Siani could sing like a song-bird.

"Come into the front row my dear," said Abraham Bowen, "I'd like you to be heard."

Whitsun Monday was warm and sunny and Lewsyn turned out in his new, grey flannel suit. His mother had starched his white shirt until it was like a board, his grey tie was knotted around his neck and his black boots shone like glass. Mari Jones admitted to herself that he did look smart.

The chapel was full from floor to ceiling by the time he arrived, and after a slight commotion, he took his usual seat among the baritones. Blod nudged Siani, "Look at Lewsyn, he's dressed to kill," she said, trying to suppress a giggle.

Though the doors and windows were open, the atmosphere in the chapel soon became stifling. Abe Bowen mopped his brow between the hymns and Lewsyn began to wish that his mother had not made the collar of his shirt so stiff. Siani's face was suffused with a pink glow and she opened the top button of her blouse to try to cool off a little. Lewsyn spotted it and wished he could kiss that beautiful neck. They sang with such fervour that they forgot the troubles and drabness of this world, and were soon transported into realms of sheer delight, which promised them a better life to come.

Tea was served in the vestry during the interval and having cooled off a little outside while talking to his friends, Lewsyn decided to go in search of Siani. She was enjoying a piece of Mrs Bowen's seed cake with a cup of tea.

"Is Mrs Bowen looking after you?" he asked, looking with envy at the plates of currant bread, Welsh cakes and cherry cake on the table.

"Not cadging are you, Lewsyn Jones?" asked Bessie, eyeing him up and down. "Done up like a dog's dinner you are today," she added.

Siani and Blod tried to stifle their giggles until in the end, Mrs Bowen relented and said, "Sit down, my boy, have a piece of my 'teisen lap' and a cup of tea to revive you."

They all collapsed into laughter and Lewsyn finally managed to undo his shirt collar and joined in the fun.

"Don't take any notice of my Mam, you're looking very smart," said Blod, trying to be serious, "I'll go to the urn myself to get you a nice cup of tea."

Flushed and happy, Siani's eyes shone as she looked up at him. His heart missed a beat and he whispered to her, "Can I walk you home tonight after the Cymanfa?"

With a smile on her lips, she nodded agreement and Lewsyn squeezed her hand beneath the table. He felt so elated that nothing could rattle him, not even the black looks directed at him by his mother. He sang lustily in the second half and took the difficult runs and cadences in the anthem with ease.

He was one of the first out of the chapel at the end of the singing. Siani, who had to do some explaining to Blod, came out a little later and joined him before they started their walk up High Street. It was a calm, warm evening and they went in the direction of the ponds overlooking Dowlais. The setting sun cast a glow over the scene, which was accentuated by reflected light from the furnaces. They lingered for a while watching the great orb dip below the ridge of the hills. He took Siani's hand and said quietly, "Does the peace and tranquillity of this moment make you feel better?"

She nodded and smiled. "At last, I'm beginning to feel that it's good to be alive," she murmured.

"Let's meet tomorrow night by the stile, and we'll go for a walk towards the new reservoir."

"All right," she said softly, and he kissed her gently on her lips.

* * *

In the cool of the evening, they wended their way towards Pantysgallog and saw the sharp silhouette of Penyfan in the distance. Overhead, skylarks poured out their song in the clear, pure air. Lewsyn looked at Siani closely and said, "The colour is coming back into your cheeks, we should come out more often."

He took her hand to help her climb a steep bank, which led through a grove of white hawthorn blossom and silver birch saplings in early leaf. He stopped, as nearby he heard a blackbird sing, "Listen Siani, he's singing to his mate," he said, and he gently took her hand to his lips.

They continued their climb to the top of the ridge through fresh, green ferns and tender, tufted winberry bushes. Below, they saw the Taff Fechan valley in a deep ravine, and in the distance, glistening in the setting sun was the massive reservoir. "I never dreamt it could be so beautiful," she said to Lewsyn.

He put his arm around her and held her to him. "Another magic moment for us both," he said. He looked into her eyes, then added, "I want to make up for everything that's happened to you, Siani. Will you let me do that?"

She buried her face on his shoulder and stifled a sob. "There's still a lot of pain left inside me, Lew, but I'm glad I joined the choir and I'm glad you are my friend.

They had been walking out together for three months when Llewelyn Jones decided to speak to Lewsyn. "You're eighteen now, my boy, and your mother tells me that you're courting Siani Davies," he said, looking slightly embarrassed.

Lewsyn wondered what was coming next, while his father coughed and searched for his words before coming to the point. "Aren't there any other girls in the choir who take your fancy? I mean nice girls who would know how to run a home properly."

Lewsyn could feel his temper rising, for he resented his father's insinuation that Siani was in some way inferior. "What do you mean Dad? Are you saying that Siani isn't good enough for me?" he gasped.

Well, apart from all that's happened, she's still working on the tips, and your mother says that such girls don't make good wives and mothers."

Lewsyn exploded. "Damn it all, Dad, she can't help that she has to work like a slave out there in all weathers. She's got a consumptive sister and she's struggling to keep the family out of debt. Is that what you've got against her?"

"Don't raise your voice to me, my boy. Your mother and I are just warning you for your own good," Llew said sharply.

Lewsyn realised that it was his mother who was making trouble for him, so he continued, "Why doesn't Mam bring up the matter of her trial as well, because that's what lies behind all this? Siani was *innocent*, more sinned against than sinning, and just remember what the Rev. Theo Evans had to say about her."

"Try to understand, Lewsyn, that your mother and I have a duty to protect you and to do our best for you."

"You can tell Mam, that I don't need your protection against Siani. I love her, I think she's the best and most beautiful girl in Dowlais, and I'd be proud to have her as my wife," he said, his eyes ablaze.

Chapter 17
1874

After a long winter of convalescence and cosseting, Lucy was feeling much better. George Williams was relieved, because the last thing he wanted was for her to become an invalid. He continued to hope that she would make a complete recovery, and in due course would be able to bear him a son.

"I've asked Dr White about taking you away for a change of air and he's advised us to wait until Whitsun. The weather will have warmed up by then. Where would you like to go dearest?" he asked.

She smiled at him and without hesitation she said, "Llandrindod Wells."

George smiled and teased her, saying "Another honeymoon?"

"Oh, yes," she said with more enthusiasm than George could ever have hoped for. Though she was gentle and fragile, Lucy had a will of her own and George had no doubt that she now realised the importance of producing a son and heir.

They made their preparations, and this time she was even more profligate with George's money. Blouses, skirts, dresses, jackets, hats, shoes and fine wool mantles, filled her large portmanteau. He did not care as long as she was happy, and he himself looked forward to getting away from the grinding work of the balance sheets and ledgers which underlay the Dowlais Company's financial stability.

Their suite was the best in The Pump House Hotel and Uncle William had written to the proprietor to ensure that they were placed in the lap of luxury. When they arrived, they found their sitting room had been decorated with roses and orange blossom and a magnum of champagne had been put on ice. George considered that Uncle William had been very generous in ordering that their account should be sent to him. Their accommodation, including the taking of saline waters and the services of a chambermaid, amounted to £2-16-0 a week, and a room for Lucy's personal maid cost £1-1-0!

This time, Lucy was more zealous than ever in taking the waters, which was a good sign, so George thought. Some days she drank as many as five glasses and confided in George that Dr White believed that the sulphur in the water would be excellent for her blood.

Her elegant clothes and delicate beauty did not go unnoticed, and they soon had a large circle of acquaintances, including a cabinet minister and his wife. It pleased George that she had once more regained her vitality and confidence, that she enjoyed the lavish balls, and danced until well into the night without any ill effect. Life had become sweet again.

They returned to Dowlais at the end of June, rejuvenated, and once more Lucy bubbled with enthusiasm to her parents about the benefits of taking the waters saying how much better she felt. Her high spirits moved Uncle William to decide to take a break himself.

"I think I'll go there for a couple of weeks in the Autumn. My gout has been playing up and it's time I had a rest," he said wearily.

"Go with my Mama and Papa, they love it in the Autumn when the colours of the trees around the boating lake are at their best," said Lucy excitedly.

"George can hold the fort here for a couple of weeks, I daresay, but at the rate at which trouble is brewing, it will soon be a case of manning it against the bunch of agitators who are getting ready for another fight. We'll be ready for them this time!" He gave George a knowing look, which signified that he had further important news for him.

Later that week, Uncle William called George into his office and told him of a scheme that was being devised by the Employers' Association whereby wages would fluctuate in accordance with the price of coal in the market place. "If we can get this adopted, it may help in avoiding strikes in future." he said, then added that they had an excellent leader in Lucy's relative, W.T. Lewis of Mardy House, Aberdare.

"Will the men agree to such a scheme?" George asked anxiously.

"They will eventually, but they'll have to be beaten into submission," Uncle William said grimly. George nodded agreement.

It was early in September that Lucy began to lose her colour and went off her food. At first, she blamed the heat and the foul air of Dowlais, and then admitted to George that she might be pregnant. He was delighted and could hardly contain himself at the prospect of becoming a father, but recent experience taught him to be cautious.

"You must see Dr White as soon as possible and take great care of yourself," he emphasised. Secretly, he was worried, for with Uncle William now away, once more he had greater responsibility and more work thrust upon him. So he decided to speak to Lud White in confidence about his wife.

"For God's sake, look after Lucy, even if it means keeping her in bed most of the time, I don't want anything to go wrong this time," he emphasised.

"I'll do my best. I think she herself now realises how much a child means to you both," he admitted. "I'll be as firm as I can with her."

Lucy's nausea took its toll and once again she began to look drained. When Uncle William returned in robust health from his holiday at Llandrindod Wells, he commented upon the change in her. "Is she pregnant?" he asked in his usual forthright manner.

George was happy to reassure him that she was, and that Lud White was going to keep watch over her.

"She couldn't be in better hands," Uncle William agreed.

Lucy was waited upon hand, foot and finger, and George steadfastly refused all invitations to dine with their friends. "I don't want you to get upset or over-excited, I want you to lead a quiet life," he told her firmly.

"But I find it so boring on my own for most of the day," she protested. "I've read so many novels that I've lost count and my eyes ache."

He took no notice because he had other problems to think about. His work was becoming ever more stressful due to narrowing profit-margins, and the unwillingness of the men to consider a further wage cut. "Life can be very hard," he moaned, as he poured over balance sheets and ledgers for hours on end, while Uncle William urged him to find places where economies could be made.

By mid November, Dr White was satisfied that Lucy was out of danger and gave way to her insistent demand that she should be allowed to go out and socialise a little in the run-up to Christmas.

"I'm not a hot-house plant, and if I can't go out, I'm sure I'll have an attack of the vapours," she told George finally.

To placate her he agreed to tea parties only, "No dinner parties," he warned. It pleased her that once again she could entertain her friends and be entertained at their homes. She was so happy she began to plan a nursery and made up her mind that she would order a layette from Mr Morgan's store in Cardiff. "Only the best will do," she said to George, who agreed absolutely, while cautioning her to ask her mother to accompany her.

With the approach of Christmas, she decided to go to Cardiff with her mother. Everything went well, and they travelled back to Merthyr Tydfil brimming with self-satisfaction. Not only had they purchased many handsome gifts, but most important of all, the order had been placed for the new layette. Lucy was overjoyed at the prospect. "Your Dada and I have decided that the layette will be our present to the baby" her mother had said.

George could hardly disguise his pleasure when she gave him her news on her return. "At last things are working out well for us, but no more outings before Christmas, dearest, I want you to take life easy," he said, enfolding her in his arms.

All was not well at work, where the announcement of a 10% reduction in wages, due to the falling price of coal, drove the men into a frenzy of trade union activity. George noticed that whenever he appeared, men stopped talking, or muttered to each other behind their hands and avoided eye contact with him. The atmosphere was poisonous, but the zeal and determination which Uncle William demanded of him, enabled him to rise above such pettiness and he pursued his duties in the Wages Office more rigorously than ever.

"He's a Company man to his finger-tips," Johnny Davies, one of the clerks, commented, after George peremptorily issued discharge notices to workers who went on an unofficial strike while negotiations were taking place. "There's nothing left for them now but the parish," he commented, and believed that his boss had no idea of the hardship caused.

Later that week, George's preoccupation with his work was rudely shaken when a maid was sent from Caeharris House to the Wages Office with an urgent message for him to come home. "The mistress is ill again, sir, she's asking for you," the girl said breathlessly, having run all the way to the office.

He did not wait for any further explanation, but left immediately, calling to the Chief Clerk, "You're in charge here until I come back." "Girl, run across to Dr White's surgery and ask him to come at once," he barked, before he jumped on his horse and rode home.

He found Lucy lying on the bed, groaning loudly in circumstances almost identical with her previous miscarriage. He paced the floor utterly distracted, and when Dr White arrived, he rushed downstairs and begged him, "For God's sake, Lud, try to save the baby this time." He poured himself a large whisky, offered up a silent prayer and waited anxiously.

It was about an hour later that the doctor emerged saying, "It's bad news, I'm afraid, she's miscarried. I did my best but it was a hopeless case."

George buried his face in his hands and wept. "I don't understand it," he groaned, "she's had the best possible care and yet this happens."

"There's something about her case that perplexes me," Dr White admitted, "the excessive blood loss for one thing. Would you like me to have a second opinion."

"Do whatever is necessary. My first concern is Lucy's health, but I **would** like to have children, Lud."

"You'd better go to her, she's very distressed," the doctor warned. "I know it's hard for both of you, but it's a situation that has to be faced."

George felt a wave of despair sweep over him as he climbed the stairs. He knew that Lucy would be as disappointed as he was, but he felt it his duty to console her and give hope. She lay prone on the bed, unable to look at him, so he took her hand gently and put it to his lips. Her sobbing increased, as he got down on his knees and turned her to face him. "Dr White is going to help us both. He's going to bring another doctor to see you to find out why this happens. Rest now, my darling, and we'll talk later," he said, kissing her hand and doing his best to comfort her.

He stumbled blindly out of the house in the direction of the Works Office where he had to see his Uncle William. He felt like a man in a trance and dreaded breaking the news to him.

"It's another body-blow, George, I'm sorry for you both and bitterly disappointed myself. We'll await the outcome of this other medical opinion," he said tersely. "Go home to Lucy, she needs you, we'll discuss our proposed strategy for dealing with the forthcoming strike some other time."

George left a message for the chief Wages Clerk that he would be out of the office for several days for personal reasons. Lucy remained in bed and Dr White's anxiety increased. "The fact that she's still bleeding worries me, George. I've sent an express letter to Dr David Roberts in Cardiff who specialises in problems relating to births. Since she can't be moved, I've asked him to travel up as soon as possible."

"Whatever you say, Lud, regardless of expense," said George, who was worried out of his mind, but he tried not to show Lucy or anyone else.

The consultation was a lengthy one, the outcome being that Dr Roberts decided to give her digitalis to staunch the bleeding. "It will have to be carefully controlled, but it's worth trying," he said.

George thought he seemed remote and uncommunicative, but he was prepared to put up with that as long as he could help Lucy. By the time of his next visit she seemed to have improved, though she was still weak. Again, he gave her a thorough examination and conferred with Dr White. They looked grave when they called George to the bedroom to hear their diagnosis.

"Mrs Williams," Dr Roberts began, "you'll always have to be careful about your health, I'm putting you on a special diet to overcome your chronic anaemia. I think you have a blood disorder which may make it impossible for you to sustain full-term pregnancies, and even if you could, there may well be further problems."

George and Lucy looked at each other aghast. "Are you sure of that?" George asked, visibly shaken by his blunt, insensitive approach.

"As sure as I can be of anything. I've encountered other cases similar to this one where it has been so," he said brusquely. "Dr White will explain more fully the risks involved," he said, and then they both left the room.

George saw them out and returned to Lucy who was in floods of tears. "Don't take it to heart, dearest, there are other doctors we can consult. I'll ask Lud White to arrange a consultation for you at Harley Street in London," he said, holding her in his arms.

Lucy, for her part, was inconsolable. "I don't know whether I can face it, dearest. I know how much you want a son," she sobbed.

"As long as I have you, that's all that matters," he said, kissing her tear-stained cheeks.

When George approached him, Lud White added an even stronger warning. "Dr Roberts has pointed out that Lucy could pass on the problem to any children she might have, especially if they are sons. By all means, take her to Harley Street, but if his diagnosis is confirmed, you should be in no doubt about the consequences."

George was stunned: the prospect of having weak, sickly children appalled him. He had counted on strong, healthy sons who could maintain the industrial dynasty of which he himself was a part. He concealed this information from Lucy but there were times when he could neither eat nor sleep and wondered how he could continue to work under such strain.

"I'll take her up to Harley Street in the New Year," he decided, "and if Dr Roberts's diagnosis is confirmed, I'll have to face the prospect of a childless marriage."

Yet again, he felt compelled to unburden himself to Uncle William who commiserated with him and blamed himself for having manoeuvred him into the marriage. "Try not to worry too much, my boy, because time may provide the answer to your problems. You are like a son to me, and in due course you may find consolation in a similar way."

George said nothing, but secretly felt cheated if he could not produce a son of his own. A cloud of gloom had descended over Dowlais and he could feel it in his bones, despite the approach of Christmas. Relationships between masters and men were in a state of deadlock and life had turned sour for him both at home and at work.

The only cheerful note was that of the high-pitched voices of the tip girls whose banter and singing he heard in the early morning as he rode to work. They seemed totally unaware of the threat of a stoppage and plied their shovels, clearing the trams of their contents as though they were going on forever. George noticed that young mothers were to be seen suckling their babies while they were on the tips. He had to look away, and was sickened by the thought that they could breed like rabbits while poor Lucy had failed to produce.

"It's an unfair world," he told himself and he gradually sank further into a depression in which he tried to drown his sorrows by drinking heavily throughout that miserable Christmas period.

It was Uncle William who shook him out of it when he told him at the end of December that the colliers throughout South Wales had given notice of an indefinite strike. "It's going to assume mammoth proportions and the Company will come under enormous pressure," he warned.

Fear gripped George like a vice and he begged his uncle to do his utmost to get one of the other under-managers to handle tip permits when the time came. "I've had enough, I can't face that problem again," he complained.

"Come now, show some fighting spirit," said Uncle William. "In due course, you'll be invited to attend a secret meeting at Dowlais House, and I hope you won't let me down."

"I won't let you down, sir," he promised.

Chapter 18

On the Saturday before Christmas, Lewsyn and Siani walked up the tramroad in Dowlais, both feeling acutely aware of the menace of the impending strike.

"What are we going to do?" she asked as she sensed a wave of panic sweeping over her.

"It will have to be the pawnshop, yet again," he said, recalling their first encounter. "Until that happens, let's make the best of things," he added as he slipped his arm around her waist.

"Do you remember the coconuts last Christmas? I think that was the turning point for me, I realised how kind you are."

"I won them at the Fair and gave them to Will and Mag so that I could come to see you," he confessed. "This year, let's meet at the Coffee Tavern on our own for an hour on Christmas Eve. Will you come?"

"Ben and I will have to go shopping in the market, but I expect we'll have bought what we can afford by about half-past seven."

"Good. Ask Ben to take it home and stand guard over it until you get back."

Siani arrived on time carrying a large basket. "Any mistletoe this year?" Lewsyn asked mischievously.

She blushed and gave him a knowing look. "Go and ask Mr Rowlands," she said.

He squeezed her hand and carefully took from his pocket a small brown box, which he placed before her.

"Nadolig llawen, Siani fi," he whispered.

She looked at it incredulously. "For me?" she gasped.

"Open it and see."

Her eyes sparkled with delight when she beheld a heart-shaped gilt locket on a dainty chain. "Oh, it's beautiful! The loveliest gift I've ever had in my whole life!" she said, fingering it gently.

"I'd like to see you wearing it when you come to choir practice," he said, smiling at her.

"I will, and I'll treasure it always," she added as she wiped away a tear.

They talked, and promised each other that whatever lay ahead, they would remain loyal and true. On their way home they walked along Victoria Street, and before parting he gave her a long lingering kiss. "Wear the locket to remind you of my love for you," he whispered, "and happy Christmas, sweetheart."

Despite the ever-present fear and threat of hardship in the background, Siani, Ben and the others made the most of the last, good square meal they might have for a long time to come. "We'll manage somehow," was her reassurance, and they all believed they could rely on her.

*　　*　　*

After Christmas, at Llew Jones's house in Ivor Lane, he, his wife and five children, braced themselves for the gathering storm. "Union funds are at rock bottom, and unless I have help from the Buffs, there's only the parish to fall back on," he warned.

"Perhaps you can understand now, Lewsyn, why I was so worried about you squandering your money," Mari Jones said bitterly.

He showed no remorse and retorted, "Money is for spending. Don't worry, we'll beat the Masters, whatever it takes, and anyway, my suit will come in handy for the pawnshop," he added flippantly.

Heavy snow in January 1875 transformed Dowlais into a white, treacherous wasteland. The gaunt spectre of lifeless mills and furnaces, silent pithead machinery and endless queues at the pawnshop, added to the all-pervading sense of desolation. Then the strike was turned into a 'lock-out' by the ironmasters, which heightened fears of what this would bring.

Llew Jones and Lewsyn received an order from the Board of Guardians to report to the stoneyards if they wanted to qualify for poor relief. Mari was frantic with worry that they would catch pneumonia working in sub-zero temperatures after being used to the heat of the ironworks. "Llew, your chest is wheezing like a bellows," she said on his return from breaking stones in Brecon Road.

"Don't fuss, woman, I have to do it if we want food in our bellies," he grunted as he brushed the snow off his coat.

By the end of his second week of stone-breaking, he had developed a graveyard cough. "I'll go there on my own," Lewsyn said grimly. "I'll tell the ganger you're bad in bed."

With his boots wrapped in sacking and another sack on his back to keep out the cold, he set out next morning prepared for a confrontation with Shad Lewis, the ganger. He handed Lewsyn two sledgehammers saying, "Your father's late this morning."

"My father's not coming. He's got bronchitis."

"Tell him to see the parish doctor or else there'll be no money for him on Saturday," Shad snapped.

"For two pins, I'd flatten you with this hammer," Lewsyn shouted, mad with rage.

"You dare lay a finger on me and you'll end up in gaol," Shad warned.

Lewsyn spat on the ground and turned away. For the next two hours he pounded away at pieces of limestone, muttering to himself, "I wish this was Shad Lewis's head I was battering." By the end of the day, his hands were cut and bleeding, and he could barely stand. When the hooter sounded, he threw down his hammer and disappeared into the darkness swearing vengeance.

His mother had a bath ready for him when he got home. "How's Dad?" he asked anxiously.

"No better. What did the ganger say?"

"That you should call the parish doctor."

"Oh, no! I'll doctor him myself. What he needs is food and rest," she said firmly.

Lewsyn decided not to give her the full story, but began to think of another solution, which he mentioned later. "Mam, I'm thinking of taking Sam and Tim with me to the Works Office tomorrow to see if they can pick cokes on the tips to bring in a few pence."

Mari Jones was aghast. "You'll do no such thing, they're only eleven and nine. Who's going to look after them out there?"

"They can go with Siani and Ben, they've got a permit."

Her voice became shrill. "Certainly not! They mustn't have anything to do with them."

Lewsyn said no more but went out to close the chicken pens and pigsty, and took his brothers with him. "Be prepared to get up early tomorrow, you're coming with me to the Works Office, but don't tell Mam," he warned.

As luck happened, they were the first to arrive there. "What is it, Lewsyn?" asked Johnny Davies, one of the clerks. "Mr Williams hasn't come yet, he's not well."

In that case, perhaps he'll have some sympathy for my father who's got bronchitis. We've hardly got a bucket of coal left in the house, and I'm desperate for a permit for my brothers. Do your best for them, Johnny, you know we haven't troubled you until now."

They looked perished and he felt sorry for them. "True enough, boyo. If Mr Williams hasn't come by seven o'clock, the chances are that we'll close the office. Perhaps I can get a temporary note for them. Will that help?"

"It will be a godsend," said Lewsyn, as Johnny got ready to deal with the next applicant.

The three brothers stood outside stamping their feet, trying to keep warm, and all the time dreading the appearance of His Lordship – George Williams. Johnny slammed the shutters down at seven o'clock and the long queue of applicants faded away, left to their own devices.

Lewsyn went around to the side door at which Johnny Davies appeared later and slipped a note into his hand saying, "It's a good thing you come to Bethania Chapel and that I can trust you."

"Thanks a lot Johnny, the boys can get started right away," he said, and off they went. They clawed their way up the slopes, to the part where Siani had said yielded the best pickings. In the half-light of the morning, they came upon her and Ben on their hands and knees chipping away at frozen banks, loosening precious nuggets of coal and coke and putting them into wicker baskets.

"Lewsyn!" she called when she saw him, her breath freezing on the icy air. She and Ben dropped their mandrels at once and turned to him.

"Can I leave Sam and Tim with you? I've got a temporary permit for them," he said, holding it up. "Will you show them what to do and make sure they get home safely? I've got to get back to the stoneyard now."

"Leave them to us, Ben and I will help them," she assured him.

He blew her a kiss and went off. As he tramped back to Brecon Road, his thoughts centred on Siani. "I'll make up for all this one day, I'll buy her a real gold locket and I'll ask her to marry me," he decided. He stepped into the stoneyard, his head held high and grabbed a sledgehammer.

"Lewsyn Jones, docked one hour's pay for being late," Shad Lewis barked. "Stuff it," he said under his breath.

Chapter 19

"This strike is likely to drag on," Uncle William admitted, "and this time, the Employers' Association won't give an inch until they've won the battle completely."

George swore quietly under his breath. "The sooner the better I take Lucy to London to have her consultation," he thought, "it seems as though my problems at work are bound to get worse."

Since her last miscarriage, Lucy had become depressed and had withdrawn into herself. The handsome gold locket he had bought her for Christmas had been set aside with the rest of her finery. She still had a ghastly pallor and was very listless, so George was not looking forward to the journey.

Immediately after Christmas, they set out and took her personal maid with them. Even though they travelled first class, the jolting of the carriages made Lucy sick. They rested overnight at a comfortable hotel near Paddington Station and George prayed that she would be well enough next morning to keep her appointment with the eminent Harley Street specialist, Dr Thomas Nash, who had been recommended by Lud White.

The consultation was a lengthy one and George paced the waiting room impatiently until he was called in. Dr Nash, a tall, distinguished-looking man in his fifties, chose his words carefully. "Dr White has briefed me about the background to Mrs Williams's case and I have examined her thoroughly. Bearing in mind her difficulty in conceiving, her very fragile condition and her miscarriages, I have to tell you, sir, that in my opinion, it would endanger her health to have children."

George gasped, then waited for him to continue, but there was a long silence. "Is that all you have to say? We didn't travel all this way just to be told that!" he protested. Putting his arm around Lucy who was crying on his shoulder, he pleaded, "Surely, there is something you can do for her."

"I'm afraid you've come to the wrong person if you want false promises or misleading information. I'll communicate my findings in detail to your doctor, and your wife will, no doubt, tell you more about the consultation. Good morning, Mr Williams, the nurse will see you out."

Lucy was so distressed that she had to be revived with smelling salts in the reception room while George was paying for the consultation. Though he strove hard not to show it, he was beside himself with disappointment. They drove back to their hotel in silence and she went straight to bed. George himself had to have a large brandy to recover from the shock. "We'll have to go back to Merthyr and get on with life, such as it is," he thought miserably.

* * *

Uncle William stood with his back to the fire and his hands behind his back. Every line etched on his face gave emphasis to his disappointment about the news George had just given him. To make matters worse, he himself was now under attack by desperate men who were baying for his blood. "I've had to have police protection, you couldn't have been away at a worse time," he complained. "And you might as well know that we've had a managers' meeting and we've allocated all the extra duties. On the grounds of your experience, you've been put in charge of permits again. Don't complain, because you should have been there to speak for yourself," he said sharply. "I don't want a repetition of the 1873 farce, remember, so start as you mean to go on."

George felt under attack from all sides, and in his present black mood, he needed no further goading. With malice and desperation he told himself, "I'll make every whining collier earn every ounce of coal he gets from our tips. I'll have them licking my boots before I finish with them."

Each day in January 1875 was a testing day. George took a perverse delight in seeing the ragged, down-at-heel strikers come in, cap in hand, pleading for permits. His sour looks and nasty sneers did not go unnoticed; his mannerisms became the subject of comment, for he would twirl his moustache, drum his fingers on the table and purse his hands together as though in prayer.

"St. George is at it again, trying to slay the dragon," said one wag, "but this Welsh dragon, breathing fire and brimstone will eventually slay him."

Once the applicants got what they wanted, they would have a good laugh at the conceited fool who flaunted his power so flagrantly.

"Bide your time," said Joe Griffiths, the union leader, to some of the men from Trecatti drift, "we'll make him squirm before we've finished with him."

Very different were the tip girls who appeared before him. Some of them displayed a brashness, which he found most disconcerting. They stared at him, bold-eyed and unafraid, so that he was at a loss to know how to treat them. As employees of the Company, theoretically they qualified for a permit, but when he tried to cross-examine them, it was like coming up against a battering ram. They even referred to the tips as 'our tips'.

"They're a brassy lot of ruffians, with one exception: Siani Davies," he decided. When he had questioned her, she had lowered her eyes and wrung her hands, and had looked such a picture of dejection that she did not have to convince him of her need. There was something about that girl which set her apart from the rest. He had heard about her trial and her poor family background, but in spite of it all, there was something about her which appealed to him.

He worked long hours grappling with the permit system, yet whenever he passed by, the tips seemed to be crawling with people grubbing for coal. Uncle William was not pleased and called George into his office. "You've created another human ant-heap out there," he snapped. "Do something about it, and soon."

George realised that his reputation as a manager was now at stake. "Is that what you think, Uncle? I've given permits only to deserving cases. They'll soon find out that as the pickings dwindle, I'll tighten my grasp upon them like a vice. I'll squeeze the life-blood out of their bodies!" he exclaimed.

Uncle William was bitter in his condemnation of the strikers. "Some of them are trying all manner of tricks in order to qualify for poor relief. The poor rates are soaring and Mr Clark is having a rough time as Chairman of the Board of Guardians, when all he's trying to do is to implement the law."

The vehemence of his feelings was not lost on George. "I sympathise with him. There seems to be a spirit of defiance in the air, but they won't get away with it, I'll show them who's boss," he said fiercely.

"That's the spirit!" Uncle William said, slightly reassured, "more of that is what we need."

Chapter 20
February 1875

Siani and Ben plodded down the tramroad in the direction of the tips and she confided in him her fear that Lewsyn could end up in the workhouse. "The Guardians are tightening up on allowing young, unmarried men to have parish relief, and are sending them to the workhouse instead."

"That's terrible!" Ben said, completely outraged.

"Not only that, Roger Williams, the Relieving Officer stopped Llew Jones's relief because he hadn't been able to work in the stoneyard, so he's gone back, even though he's still wheezing and gasping."

Ben darted an anxious look at her. "They've been unlucky; if I were a bit older, I'd have had to take the Labour Test just like them. What's Lewsyn going to do?"

"He's talking about trying to get a permit and joining us out here." Her brow was furrowed and her lips were pursed and eventually she admitted, "I don't fancy his chances because it was only by luck he had a temporary note for Sam and Will, until they pushed it too far and were stopped altogether."

*　　*　　*

Lewsyn Jones stood outside the Wages Office in the half-light of a cold February morning waiting for George Williams to arrive. His well-worn cap was pulled down over his ears and the collar of his patched coat was pulled up to his chin to act as a windbreak. His badly-chapped hands were stuffed into his coat pockets, and around his waist he had a piece of thick twine, which not only kept his coat closed, but acted as a support for his loose, slack trousers. He had lost so much weight that he looked like a human scarecrow. He stamped his feet on the cobblestones in an effort to keep warm, and then realised that the pads of paper he had put inside to fill up the holes had worn away. He looked miserable and felt wretched. After a while, he banged on the shutters of the office window and shouted, "How much longer do we have to wait?"

"Calm down, Lewsyn," said Johnny Davies who appeared at the grille, "Mr Williams should be here any minute."

There was a further wait before the sound of a horse's hooves signalled his arrival. Lewsyn watched him closely. He dismounted, handed the reins to a stable boy and sauntered across the yard to the office. His nut-brown great coat with its smart epaulettes and his highly polished leather gaiters were the essence of style and affluence.

Lewsyn's stomach rumbled noisily and there rose within him such a sense of anger and outrage that he could have spat at him. "I bet he's been gorging himself on a damn good breakfast, while we've been standing out here almost fainting with hunger," he thought.

In due course, his turn came to appear before George Williams who sat centre-stage in his office, flanked by two clerks. He made no effort to raise his head while Lewsyn stood before him, cap in hand, but seemed totally immersed in columns of figures, which he traced with his finger. Lewsyn watched him and wondered whether they were profit and loss figures. He noted his modish waistcoat and smart check trousers, and thought "He's making damn sure we know that he's a toff."

At last, George looked up with a bored, disdainful stare and said, "Outline your circumstances."

Lewsyn gave the facts and emphasised that this was his first application to scavenge on the tips.

"Second one," Isaac Evans, the senior clerk, said in a thin nasal tone. "He had one previously for a day, sir, but his brothers abused it so we had to confiscate it."

Lewsyn glared at Evans whose long, cadaverous jaw reminded him of a corpse.

George Williams turned to Johnny Davies, "Did you give it?"

"Yes, sir, for one day only, when you were away. It was a deserving case."

A look of resentment and suspicion came across George Williams's face and he snapped, "Deserving or not, it was misused. Application rejected."

Lewsyn's temper exploded like a rocket. He leapt forward, grabbed the lapels of Isaac Evans's coat and shook him like a rat, then pushed him to the floor. George got to his feet only to be confronted by Lewsyn's fist under his nose.

"If you don't give me a permit, you'll feel the weight of this," he shouted.

George backed off and thundered, "Get out of here before I call the police."

Lewsyn lunged at him and it was only the quick thinking of Johnny Davies that stopped a fight developing. He came between them and hissed at Lewsyn, "Bydd yn dawel! Ewch adre!" (Be quiet! Go home!).

Thwarted and angry, he shouted, "Keep your bloody permit! I'll chop up the furniture for firewood before I'll come back here!" and he slammed the office door so hard on his way out that it shook the whole building. Lewsyn's mind was reeling from this encounter and without knowing what he was doing or where he was going, he went in search of Siani.

"You didn't threaten Mr Williams, did you?" she asked, on hearing his story.

"I did and I meant it. If Johnny Davies hadn't come between us he would have caught it. He's nothing but a pompous ass, drunk with a sense of his own power and I hate him," he growled.

Ben looked alarmed. "If I were you, Lewsyn, I'd make for home, in case he reports you to the police and they come after you."

"I'd rather stay here with you," he said, as he watched Siani chipping away at the side of the tip. "Can't I give you a hand?"

"No! You'll get us thrown out as well. Call in to see us tonight and we can talk about it then," she said, trying to placate him.

Reluctantly, he left, swearing that he would get even with 'bloody George Williams' no matter how long it took.

Siani's Uncle Joe called that evening, shortly after Lewsyn arrived. "You're just the man I want to see," said Joe, "I'm looking for volunteers." He went on to explain in a conspiratorial tone how he was organising a run on the workhouse.

"The Board of Guardians are frightened of losing control. They are meeting every day and don't know what to do next. Our union is looking for about forty young men willing to go inside so that all the rest of the strikers can qualify for outdoor relief."

"Put my name at the top of your list," Lewsyn said instantly. "I've got nothing to lose after what happened to me this morning with George Williams."

Fear gripped Siani's heart and she put her hand on his arm, "Don't go Lewsyn," she said, "think of the consequences."

"That's just what I'm doing. If we can paralyse the Board of Guardians, we'll win the battle. They won't be able to refuse relief to thousands if we jam up the workhouse."

Every nerve in her body cried out against his decision, but he remained adamant. "My mind is made up, Siani, I'll be ready when Uncle Joe gives me the call."

Chapter 21
1875

The frantic hammering on the heavy front door of the grim, forbidding workhouse was loud enough to awaken the dead. Nine hundred men converged upon it in the early hours of Wednesday, 27th February, demanding admission. Among them were Lewsyn Jones and his best friend, Moses Williams, a farmer's son from West Wales, who was intelligent and well-respected.

"Let us in," they shouted as they pounded the door of the porter's lodge, rattled its windows and kicked the massive, prison-like, double doors under the archway. The pandemonium awoke Joseph Lloyd, the Master, who came scurrying half-dressed from his nearby house, to the porter's lodge, where he found Jack Bowen cowering under the counter.

"This place is swarming with men, hundreds of them," Jack squeaked, "just look through the window. They've climbed over the gates and railings and there's a solid mass of men in the front. What can we do?"

Joe Lloyd looked petrified. "Get the police, go through the mortuary and jump over the cemetery wall, and be quick about it. Tell them there's a riot going on here, and ask them to send as many officers as possible."

Outside, the barracking continued. "Bread! Bread! Bread! Give us bread not stones." The attack now centred on the lodge, where after a few hefty shoves, the windows fell in, and the mob surrounded the Master. "Get hold of him boys and push him out into the yard," shouted Joe Griffiths.

Lewsyn and Moses grabbed him by the scruff of the neck and marched him out so that more of their comrades could pile in.

"Now open the main door, boys, to let the others in," shouted Lewsyn, and the heavy iron bars were lifted, releasing the doors and admitting hundreds of baying young men to the inner yard.

Oil lamps flickered in the narrow windows and inmates gawped at the mêlée going on in the circulation yard all around the workhouse. The Master found himself being frog-marched into the Dining Hall where the rebels occupied the long benches and tables and banged on them demanding, "Bread! Bread! We want bread!"

Four powerful policemen arrived, and brandishing their truncheons, they forced their way through the mob to the Master who was pinioned to a chair by some of the rioters. His ashen face revealed his abject fear as he pleaded with the officers, "Get them out of here!"

"How many vacant beds have you got for them in the House?" asked the Sergeant. "They're demanding admission."

"I'm not sure."

"Make up your mind, if you want us to get rid of this lot," he growled.

"What about forty? I think I could manage that."

Sergeant Flint got to his feet, banged on a table with his truncheon, and bellowed, "There's room for forty men in this House. Open the door, Constable Wilkes, the last forty to remain in this Hall are those to be admitted, the rest of you go to the Relieving Officer for notes to have bread."

There was a mad rush to the door and in the scuffle which followed, Constable Wilkes was pushed to the floor. Sergeant Flint drew his baton and lashed out right and left.

"You cruel bastard," yelled Lewsyn, lunging at him, only to be felled by one swift blow which laid him out stone cold.

"Lock the door, Wilkes," shouted the Sergeant, stepping over Lewsyn's body. He turned to the Master saying, "We've done what is necessary, the rest is now up to you. I'll leave two of my men to help you sort things out, while Constable Wilkes and I clear the yards of any stragglers.

The Master set about dispersing the new arrivals throughout the workhouse. When Moses' turn came, he pleaded "I've got to look after him," pointing to Lewsyn. "Let me stay with him at least until he comes around."

"In that case, you can carry him into the Old Men's Ward and wait for him to surface. I've got enough to do as it is," said Joseph Lloyd testily.

An hour or so later, Lewsyn began to stir. "Oh my God! My head's splitting! Where am I?" he groaned. He looked around at the bleak, bare, unfamiliar walls, smelt the stench of urine rising up from the sodden floors, and retched.

"We're in the workhouse, boyo, and you've been knocked about a bit. Try to rest, I'll keep an eye on you," Moses said.

Lewsyn drifted back into semi-conciousness, not caring whether he was alive or dead. He was next awakened by the clanging of a bell calling the paupers to breakfast. With difficulty, he climbed out of bed, helped by Moses, took one look at the grim ward with its decrepit occupants, and made for the stone stairs. When they reached the Dining Hall, prayers had just ended, so they joined the queue for food and jostled with the other paupers who complained of feeling ravenous.

The Master stood stolidly alongside a copper boiler, ladling gruel into tin bowls and handing them in turn to each pauper. Lewsyn took one look at the slimy, grey mixture and felt a wave of nausea creeping over him.

"I can't eat this stuff," he said, thumping his bowl on a trestle table and tossing his tin spoon on the floor. He looked around and saw many of the half-starved paupers polishing their bowls for the last traces of this obnoxious concoction, and decided he would make an early protest. He seized his bowl and spoon and he flung them on to the stone floor with a loud clatter. Immediately, a sea of upturned faces surrounded him and Moses got up to retrieve the basin from two paupers who were squabbling over the gruel on the floor.

The commotion caught the eye of the Master who left the Matron to distribute the rest of the gruel, while he came to see what was happening. "What is going on here?" he snarled, looking at the disgusting mess on the floor.

By then, more paupers had gathered around and Lewsyn saw their pinched, grey faces, their ugly workhouse clothing and the fear in their eyes. He felt his gorge rising and he shouted, "This food isn't fit for pigs!" Yet again, he threw his bowl on the floor, and this time gave it a hefty kick, which sent it spinning down the Hall.

The Master looked as though he was about to have a fit, and the onlookers were aghast, but Lewsyn viewed them all with an insolent smirk on his face. "Jones! Hughes! Come here at once," Joseph Lloyd barked to two attendants across the Hall. "Take him to the punishment cell," he shouted, pointing to Lewsyn. They pinioned his arms behind his back and dragged him kicking and shouting through the rear door.

"It's bread and water for you for twenty-four hours, you cheeky devil," said one of them, before bundling him into a small cell and slamming the door.

Lewsyn had ample time to consider the situation while lying on the foul mattress, which was the only item in the room. He thought of the treatment being meted out to the strikers, and to the inhuman, degrading treatment of paupers, and concluded that this was his chance to protest. "If I leave it too long, I'll be too weak to do anything at all," he thought. "Once I get out of this cell, I'm going to wreck this bloody place," he finally told himself, throwing all caution to the wind. Before his release next morning, he had worked out a plan, which he was determined to put into action.

In the labour yard, he made a pretence of putting stones into an iron ring and tapping them with a sledgehammer to the required size, but actually spent more time banging his hammer on the ground so that he could talk to Moses without being overheard by any of the supervisors.

"You see that room above the porter's lodge, the one with a big arched window like they have in Dowlais Church, I've heard that's where the Board of Guardians meet," he said through his teeth.

Moses looked puzzled and wondered what he was getting at. "Oh yes, what about it?"

"I think we should pay it a visit."

"What for, Lewsyn, you surely don't think they'll take any notice of us?"

"Get our boys together when we have our dinner break, then we can talk about that beautiful Board Room," he said mysteriously.

The overseer came striding towards them. "Here, you two, get on with your work," he shouted, glaring at Lewsyn. "If you're not careful, you'll go back to the cell. You've done very little work all the morning judging by the small pile of stones you've cut."

"I'm just too weak to lift the hammer. Workhouse food doesn't agree with me, sir," he said feebly.

Moses stifled a laugh and looked away. Later, while they were eating their allocation of bread and cheese for dinner, Lewsyn quietly outlined his plan, shielding his face with his hand so that his lips could not be read nor his voice overheard.

"I reckon that if we stay in this 'prison' much longer, they'll starve us to death," he said, throwing his black rye bread on to the floor. "Before we leave, I think we should give the Board of Guardians something to remember us by, and make them too terrified ever to put young men like us into the workhouse again."

"What do you have in mind, Lewsyn? I'm itching to have a go at them," said fiery Dai Dando, diminutive in size, but with the heart of a lion.

"I'll work out the details of my plan with Moses, but first you've got to promise absolute secrecy and total commitment," he said, his eyes scrutinising their faces and arousing in them intense speculation.

"You can depend on us. Why do you think we're here?" said Dai, getting quite excited.

"All will be revealed in due course, but when the call comes, I must be able to rely on you, regardless of consequences," he emphasised.

Lewsyn and Moses were given the task of cleaning the latrines as punishment for insubordination of the overseer in the stoneyard, and persistent talking. "That will teach you to keep your mouth shut," he said, not realising they were only too glad of such a chance to talk freely.

They embarked on their grisly task with glee. "Now then, this is how we set about it," Lewsyn said, muffling his nose against the stench. "On Sunday morning, in the Workhouse Chapel, some of the boys must fall sick. While they're writhing on the floor, complaining of stomach cramps and diarrhoea, and demanding to use these latrines, others will slip out and go to the porter's lodge to keep him occupied and tie him up. We'll lure the Matron outside and seize her bundle of keys, then the 'heavies' in the back row can come out. We'll lock the chapel door, and we'll hide the Matron somewhere out of the way. Meanwhile, we'll have hidden our sledgehammers in the bushes near the laundry, and we'll make for the Boardroom. The rest will be sheer pleasure! We'll reduce it to rubble and then we'll scarper."

"Lewsyn, you're a genius!" said Moses, his weather-beaten face wreathed in smiles at the prospect of this gesture of protest.

Lewsyn continued, "We'll have to go over this plan until we know it like the palm of our hands. You'll have to organise our boys, because you know them better than I do, and because I'm regarded with too much suspicion by the Master. Can I depend on you Moses?"

"Absolutely, I'll handpick them," he said emphatically.

For the next few days, Lewsyn seemed to adopt an air of relaxed unconcern, though he knew that the rest of the young, able-bodied victims were seething with excitement, and eagerly awaiting the Sunday service in the Workhouse Chapel.

The plan went into action. On Sunday morning, before breakfast, four, miserable looking, able-bodied young men stood outside the Master's office complaining that they were unwell.

Joseph Lloyd glowered at them. "What's the matter with you?" he snapped.

"Diarrhoea," each one reported.

"It was that soup we had last night. The fat on the bones was rancid," one of them complained.

The Master scratched his head, narrowed his eyes, and rounded on them. "I don't suppose you're trying to avoid chapel this morning are you?" he sneered. "Go to the Dining Hall and have a bowl of gruel, that will put your right."

His suspicion that they were trying to dodge chapel confirmed his resolve to get them there. "Round up all those young strikers and make sure that they're in chapel this morning," he barked to the orderly, before going into the Dining Hall to say grace.

"I'll see that they're there, even if I have to leave out some of the imbeciles and infirm. You can depend on me, sir," said the beery Billy Tooze, whose hangover was too bad for him to put up with any troublemakers.

Lewsyn's plan went into action neatly, and the 'belly-achers' were put in pews just behind the feeble-minded old women who were cackling like geese. Billy Tooze took his position in a corner near the door, where he hoped he could have forty winks and nurse his headache.

To start the service, the Master approached the lectern and read the lesson with great fervour in Welsh and

English. He chose St. Matthew's Gospel, Chapter Five, emphasising the words 'Blest are the pure in heart, for they shall see God', which the Rev. Erasmus Richards, a powerful preacher with a stentorian voice, took as his theme. He soon got caught up in Welsh 'hwyl' and in a raucous, spine-chilling crescendo, warned his terrified congregation of the consequences of immorality, sloth and greed.

He was at the peak of his performance when Dai Dando and his mates started to writhe on the floor. As those assembled stood for the singing of 'Fight the Good Fight', Dai and Co. made for the door, saying, "Let us out, we can't hold it any longer,"

Billy Tooze was half-asleep, so Dai put his hand in his pocket and snatched the door key. It seemed that Lewsyn's plan was working like clockwork. The heavyweights in the back rows followed suit.

The one problem proved to be the Matron, who on seeing so many young men running out of control, started to wail like a banshee. Lewsyn put his hand over her mouth, pushed her outside, divested her of her keys and locked the door. He bundled her into a large laundry basket full of dirty linen, and pulled the iron bar across to lock it firmly. Moses, leading four others, had gone to the porter's lodge, where they terrified Jack Bowen with their threats and tied him up.

The heavyweights charged up the stairs to the Boardroom, with their sledgehammers at the ready, and once inside, set about mass destruction of windows, doors, tables and chairs. It was all over in less than ten minutes. The effect was catastrophic, and the room was one mass of broken glass and splintered wood.

Lewsyn surveyed the scene with satisfaction. "Make for the walls by the graveyard, now, boys," he shouted, and there was a stampede down the stairs into the yard, past the mortuary, towards the boundary wall.

Just as they neared the wall, they heard the shrill sound of a police whistle. "Someone must have sent for the police. Jump to it," shouted Moses.

Lewsyn looked over his shoulder to see if anyone was left behind, and was in the act of climbing over when his left leg was seized in a grip of iron. He lay astride the wall unable to move, then from his pocket he pulled out a short iron bar from the stoneyard, which he brought down sharply on his assailant's nose. There was a loud groan and he got away.

Most of his mates, including Moses, had disappeared, so he dodged about among the gravestones, keeping an eye open for likely pursuers, while in the distance, he heard a fearful hue and cry coming from the workhouse yard. He headed towards Pontmorlais where he crept down a narrow alley, which led to Bethesda Street, beyond which was Chinatown. "If only I can get there, I'll be safe for a while," he told himself.

The service in Bethesda Chapel was running late and he could hear its powerful singing, which gave him fresh heart. With enormous relief, he slipped into the maze of alleyways in 'China' and ran on endlessly, weaving this way and that, until he thought he had reached the heart of this famous fortress of crime. He sat down on a low wall, puffing and panting, and began to realise the enormity of what he had done. "I'd better look for a place to hide my head, I'll be hunted down after this," he admitted to himself.

Chapter 22
March 1875

"Assault on police officer! Workhouse wrecked!" These were the headlines Sally Owen brought back to Lewsyn Jones in the hovel where she lived in one of the back alleys of 'China'.

"I thought you'd like to see The Observer to know what's going on," she said, with a smirk on her face. Sally was well-versed in crime and her lodging house was secretly recognised as a safe haven for criminals.

Lewsyn could feel his heart pounding when he saw his name on the front page, at the head of the list of wanted men. There was even a reward of £20 guineas on offer for his capture and he was described as 'Dangerous'. "What am I to do?" he said, darting an anxious look at Sally, "I never intended that it should come to this." He recalled his own words, 'regardless of consequences' and only then realised how rash he had been.

"The choice lies with you," she said, "you can either give yourself up and go to gaol, or lie low here and join our gang, doing a bit on the side, as we call it."

Lewsyn said nothing but continued to observe Sally while he weighed up his own position. She was a coarse, common, blowzy woman who in the past had earned a living as a prostitute, but now her ugly features and thickened body no longer attracted much custom. At fifty years of age, she could not compete with the younger molls who plied their trade from 'China'. She recognised this and took in lodgers, like Lewsyn, who were in need of a hideout due to their criminal activities.

Faced with the stark choice, he accepted Sally's offer to hide under the rafters. "I'll pay you back, Sal, as soon as it's safe for me to get out and about, but first, I'll have to try to disguise myself."

She nodded agreement, then added, "Talk to Hoppy, he'll tell you what to do."

Hoppy, or Ted Thomas, to give him his real name, stumped across the room on his wooden leg to scrutinise Lewsyn. He was a fearsome looking creature with gnarled and craggy features, long, dark hair, rotting teeth and a wild glint in his eyes.

Lewsyn instinctively drew back as Hoppy looked at him closely. "So you want a disguise do you? That won't be easy with your colour hair," he rasped. "You'll have to dye it and wear a hat. Get rid of those workhouse clothes, the coppers will recognise them a mile off. Ask Sal to lend you some togs, she's got a good stock of cast-offs, suitable for all sorts. And changing your name might help," he added as an afterthought.

Lewsyn balked at the very idea. He had always been proud of his name, which his father had chosen for him after a local hero, Lewsyn yr heliwr. "Hell and damnation," he muttered to himself, "I've made a mess of things to land up here with people like these." His heart lurched when he thought of Siani who had begged and pleaded with him not to volunteer for the workhouse. What must she be thinking of him now? He swallowed hard and promised himself that he would leave this pest-hole as soon as it was safe to do so. His heart ached when he thought of her, and no matter what risk he had to take, he knew he would have to see her; these last two weeks had seemed like an age.

*   *   *

"How do you make a living, Hoppy?" Lewsyn asked, when his fellow lodger came back from a drinking spree, one night.

Hoppy fixed him with a gimlet eye, "Quite simple, my boy. I relieve the well-to-do of some of their most treasured possessions and I pass them on to ready customers."

Lewsyn blinked and wondered whether the drink was talking. "You can't be a burglar, so what do you mean?"

"Quite right, my boy, this peg-leg would get in the way, and at fifty years of age, I'm past it. No, I rely on fit young men like you, who can climb walls, run like hell, and are not too squeamish about tapping a bobby on the nose. What about it Lew? Are you ready to come in with me and Sal?"

Lewsyn felt his stomach turn over. Here was the catch and now came the reckoning. "Count me out, burglary is not for me," he said sharply.

"I'm surprised, I thought you'd jump at the chance," Hoppy sneered. "But perhaps you didn't know that the police use me as an informer about new arrivals in 'China', not that I've mentioned you as yet. When I was asked, I simply told the bobbies I had seen a redheaded rapscallion jumping from Jackson's Bridge into the swollen river on Sunday morning. They've been dragging the river downstream looking for a body."

Lewsyn's blood turned cold. Hoppy's calculating stare filled him with dread as he added, "Think about it, my boy."

That night, he lay under the draughty rafters, twisting and turning on a louse-ridden palliasse, wondering how he could get out of the trap they had set for him. If he were to make a run for it now, he'd be hunted like a wild animal, so he decided to bide his time, and consoled himself that as soon as he had a chance to escape, he'd make for Siani's house.

Sally dyed his hair black and kitted him out with a sombre black suit and a black hat, which made him look like an undertaker's assistant. "You're tall enough to carry it off," she said, "and with a black muffler to hide your face, you'll get by unnoticed."

Hoppy produced a black portmanteau saying, "You'll need this for the swag. There's a lot of silver in the house you'll be visiting, and Jaco will want to hand it to you fast. He's coming this afternoon to take you to the coffin shop where he works and he'll show you the lie of the land, ready for your first big job tonight. Don't try any tricks on him, because he's a professional, and he'd cut you to ribbons before you knew what was happening."

Lewsyn felt sick, yet he knew that he'd have to go through with the pretence, though every nerve in his body cried out against it.

"Sal, give Lewsyn a drop of the hard stuff to steady his nerves. He's looking rather pale," Hoppy said quietly, as it got dark.

"I'll have to go to the vaults, you drank the last dregs of the whisky last night," she complained.

"All right, here's some money, go get some more and be quick about it," he said, handing her a florin.

As soon as she left, Lewsyn watched for his chance and edged towards the door. Hoppy fixed an eagle eye upon him, and in a flash, drew out a long, sharp knife, ready to stab him. Lewsyn grabbed his wrist and held it in a vice-like grip, then lifted his arm vertically and sent him sprawling on the floor.

"I'll get you for this, I'll tell the police you attacked me, you ungrateful bastard," Hoppy shouted as Lewsyn fled.

Not daring to take his usual route, he clambered up a bank of putrefying garbage too steep for Sally to try to negotiate. Stealthily, he made his way towards the Iron Bridge where, to his horror, he spotted two policemen. He retreated hastily behind the brewery wall and sought refuge in an outhouse amid sacks of grain until it got completely dark. There he lay, imagining the tale of woe that Hoppy was spinning to the police at that moment, but uppermost in his mind was his need and determination to escape and to see Siani.

"I've got to get back to Dowlais tonight to explain to her why I must remain in hiding," he told himself repeatedly.

Eventually, when he was satisfied that the course was clear, he slipped out into Wheatsheaf Lane and followed his nose towards the bakehouse where the smell of newly-baked bread made him acutely aware of his hunger. "My luck is in," he thought, when he saw the horse-drawn baker's van standing outside the rear door of the bakery, "they won't miss a loaf," he decided and groped inside the van. But it seemed to be empty, so in desperation, he jumped into the driver's seat, took the reins, made a clucking noise through his teeth, and got the horse to move in the direction of High Street. The animal obeyed his commands, hoping that it was on its way back to the stables at the end of a long day.

"This is the way to avoid the police, they'll think I'm the baker," he told himself, while pulling his collar well up to cover the side of his face.

The horse trotted along willingly and seemed to know where it was going, but by the time it reached Pontmorlais, it began to slow down. No amount of persuasion would make it start the steep climb to Penydarren, let alone Dowlais, and in blind panic, Lewsyn led it down the tramroad, knotted the reins to an iron railing and fled.

"Thank God to be rid of that encumbrance," he said, as he made his way through a maze of side streets and short cuts. Fear drove him on and by the time he reached Nant Row, his heart was hammering against his ribs. He saw the faint glow of an oil lamp in No. 2, and his spirits rose. "Siani is waiting for me, I know she is," he told himself desperately.

He tapped lightly on the door and waited until she opened it a crack. "Let me in, Siani, it's me, Lewsyn," he murmured. But for his voice, she would not have recognised him and she gasped at his changed appearance and haggard looks.

He threw his arms around her. "Let me hold you! If only you knew how much I've longed for this moment," he said, as he buried his face in her hair and sobbed.

She led him to the fireside and stared at him in bewilderment. "What's happened to you, Lewsyn, and what are those strange clothes you're wearing?"

Gradually, his story unfolded. "I'm on the run and this may be my only chance of seeing you for some time, my darling," he said, enfolding her in his arms.

"Oh, I've missed you," she murmured, "and now you're going from me again!"

"I'll stay with you until dawn, and then I plan to hide in one of the wagons taking stone down to Cardiff docks."

"Take those awful clothes off while I get some food for you," she said with a shudder.

Time passed while they talked and gradually they relaxed and slept in each others arms by the fireside. He awoke early and became conscious of a tremendous desire for her. She instinctively sensed his passion, and unable to resist it, gave herself to him with total abandon. "I love you more than anybody else in the world, my darling Siani," he murmured. When all passion was spent, he said, "Promise you'll wait for me, I want to marry you, my sweetheart."

"I'll be here, Lewsyn," she said, and he gave her one last lingering kiss, before he slipped out into the darkness and an unknown life beyond.

Chapter 23
March 1875

The strike was deepening and the members of the Board of Guardians were becoming desperate men. Young boys like Ben, now sixteen years of age, were being offered stone-breaking on the parish roads, and when that was no longer possible, they were being sent to the workhouse. He knew that his turn was coming soon, and that if he turned it down, the poor relief for the whole family would be in jeopardy. He lived in a state of constant terror, and every morning when he went to Brecon Road stoneyard, he dreaded being told that there was no work for him.

He kept his fear to himself for as long as he could, not to worry Siani, but now a final warning had been issued, which meant that by the end of the week the stoneyard would close because the stock-piles were so massive, and the demand for stone was so low, that the Guardians could not sell it. "It's workhouse or starve, so I'd better tell Siani my position," he decided.

When she heard of his dilemma, she came out in a cold sweat. "You're not going to any workhouse. Look what happened to Lewsyn when he went there – his life was ruined and God knows when I'll see him again." Siani began to cry and Ben felt guilty that she was so upset.

A few days later, they had another shock, Joe Griffiths called a meeting of Dowlais Colliers to inform them that the Dowlais Iron Company had come up with an offer: they would provide work for twenty-five colliers at pits from which they had been locked out. Siani thought that Ben must have got things muddled and urged him to attend the union meeting to find out.

Joe Griffiths addressed the packed meeting in the large upstairs room in The Colliers' Arms. "This offer of work to twenty-five colliers when there are thousands on strike, is nothing but a ploy to break us down by getting some of us to black-leg," he thundered. "Remember that if they succeed, our solidarity will be smashed and they'll have a stranglehold on us. We'll have to accept whatever settlement they wish to impose."

Llew Jones looked very uneasy. "If we all stand firm and reject this offer, what will happen then?" he asked.

"Now Llew, you're talking sense," said Joe, "because if we stand together, there'll be a stalemate." He looked around the room at the mass of worried faces. "I don't suppose any of you want to dance to the bosses' tune do you?" he shouted. There was a blank silence during which they all looked at each other uneasily. "I thought not, because you can pass the word around that black-legs don't live long in Dowlais."

Ben could feel shivers running down his spine. Cries of "Throw it out! Tell them to keep it!" reverberated around the room.

Moses Williams got to his feet and put a question to the chairman. "Since we are going to reject this offer, what about us sending a deputation to the Board of Guardians to hear our case? They are likely to use this offer as a stick to beat us with, and they could refuse relief to thousands on the grounds that there's work available for us and that we should take it. We all know who their Chairman is don't we?" he said, jabbing his forefinger in the direction of Dowlais House.

Angry shouts, loud oaths and gasps of shock at the sudden realisation of the danger they were in, re-echoed around the room. Only with difficulty was Abraham Jenkins, the chairman, able to restore order to the meeting. "He's right, boys, we'll be caught in a cleft stick. This offer is meant to paralyse us. Joe and I have been talking and we think we should ask the Cyfartha and Plymouth lodges to come with us to present a united deputation to the Board of Guardians."

The meeting rallied behind him and the gathering of haggard, half-starved colliers and ironworkers pledged a fight to the finish. Before the meeting closed, Joe gave a spine-chilling warning, "Anyone who gives in and black-legs will be tarred and feathered, his windows will be smashed in, and his family will become outcasts. I can assure you that what happened to Mr Clark's beautiful boardroom in the workhouse will be nothing compared with what we'll do if they refuse us poor relief. We'll burn the bloody place down!" he shouted to loud acclaim.

After the meeting, Ben walked home with Uncle Joe, his small, pinched face creased with anxiety. "What am I to tell Siani? She's worried to death, especially as Alys seems to be going down with consumption."

He put his hand on Ben's shoulder. "Tell her we've got to put up a fight and we'll try to save you from the workhouse at all costs."

They parted company before reaching Nant Row and Ben decided that he would have to put on a brave face, not to worry Siani too much. Apart from nursing Alys, who had taken to her bed, Siani was not feeling well herself. Her colour was poor and she complained of feeling sick.

As soon as he entered the kitchen, David demanded a full account of the meeting, but Ben prevaricated. "I'm not supposed to say what goes on in union meetings. Uncle Joe spoke well, and on the way home he told me not to worry about going to the workhouse."

"Thank goodness for that," Siani said. "Did he say whether we'll be able to have money from the parish?"

Ben hesitated. "He said it's all to be sorted out, and in the meantime we'll have to grin and bear it."

She snorted. "If you can't get work to qualify for relief, then how does he think we're going to have money to put food in our bellies? We can't live on fresh air!"

Ben hung his head and Siani knew by him that he was not giving her the whole truth. "I tell you what, you and I will have to try for a permit to go back on the tips. We've got to have a fire in the grate and we must make sure of some money coming in."

He gave her an anguished look. "I wish I could come with you, but things are bad, Siani, and it's not safe for me to go anywhere near the Dowlais Office."

She could tell by the catch in his voice that he was near breaking point. The last thing she wanted to do was to grub for coal, because she felt so off colour, but she knew that for all their sakes, she would have to do it. "Dave, will you come with me to gave a hand? If we can get a permit, Ben can sell some on the side as he used to."

David, though now thirteen years of age, was small and wiry, and jumped at the chance of helping. "I'll do anything for you Siani, I'll work as hard as our Ben, you'll see."

Siani saw a tear trickling down Ben's face and she swallowed the lump in her own throat as she thought of the prospect before her.

*　　*　　*

On a blustery March day she and David stood once again outside the Works Office. The prospect of appearing before Mr George Williams filled her with dread. She had heard that he had tightened up the system and hardened his attitude. When they entered his room he did not bother to raise his head, but simply barked out, "Name?"

"Siani Davies, sir, and this is my brother, David."

Slowly, he raised his head, and looked at her closely. "I've seen you before," he mumbled.

"Yes sir, I was a tip girl, but now because of the strike, I'm out of work. Please sir, my parents are dead, and I'm the eldest of six children. We've got no coal in the house and my sister, Alys, has consumption."

He listened to her light, lilting Welsh accent and stroked his whiskers thoughtfully. The girl still had the most beautiful eyes he had ever seen, but there was something different about her now. "You know I'm cutting down on permits," he said curtly.

"Yes sir, I wouldn't ask, but my brother Ben is being threatened with the workhouse and the family relies on me for everything."

The feline quality of the girl and the directness of her gaze disturbed him so that he found it hard to refuse her. He grappled with his feelings, then said tersely, "You'll have a permit for a week, to be reviewed."

Siani's face lit up and he noticed that there was a sharpness and a quickness about her eyes. "Thank you sir," she said, as she turned to go.

He could hardly believe that he had given in so easily and wondered at the effect she had on him.

She and David worked like beasts of burden all that week, in case it was the last permit they would ever have.

At home, Ben kept an eye on Alys and took the youngsters to the soup kitchen each day. The strike was biting deep and the battle for survival was almost unendurable.

"When is the meeting taking place with the Board of Guardians, Ben?" Siani asked. "Parish relief is barely enough to keep a sparrow alive, let alone hungry people like us."

He looked away. "It's already been held and it's deadlock. They're offering work in the Dowlais pits to strikers, and if we refuse, there'll be no money at all for us from the parish," he said miserably.

"How can they do that? she gasped.

"They say the law is on their side and thousands of men have already been refused relief. It's a way of breaking the strike."

Siani's worst fears were being realised, though she dared not admit it. "What have I done to deserve all this?" she asked herself. "Where is Lewsyn? Why doesn't he send word to me?" The anguish was so great that she put her head on the table and cried. Ben looked on, feeling helpless and full of guilt.

On the last day before their permit was due to run out, she and David were dragging a big basket of coal up the tramroad in the gathering dusk, when they heard the clippity-clop of a horse's hooves. David rested for a moment saying, "That's just what we could do with to carry this home."

Alongside them appeared George Williams, looking down at them. "Hey there Siani Davies! I want to see you in my office tomorrow after work," he called, before giving her a strange look and galloping away.

Her mouth suddenly became parched and her legs buckled beneath her. "That's it! He's heard about our Ben selling a bit on the side and he'll stop our permit tomorrow," she said to David. She could barely find the strength to continue her journey and wept quietly at the inevitability of their fate. "Say nothing to Ben, it will be time enough to let him know when the axe has fallen," she said.

They finished earlier next day and David had to drag a smaller load home on his own. "Tell Ben I'll be a bit late and that he's not to sell an ounce of this," she warned.

She reached the Works Office and began to panic. Johnny Davies, the clerk, seemed surprised to see her. "What are you doing here?" he asked. "I thought you were working with David."

"Mr Williams wants to see me. I think it's about my permit," she whispered, giving him a worried look.

"I'll go and tell him," he said, and disappeared into the inner office.

To her surprise, George Williams emerged. He turned to Johnny and said brusquely, "You can go now, I'll lock up." Then he called to Siani, "Come this way." He seated himself behind the desk and scrutinised her. "Do you know why I've sent for you?" he asked.

"No sir, unless it's about Ben, my eldest brother," she stammered, her colour rising.

He fingered his moustache before saying, "I won't be giving anymore permits for picking coals, the tips are now far too dangerous."

Siani opened her mouth to protest, but he continued, "Would you like to earn a little money doing something easier and cleaner?"

She looked at him alarmed and wondered what was happening, until he said, "I'm thinking of offering you work here as a cleaner at 2/6d a week. You would have to come after the staff have left, at this time of day.

Siani was struck dumb, and looked bewildered. He sensed the turmoil within her and went on to say, "Your little brother can still forage for a bucket of cokes each day, if he can find any in safe places."

She looked at him, her eyes wide with concern, "You are very kind sir, but would I be taking anyone else's job?" she asked uneasily.

"I decide who works here," he said sharply, "do you want this job or not?"

Her mind was in a whirl but she found herself saying, "Thank you, sir, I'll come whenever you require me."

"You can start tomorrow at this time," he said, getting to his feet and opening the door for her to leave.

She thought she detected a faint smile on his lips as she brushed past him. She went over it in her mind, "Why did he ask me? It's a good offer, but there's something about it that I don't understand," she told herself on her way home.

Chapter 24

Ben was fed up with waiting for Siani to come home. As soon as she set foot inside the kitchen he shouted, "Where have you been? Why can't I go out with my barrow?"

She gave him a stern look, "Mr Williams sent for me. He's going to stop the permits, so we'll need the coal for ourselves."

"He's playing the bosses game, tightening the noose around our necks," Ben complained.

Siani slumped wearily on the settle and young David waited for her to speak. She looked at him appealingly, "Do you think you could manage to carry a basket a day on your own?" she asked.

"I'll try, and if I can't manage it, I'll drag it on a sledge with a rope around my waist," he said.

Siani's eyes misted over. "You're a good boy, Dave," she said, willing herself not to cry.

"What use is that?" asked Ben, infuriated because he would not be able to make money out of it.

"It's all I was promised, but I can have a little job cleaning the Works Office for 2/6d a week."

Ben's jaw dropped. "Do you mean to say you'll be a cleaner? Whose job are you taking?"

"Nobody's. Mr Williams thinks this is the time to clean them, while the Works are on stop, and he's asked me to do it."

"Are you going to take it?" Ben asked hesitantly.

"Yes. It will keep you out of the workhouse won't it, Ben?"

He averted her gaze and bit his lip.

By the second week in April, the offices had never looked so clean. Layers of dirt had been removed and even the windows looked cleaner.

"It's a treat to be able to look out to see what's going on," said Johnny Davies.

"I suppose that when the furnaces are going full blast, Mr Williams sees little point in having the place cleaned. The filth that comes out of them is terrible; it's impossible to keep our windows clean at home, but I'd gladly put up with it if only a settlement could be agreed."

"The strike is getting nasty now, Siani," Johnny said gravely. "Even the poor relief for heads of families in the stoneyards is only a loan, which is terrible when you think of all the hard work they have to do for it."

"Yes, we've had three long months of it, and no sign of a settlement. Our Ben has been offered the workhouse yet again, because he's a single man, but I won't let him go. The money I earn here is a godsend," she said quietly.

"Mr Williams is not so bad once you get to know him," Johnny assured her. "Try to hold on to this little job for as long as you can, because you are more protected here than out on the tips."

George Williams himself was more than pleased with Siani's progress; his desk was polished, the fire grate was black-leaded and the tiled floor was exceptionally clean. He noticed that she herself came to work looking very presentable in a trim black dress and black shoes, above which he caught an occasional glimpse of a well-turned ankle. From the first time he set eyes on her, he found himself attracted to her more than he was prepared to admit. Now he began to find her almost irresistible.

He usually worked later on a Thursday evening going through the accounts, though there was now less work in that respect, due to the strike. He could hear Siani moving chairs in the outer office and decided to find out what she was doing, so he opened the door suddenly and found her on top of a chair trying to clean a high cupboard. She nearly toppled over with the shock of being taken unawares, but he quickly leapt forward to save her. The lovely outline of her slim body and a quick glimpse of her shapely legs set him on fire. Before Siani knew it, she was in his arms and was paralysed with fright.

"Relax, my dear, you are safe with me. I think you are beautiful," he said, caressing her hair, her face and her breasts. She tried to release herself from his grasp, but he continued, "Now that you know how I feel about you, we must get to know each other better." He kissed her passionately on her lips and was most reluctant to set her free.

Siani was in a state of panic and made for home, telling herself that she could not possibly stay there any longer. "There's only one thing a man like him would want from someone like me, and I'm not falling for it," she told herself. "Lewsyn would kill him if he knew that he was trying to take advantage of me. I wish he'd come back, I need him," she moaned.

The problems that faced her when she got in soon reminded her that she could not afford to be too high and mighty. Alys had had a relapse and the youngsters were squabbling over the last crust. In bed that night, she decided that George Williams would have to be kept at arm's length, because she needed her wages at all cost. She also decided she might be better off going in early in the morning to do some of the work so that she would not see much of him.

For his part, George was bored with the strike, bored with the tip permit system and bored at home. Spring was in the air and he felt restless. "I could do with some excitement in my life," he thought, as Easter approached. Taking a holiday was out of the question while the state of emergency still prevailed, but he tried to persuade Lucy to come out for a drive in their carriage in the hope that fresh air would bring colour to her cheeks and would sharpen her appetite. The first two runs down the valley to Abercanaid to see her parents were quite successful, and she even felt sufficiently stimulated to order a new spring bonnet. But she soon lost interest, took to her couch and refused to go out at all.

George tried bribery, and even promised to take her to Llandrindod Wells when the strike was settled. The very thought of it threw her into a frenzy and she accused him of being insensitive. "Are you anxious for me to become pregnant again? I can't face the agony and disappointment of it," she wailed.

He realised that he had touched a raw nerve, and that for the sake of peace, he would have to pander to her whims. But beneath his placid exterior, emotionally he was craving for stimulus and satisfaction. He had often considered that there were many women in Dowlais who would be only too pleased to satisfy his needs, but he had to avoid scandal; he had no wish to hurt Lucy or to damage himself in the eyes of Uncle William.

The one person he fancied was young Siani Davies, who he believed was ripe for the picking. He often wished she would make herself more available, because recently he had seen less of her as she worked more time in the morning and less in the evening. He decided to put her wages up by a shilling a week because she was doing so well, and hoped it would be an inducement to her to spend more time when he was there.

In the evening, she still concentrated on the upper floor where his uncle's rooms were fitted out on a much grander scale. She enjoyed polishing his mahogany desk and his tall glass-fronted bookcase, but in particular, she took pride in polishing his black leather couch, which was placed beneath the window.

She had almost finished her work there one evening, when she heard the door creak and she turned her head to see George Williams come into the room. He went to the bookcase to replace a ledger and then smiled at her. "You're doing a good job of work up here, that leather couch looks most inviting," he said. She looked away, but he tilted her chin with his forefinger, kissed her and led her towards the couch.

She resisted him. "Please Mr Williams, I'd rather not," she protested.

"Come, my dear, all I want is a little cuddle," he said, slipping his arm around her waist.

He quickly covered her face and neck with kisses and had her firmly within his grasp. His passion finally got the better of him and he ripped her bodice open, eased her down on to the couch and tugged at her underclothing.

Siani screamed when he bent over her, and instinctively she brought her knee up and caught him directly in his crotch. He threw his head back and howled with pain. She leapt upon him and clawed his face in a wild frenzy, then fled.

"You little bitch!" he yelled, and he heard her running down the stairs, then trying the outer door, which he had locked in case of trouble. The next thing he heard was the sound of shattering glass, and he later found that she had kicked the office window out, in order to get away. "She'll pay for this!" he growled and went to his office to recover.

Siani ran home non-stop, not daring to think of the consequences of her actions. When she reached home, she was in a state of collapse. Ben and David looked at her in bewilderment, "What is it Siani?" Ben asked.

"George Williams was going to rape me," she said, choking on her words, "go and ask Mrs Bowen to come."

Ben ran off at once and Siani gradually unfolded her story, as she wept on Bessie's shoulder. "I've marked him, Mrs Bowen, perhaps he'll report me to the police," she said, trembling with fright.

"He won't do that, he'll be too ashamed, he asked for what he got," Bessie Bowen said, trying to calm her down. "Some of these bosses seem to think they can do what they like with people. The main thing is that you got away from him and you are safe here with me."

"I can't go back there ever again. How are we going to manage, Ben?" she moaned.

"Don't worry, we won't starve, I'll go to the workhouse rather than see you fall into the clutches of that man," Ben said bitterly.

"I wish Lewsyn would come home," Siani cried, "he'd look after us and he'd soon deal with George Williams."

"Have patience," said Mrs Bowen, "he'll come in good time," though secretly she wondered whether it would ever be safe for him to do so because he had such a bad reputation.

The few shillings Siani received from the parish were barely enough to keep body and soul together. Ben and David scoured the countryside for wood, and even went as far as raiding the Crawshay tips for cinders. By the end of April, like many others, they were in rags, wore odd shoes stuffed with paper, and survived mainly on bread and dripping.

In Dowlais, tempers were frayed and there was talk of rioting. Siani felt sick when she eventually received a letter from George Williams, banning her and all members of her family from the works and land owned by the Dowlais Iron Company.

* * *

Early in May, Joe Griffiths, as lodge secretary, called a meeting to spell out his view that the union faced defeat and would have to negotiate with the Masters. It was a hopeless situation and he had an unenviable task. He needed every ounce of courage that he possessed to present the unpalatable truth that the Masters' Association remained as inflexible as ever. "In Dowlais, it's the alliance between the Board of Guardians and the Ironmasters, which has been our undoing. We never foresaw the cruel dodge of offering twenty-five of us to work at pits from which we were locked out. But for the fact that they've had to give us poor relief as a loan, they would have had a bloody revolution on their hands," he said bitterly.

He looked around the room at the gaunt, haggard faces of beaten men and sensed their misery and degradation. "This stalemate can't continue, so what are we to do? The Masters are prepared to negotiate, but only on their terms. They've lost a lot of money over the last five months, and they'll want to make sure they get it back."

There were howls of protest from extremists like Dai Dando and his followers. "Was it for this that we risked our lives in that bloody workhouse?" Dai shouted, blazing with anger.

But another reaction followed quickly. Moses Williams drew himself up to his full height and said solemnly, "I care as much about principles as anyone, and I've risked my life to fight for them, but I say the time has now come for a temporary pause so that we can gather our strength."

Llew Jones staggered to his feet looking a broken man; he was so short of breath that he could barely speak. "I think my family has suffered as much as anyone's," he said quietly, "and unless you want them to starve to death, then we must negotiate a settlement, however much it goes against the grain." He could say no more but sat down to loud acclaim.

There were howls of dissent from the extremists, but Moses shouted, "Put it to the meeting that we start negotiations."

Abraham Jenkins got to his feet. "All those in favour, raise their hands," he thundered.

Joe Griffiths and two committee members counted the forest of hands.

"Any against?"

"Five."

"One hundred and ninety nine in favour, five against. Motion carried," said Abe.

Young Ben Davies who had been following it all, heaved a sigh of relief and went home to tell Siani.

Chapter 25
May 1875

Union meetings were held weekly in The Colliers' Arms, to keep up with details about the strike settlement as it was being negotiated.

"The news is grim," Joe Griffiths warned. "The Masters insist on a twelve and a half percent wage cut and what they call a sliding scale."

There was a growl of disapproval. "What's this sliding scale?" asked Dai Dando.

"It means that wages will go up and down according to the price of iron, steel and coal in the markets," said Joe, trying to put a brave face on it.

"More than likely it will work in favour of the Masters while it lasts," said Moses, "I can see another fight ahead of us."

For the most part, the members of the union were resigned to their fate, and even Joe had lost the will to continue with the battle.

"I want a show of hands for the twelve and a half percent cut and the sliding scale," said the Chairman, emphasising the importance of the decision. It slipped through in stony silence because there was no point in arguing about it. Downhearted and demoralised, the men left the meeting secretly swearing vengeance.

*   *   *

Siani should have been more cheerful now that the end was in sight, but she looked more worried then ever and Bessie Bowen was concerned about her.

"What's the matter, Siani fach? Is there anything I can do for you?" she asked.

Siani shook her head and was close to tears. "If it's Alys you're worried about, then I think you should call the doctor," Bessie insisted.

"We stopped paying the doctor's fund after Dad died, so it will have to be the parish doctor," Siani admitted.

"Will you let me see to it?" Bessie asked.

Reluctantly, she agreed. "Alys is bringing up big blobs of blood like Mam did," she said.

Dr. Job James called towards the end of the week and could tell by Alys's wasted body and high fever that she would not last long. Siani explained about her troublesome cough causing her to bring up blood. "Can you give her a bottle of medicine, doctor?" she asked.

He took her out to the kitchen and said, "Your sister is very ill and must be given peace and quiet. Keep the younger children out of the room. I'll send a bottle of medicine to keep her calm, but keep it under lock and key," he warned.

Bessie listened to this conversation and decided to speak up. "Siani's not well either, doctor. She's been out of sorts for some time."

"Do you sleep with your sister?" he asked.

"Yes."

"Let me sound your chest," he said.

Bessie helped Siani to undo her blouse, which she took off and, meanwhile, Dr. James questioned her about her symptoms. "Off your food and sickness in the mornings you say?"

"Yes doctor."

He sounded her chest. "That's clear, thank God," he said, "now let me see your stomach."

Siani looked at Bessie Bowen, who nodded her head and urged Siani to unfasten her skirt.

He carried out his examination gently, and asked, "Have your monthly periods stopped?"

"Yes doctor," she whispered.

"Since when?"

"March."

"I think you are pregnant, my dear," he said.

Siani gulped and flopped into the armchair.

"I'll leave you now, but you can send for me if your sister gets worse, and remember what I said about the medicine."

After he left, Siani burst out crying. "Mrs Bowen, what am I to do?" she wailed.

"How far gone are you, bach?"

"It must have happened just before Lewsyn went away."

"That's nearly three months now," Bessie said, counting on her fingers.

Siani's crying became uncontrollable.

"Do you want me to speak to his father and mother?" Bessie offered.

"No, they would put all the blame on me," she said, starting to tremble violently.

"I thought you might be in some sort of trouble but there's little you can do until Lewsyn Jones comes out of hiding."

"I don't want anyone else to know about it yet. Promise me, Mrs Bowen," she pleaded.

"You can trust me, cariad," Bessie said, putting her arms around her.

*　　*　　*

Ben and David hoped to get work in Trecatti Pit when it became known that there was a need for coal to feed the Dowlais furnaces, which had been re-lit. They looked like two scarecrows when they set out to sign on. To Siani's surprise, they returned home mid- morning, and as soon as she saw Ben's face she sensed trouble.

"We're not wanted there. We queued outside the offices to sign on, but when I gave our names and addresses, the clerk said there was nothing for us," Ben said, with a tremor in his voice.

Then David added, "We spoke to Uncle Joe and asked if he'd take us on as labourers, but he said he couldn't."

Ben's face was furrowed with anxiety. "I think we've been blacklisted Siani, and I know who is behind it all."

She buried her face in her hands and thought of the all-pervading influence of George Williams and his uncle. She had hoped that his ban was only during the strike, but it was now clear that he was taking revenge on both her and her family indefinitely.

"What about trying somewhere else? Are the Crawshay Works starting up?" she asked desperately.

"No, Robert Crawshay won't accept anyone who has anything to do with trade unions. His works are shut down," Ben said.

"I wonder whether Moses Williams can tell us where to go," said David, "he may be in the same position as we are."

"I doubt it, but there's no harm in trying," said Ben. "We've got to do something quickly because our money from the parish will be stopped soon."

Moss, as he was affectionately known, was very helpful. "I'm hoping to have a start in one of Fothergill's pits down the valley. Come with me, he's not as hard and fast on the wages policy as the Dowlais bosses. We can try our luck at his Graig Pit."

"We'll be there, Moss. Just tell us when you want to set out," Ben said. "It will be a long walk but that's nothing as long as we can have work."

"I'll see you tomorrow morning at seven o'clock," he promised.

Siani sat with Alys most of the day keeping watch over her, mopping her clammy brow and moistening her parched lips. She tried everything possible to nourish and sustain her, but Alys had lost the will to fight. Since she had started taking Dr. James's medicine, she was calmer and slept a great deal, which no doubt was what he had intended.

During her long wait, Siani turned her thoughts anxiously to the boys, though she dared not count on success after their experience at Trecatti. When she heard their footsteps in the kitchen, she went out at once and knew by their faces, that they had good news. "We've got work in the Graig Pit and we're going to start labouring for Moss on Monday," Ben said jubilantly.

Siani's face lit up. "You're in good hands, Lewsyn used to say that Moss was one of the best colliers in Trecatti."

He had come back with them specially to enquire about Alys. "She's very peaceful Moss, but she's slipping away from us," Siani said, choking on her words.

"When the time comes, if you need any help, you can rely on me," he said quietly.

She sobbed and turned to him saying, "If only Lewsyn would come home, I need him. He's been gone for three months with no word."

"He'll come when he thinks it's safe, but in the meantime, I'll keep an eye on Ben and Dave in Graig Pit, you can depend on that."

The boys were reluctant to leave Siani on her own with Alys, but she insisted that they should go to work because their need for money was so great. They were heavily in debt to Mr Morris, the grocer, and they needed every penny they could get for food.

Siani confided in Ben about her fear that Alys would have a pauper's funeral, but he himself had already decided that she should lie with their Mam. "I'm going to talk to the Buffs' Secretary and I'll tell him that Dave and I will pay our arrears now that we're working. They'll understand," he said solemnly.

Dr. James made one final visit to see Alys, and when he heard the rattle in her breathing, he warned Siani that death was imminent. Bessie Bowen stayed with Siani throughout the night, and as dawn was breaking, Alys breathed her last gasp. Gently, she led Siani, who was completely distraught, out to the kitchen, and she pulled the sheet over the waxen face of the young girl, who was barely fifteen years old.

Chapter 26

In the aftermath of the funeral, Siani began to feel bitter about all that had happened in her short life. Slowly, she slipped into a depression and even talked about drowning herself in Dowlais pond. Bessie Bowen was so concerned that once again she took matters into her own hands and confronted Mari Jones.

"Isn't it about time your Lewsyn came home now that the strike is over?" she asked.

"He'll come when he's ready," Mari said, then pursed her narrow lips.

"Well, you can tell him from me that he'd better come home to do his duty by Siani Davies," Bessie added.

Mari looked startled. "What do you mean by that?"

Work it out for yourself, Mari, he was courting her wasn't he, and she's carrying his child."

Her temper flared. "I warned him to have nothing to do with that girl, she's a bad lot," she said angrily, her colour rising.

"I'm afraid the Rev. Theo Evans will have to know because he's been like a father to those children," Bessie added, knowing full well that this was the last thing that Mari Jones would want to happen.

After the younger children had gone to bed, Mari broached the subject with Llew, who was now back at work, but not in the best of health. "Bessie Bowen came to see me today and gave me an awful shock. She said that Siani Davies is in the family way and that our Lewsyn is to blame." With difficulty she continued, "She's threatening to tell the Rev. Theo Evans and says that Lewsyn had better come home soon to marry her......."

Llew looked thunderstruck and stared at Mari in bewilderment. "He's been a wild boy, I know, but I didn't think he'd get himself into trouble that way. How can we be sure that it's true?"

"That's exactly what I thought, and the sad part is that he can't come home to speak for himself. Bessie insists that we write to him to make him come home, but he could end up in goal if the police find out he's here." Mari bit her nails and shifted uncomfortably in her chair as Llew stared blankly into the fire.

Eventually he said, "Well, I suppose he'll have to come home sometime, especially if she names him to the parish as the putative father. They'll insist that he pays towards the child." He drew his hand across his forehead, saying, "This is all too much for me. I'll think about it and we'll discuss it tomorrow." Wearily, he got up from his wooden armchair at the fireside and set about putting his clothes ready for work next morning. "I hope Bessie Bowen will keep her trap shut and give our Lewsyn a chance to clear his name," he said, before he climbed the stone stairs to bed.

The more Llew thought about the problem, the more he believed his family's reputation would be endangered. Mari was all for keeping things quiet, but he pointed out that it could only be for a while. "The truth will have to come out and we'd better hear it from the lips of our own son," he said emphatically.

He sat down and wrote a short letter to Lewsyn, who was now in lodgings in Loudon Square in Cardiff docks.

Dear Lewsyn,

I'm back at work now and the iron trade is holding up well. Wages are not all that good, so that I have to work longer hours to get enough to feed and clothe us. Your mother and I would like to see you, as we believe there's something you ought to know about Siani Davies, so try and make a short visit, however brief it may be.

Cofion cynnes, (Good wishes)
Dad

* * *

When Lewsyn Jones returned from his third voyage from Cardiff to Bilbao on a coal ship bringing back a cargo of iron ore, he was delighted to see a letter in his father's handwriting awaiting him in his Cardiff lodgings. He opened it eagerly but his face fell when he finished reading it. What was his father trying to tell him? Was Siani ill or had she taken up with someone else during his absence? He was in such turmoil that he decided to risk going back to Dowlais as soon as possible. He had sent her a card from Bilbao, but whether she had received it was another matter.

There was a note of urgency in his father's letter which, combined with his overwhelming desire to see and hold Siani, made him throw caution to the winds. His heart was thumping when he set out next day and he couldn't get to Merthyr Tydfil fast enough. Passengers on the train looked at him with interest, but he hoped that his auburn beard, his long, golden hair, bleached by the sun, and his bronzed skin would act as a cover to prevent him being recognised. The long scar down the side of his face which he had acquired in a fight in Bilbao, certainly marked him out and distinguished him from the old Lewsyn, so he hoped.

As the train approached Merthyr Tydfil, the old familiar sights of sprawling tips and the coal-black river brought a lump to his throat. Then he thought of 'China' and a shudder went through him; Hoppy was no doubt still up to his old tricks and Lewsyn realised that he'd have to keep his head down until he reached Dowlais. His heart raced at the prospect of seeing Siani and yet fear of the unknown made him very uncertain of the reception he would have.

He got out of the train at Dowlais, hoisted his kit bag on his back, and with his wide-brimmed hat tilted over his face, he made for Ivor Lane. His mother was overcome when she saw him.

"My lovely boy, I knew you'd come, I've been preparing for you," she said, as she wept tears of joy. She caressed his face, marking out the jagged scar and asked innumerable questions about what had happened to him.

Lewsyn had little patience with all the fuss, and quickly calmed her down. "What did Dad mean in his letter when he said there was something I should know about Siani?" he asked.

"Perhaps you should wait until your father comes home," she said mysteriously.

"I want to know now. Is she ill? Tell me what's happened."

His mother busied herself making him a cup of tea, but he stood up saying, "I can't wait, I'm going to Nant Row to find out for myself what's been happening."

Mari Jones barred his way. "You won't go until I've spoken to you. That hussy is in the family way and you're having the fault."

Lewsyn gasped, and at once his mind raced back to his last night in Dowlais. He side-stepped his mother, shot out through the door and raced down to Nant Row oblivious to whoever saw him.

Siani was bent over the washing-board scrubbing clothes when he burst into the kitchen. She was stunned by his sudden appearance, and stared at him in amazement while she wiped the lather from her arms and stood back unsure of what to do or say.

He opened his arms wide, but she still did not move, then he advanced towards her and kissed her gently on her lips. To his surprise, she did not respond but lowered her head and wept bitterly.

"Where have you been Lewsyn, and why didn't you send me word?" she sobbed. "I've been waiting for you, hoping desperately that you'd come home."

He held her to him as she wept uncontrollably.

"I did write, so tell me what's worrying you, Siani."

She raised her head slightly and whispered, "I'm going to have your child." Then overcome by emotion, she broke down again.

"How far gone are you, my darling Siani?" he asked.

"Four months, it happened here in this room the day that you went away," she murmured.

He kissed her gently and said, "I'll look after you, my sweetheart, we'll get married and you can come back with me to Cardiff to live."

To his surprise, she suddenly recoiled. "How can I? There are Will and Mag to think of, I can't leave them," she gasped, "and poor Alys has died."

He swallowed hard and he suddenly realised that he was trapped. "I'll do anything for you Siani fach, but if I stay here in Dowlais I'll be arrested. The police are after me, I've made lots of enemies, especially when I was in hiding in 'China'. I'm risking my life by coming her today."

A shudder went through her and she raised her tear-stained eyes. "Then it seems we'll have to live our lives apart," she murmured.

"Not if I can help it," he said, clinging to her. "I'm going to stand by you Siani, we'll have to find a way out. I'll go back to Butetown, but I'll give you the address where I lodge."

She gave him a pathetic look. "Promise you'll come back, Lewsyn, because I love you. Any day now the word will get out that I'm having a baby and I'll be treated like a leper," she cried.

"If you come with me, I'll treat you like a princess," he said, kissing her passionately.

She made no reply.

Chapter 27

Word soon got out that a bronzed young man like Lewsyn Jones had been seen leaving Siani Davies's house and had gone off towards Ivor Lane. Bessie Bowen called to ask Siani if it was true that he'd been to see her.

"Yes, quite true, Mrs Bowen, and I've told him about the baby," she sighed.

"What did he say?" Bessie asked, full of concern.

"He's pleased about it and has promised to marry me, but don't tell anyone yet," she pleaded, still feeling unsure of herself.

"Siani fach, you can trust me, it's that mother of his you'll have to be wary of. I gave her a piece of my mind, and threatened that if Lewsyn didn't show up, I'd go to see the Rev. Theo Evans."

Siani looked startled. "Please don't tell him, whatever you do, I've got a dread of what will happen. Mrs Jones isn't likely to blab because she'll want to keep clear of the disgrace, and she certainly won't want anyone to know that Lewsyn has been home."

"No matter what she thinks, Lewsyn will have to face the consequences of what he's done, and I hope he'll be man enough to do so," Bessie said sharply.

* * *

After Ben and David had bathed and had their food, Siani decided it was time to tell them the truth about her predicament. "I had a visitor today, and you'll never guess who it was! Before I say anymore, I'm going to swear you to secrecy," she added.

Ben looked up from the paper he was reading and David leaned across the table, anxious not to miss anything.

"It was Lewsyn!"

"Never!" said Ben.

"How did he look?" asked David.

"He looked different, and had grown a beard. He's been living in Cardiff and has been sailing on a cargo boat to Spain."

"Is he coming back to Dowlais?" Ben asked anxiously, peering into Siani's face.

"No, it's not safe for him, he could be arrested, but he's given me his address."

Ben looked discomfited, and Siani sensed his uneasiness. "I'm going to have his baby and he's going to marry me," she said quietly.

David gasped. "Why didn't you tell us this before? I knew there was something wrong with you when you were looking after our Alys."

She looked guilty and admitted, "Yes, I was expecting before Alys died. I've been frantic with worry because Lewsyn did not come home earlier, but I feel much better now I've seen him and talked to him."

Ben looked hard at Siani and then said, "I've had my suspicions too, and I won't be satisfied until he puts a ring on your finger." Turning to David he warned, "Don't say a word of this to anyone, not even to Moss, because, knowing Lewsyn, anything could go wrong."

"Don't say that! He risked his life by coming back to see me, and I still love him," she gasped.

"When is the baby due?" Ben asked, running his eyes over Siani.

"At the end of the year, I think," she said quietly.

Ben subconsciously began to count on his fingers. "So it happened when the strike was on, before he ran away," he murmured.

"Just about then," she admitted.

Ben shook his head in disbelief. "And you've kept it quiet all this time."

"I had to, Alys was so ill, and we had so many problems, but I managed to work through it all."

David raised his large brown eyes and looked at Siani. "Don't worry, I'll stand by you. All that matters is that you've come through it all right and that you got away from George Williams."

She shuddered and felt a lump rise in her throat so she went out to call Will and Mag in from the street where they were playing with their friends.

* * *

Mari Jones could scarcely believe Lewsyn's declaration that he was going to marry Siani Davies.

"Do you mean to tell me that you admit that you are the father of that girl's child?" she shrieked. "You should be downright ashamed to say such a thing."

Llew Jones was more understanding, but even he urged caution. "How can you be sure after being away from her for over three months?" he asked, hoping for a way out.

"It's my child, Siani has been faithful to me, there's no doubt about that. We'll get married as soon as possible."

"You won't marry her from this house," Mari screeched.

"No Mam, I'm going back to Cardiff, so you needn't worry," he said angrily and left in a huff.

Lewsyn hid in the scrubland above the railway station and once more realised that he was on the run. He had decided to wait until dusk, because he knew he was in danger in Dowlais. He was leaning on his bag trying to work out his best course of action, when he saw two policemen arrive on the platform and they began to search the waiting room and adjacent buildings.

His heart thumped and he wondered how long they had been looking for him. He watched them talking to people waiting on the platform for the next train, but they were too far away for him to hear any of the conversation. He realised that if he were to break cover now, he would be caught at once, so he decided he'd have to change his plans and go in the direction of Pant, to see if he could find wagons carrying limestone as before. "If I can find a journey going down the valley, I'll join it, no matter where I'll end up," he told himself.

His luck was in, because in the sidings at just before midnight, he saw and heard a long string of wagons being shunted out, ready for departure. He jumped aboard, slung his kit bag over the high side of the wagon and lay down flat, his head on the bag. It was a moonlit night, and away from the smoke of Dowlais, he was able to see the stars. One in particular stood out, and he wondered whether it was the North Star to which sailors attached so much importance. "Be my guiding star," he prayed, as the wagons jolted awkwardly down the track to an unknown destination.

The locomotive hissed and hooted and gradually chugged its way through Dowlais and down the valley past the town of Merthyr Tydfil. Lewsyn saw the iron and steel works from a perspective which he had never known before, and cursed the fact that he was being forced to leave them, and the woman he loved.

A mile or two further on he began to realise that this journey of wagons was making for a tunnel, and the next thing he knew was that he was plunged into total darkness, and was being covered by a deposit of soot from the engine. He lay face downwards on his bag and offered up a silent prayer for his safe delivery from such a long, noisy, frightening experience.

To his great relief, the train emerged safely from the tunnel and came to a halt at the little station of Abernant, above Aberdare, the name of which he was able to identify in the moonlight. He realised he had to be quick-thinking if he were to survive, so he hoisted his bag onto his back and using both hands, he levered himself over the side of the wagon and ran off into some bushes, away from the track. He watched the journey go on its way towards Neath and heaved a sigh of relief. Unable to go a step further, he used his bag as a pillow, drew his coat around himself and slept under the stars.

Next morning, he woke early to the heavy tramp of feet going in the direction of the nearby Werfa Colliery. He stretched his stiff limbs and slowly made his way out of the undergrowth on his hands and knees, and saw the men on the early shift trudging along in a steady, black stream carrying their lamps, jacks and tommy boxes. He sat on his haunches for a while, taking stock of his situation and eventually decided that since fate had dictated that he should be in Aberdare, he should try his luck to find work there instead of returning to Cardiff. It would certainly be nearer to his beloved Siani and a covering of coal dust might even be a useful disguise for him.

He slaked his thirst from a nearby water-spout and set off to look for work at the Werfa Colliery. He told himself that there was no harm in trying, and that if all else failed, he could always go back to Cardiff. He found the colliery office and knocked on the door, which was opened by a startled clerk who looked at him suspiciously.

"What do you want?" he snapped.

"I'm looking for work. Any jobs going on top or any haulage work?"

"You don't look like a collier, wherever you come from. We have more than enough men already. Go down the valley and try in Thomas Powell's pits." So saying, he slammed the door.

Lewsyn trudged down the steep mountain path in the direction of Cwmbach. He looked down upon the valley at his feet and saw that it was green and pleasant compared with the all-pervading ugliness of Dowlais. He stopped and looked and listened; he saw long lines of wagons, full of blue-black coal gleaming in the sunshine, jostling with each other as they snaked their way down the valley to the port of Cardiff. "Coal is king over here," he told himself, "and if I want to be near Siani, yet remain hidden from my enemies, I'll have to take whatever work I can get."

On his third attempt, he finally had a job as a labourer in the Middle Duffryn Pit in Cwmbach, where he would earn five shillings a day and work a fifty-four hour week. "It's not what I want, but shortly I'll have a wife and child to support and I'll have to put them first," he told himself.

Hungry and thirsty, he called in the Victoria Inn, where he found the bar full of coal-black men who had come off the early shift, and were quenching their thirsts before going home. He looked at them with interest and thought that no disguise could be more complete; only the whites of their eyes relieved their total and utter blackness.

Lewsyn, with his red-gold hair and tanned skin caught the eye of the barmaid. "You're not from these parts by the look of you," she said, giving him the glad eye.

"No, I've come up here to look for work, he said in as non-committal a way as possible, "and now I'm looking for lodgings, do you know of any?"

"I might do, my auntie takes in lodgers, but she usually likes to know a bit about them. What's your name, then?" she asked, leaning forward to have a better view of him.

"Lewis. What's yours?"

"Rosie."

"Well, Rosie, tell me where your auntie lives, so that when I've eaten these few sandwiches, I can go to see her."

"I'll come with you, if you wait for me to come off duty in half an hour," she said, giving him a sly grin.

Lewsyn sat back and sipped his tankard of beer and speculated on whether it was wise to allow this voluptuous young woman with such brassy good looks to walk him around Cwmbach.

He turned away to talk to some of the colliers, most of whom spoke Welsh, and who welcomed him when he greeted them in their mother tongue.

"So you're looking for work are you?" said one big, burly character, who had overheard the conversation with Rosie.

"I've had an offer of labouring in the Duffryn Pit, but the wages aren't very good," Lewsyn said.

"Don't we know it?" said one small, hunch-backed fellow across the table. "Luther here is our lodge secretary, so if you're going to work for Powell, the sooner the better you join our union.

Lewsyn nodded. "I'll join as soon as I get my first pay packet. Where do you meet?"

"Here in the upstairs room, second and fourth Fridays in the month," said the big, burly Luther, downing his last drop of ale.

"Do you want another?" Lewsyn asked.

"No thanks, boyo, my missus will be making dinner for me and she'll have the bath water ready. By the way, be careful with that wench behind the bar, I know what her auntie's doss-house is like and before you know it, you'll be fleeced."

"Thanks for warning me Luther," Lewsyn murmured, and gave him a wink. In the interval which followed the departures of Luther and his comrades, Lewsyn spent his time looking around the shabby room and observing its occupants. The grimy windows, worn wooden benches and stone floor strewn with sawdust was as bad as The Colliers' Arms in Dowlais. There were few embellishments save for a murky mirror with Rock Brewery inscribed on it and a good, solid cast iron fireplace with a brass spittoon on the hearth. Since living in Cardiff, sailing to and fro to Spain, he had become used to something better and more colourful, but he consoled himself with the thought that without places like Cwmbach and Dowlais, there would be no Cardiff Docks and no voyages to Spain. He did not relish the prospect before him, but it would be worth it as long as he could see Siani and do his duty by her.

He walked down Bridge Road with Rosie and they made their way along the canal bank towards Duffryn Row. The smell from the turgid, murky waters turned his stomach, yet he noticed children playing happily nearby. "Not much traffic on the canal now," he commented.

"No, the railway has taken over most of it," Rosie said. "Some barges bring cargoes of goods to the village, and the Coop shop in Bridge Road uses it quite a lot."

They arrived at Mrs Flynn's cottage and one look was enough to tell him that she was easy-going, to say the least. A dark, plump, slovenly woman of about thirty-five or so, she eyed him up and down. "So you want lodgings do you? Well, Rosie must think you'd fit in or she wouldn't have brought you here. I'll put you up for 17/6d a week all found. How's that?"

Lewsyn looked around the kitchen, saw the pile of ashes which had spilled out from the grate on to the hearth, noticed the rickety wooden table and chairs, the lack of the usual polished dresser or chest of drawers and decided it was a poverty-stricken place. He didn't ask to see the bedrooms, because the all-pervading smell in and around the house put him off. He looked out on to the untidy garden and saw a pig-sty at the end of it, with a barrel of 'wash' nearby. His stomach turned over and he decided this place was not for him. "Before I make up my mind, I'm going to look at some other lodgings up in the centre of the village," he lied.

Rosie's face fell and she pointed out that Duffryn Row would be more convenient for his work.

"Perhaps too convenient, I'd like to get away from the noise and the dirt," he said pointing towards the colliery. He picked up his kit bag, slung it over his shoulder and called to her, "See you in the Queen Vic, sometime." He left hurriedly, thanking his lucky stars that Luther had warned him.

The lodgings he finally settled on were in a house in Phillip Row, where he shared a bedroom with two others for fifteen shillings a week. It was clean, cramped and comfortless, but was bearable, as it was far enough away from the smell of the canal. Throughout the month of July, he worked at the Duffryn Pit as a labourer, clearing the small coal and slag which colliers at the coalface threw aside. It was dreary and boring work which he hated. Sometimes, he thought he heard the timbers groan as he made his way along the roadway at the pit bottom, and his blood ran cold at the prospect of being buried alive.

At the end of his first week, he took home twenty-five shillings after stoppages for his safety lamp, tools and the doctor's fund. He looked at it in disgust, and thought of what he should have been earning in the rolling mills at Dowlais Works. "It's nothing but slavery down in that big, black hole, but I'll have to put up with it," he said wearily.

Chapter 28

One of the saving graces of living in Cwmbach was that no one knew Lewsyn Jones. He told his mates only as much as he wanted them to know, and spent much of his free time helping in the Co-op shop in Bridge Road. Luther Jones had got him involved there, for which he was very grateful. After he had unloaded sacks of flour and sugar from the canal barges, and carried them to the shop, he would sometimes be given a packet of tea or a lump of cheese for his trouble, which pleased him and saved him money.

But always in his mind was his need to see Siani, and by the end of his first month, he decided he would have to risk it, as he could hold out no longer. He walked over the mountain from Abernant to Heolgerrig and then up to Dowlais. He was glad of the fresh air, and prided himself that with his beard clipped to hide his scar and his hair cropped he could pass unnoticed in a crowd.

It was about five o'clock in the afternoon when he reached Dowlais, hot, hungry and thirsty after his long walk. He could feel his heart pounding as he turned the corner into Nant Row, saw the door of No. 2 wide open and heard Siani's voice. When she saw him, she smiled and came forward to greet him. He kissed her and looked at her quizzically to make sure she was all right. He had to satisfy himself that she was looking after herself after all she had been through.

David, Will and Mag were at the table having tea, but immediately stopped eating and started to question him.

"Where have you come from, Lew? It's ages since we saw you," said David eagerly.

He sat down in the armchair and wearily undid the buttons on his waistcoat. "Let's say I've travelled a fair distance since I left my lodgings, but I'm not saying how far." Looking at Will and Mag, who were staring at him in bewilderment, he added, "No one is supposed to know that I'm here, so say nothing."

They nodded their heads and resumed eating. Siani brought him a cup of tea and as she did, he noticed that she was beginning to show that she was expecting a child, which secretly brought him great pleasure.

David continued to chat about his work and explained how he and Ben had a long walk each day down to Graig Colliery where they worked with Moss Williams. "Can I tell Moss I've seen you?" he asked.

"Yes, but ask him to keep it secret, tell him I'd love to have a talk with him sometime."

Soon, Will left the table to sit on his lap. "We're going to the circus up on the Waun, are you coming with us?" he asked plaintively.

Lewsyn looked at Siani who explained that David was taking the youngsters to stand outside the tent in the hope that they could peep inside to see what was going on.

"No, I think I'll stay here with Siani," he said with a smile, and he put his hand into his waistcoat pocket and pulled out two halfpennies. "One for you and one for Mag to buy some sweets," he said to Will who beamed at him.

Siani hastily washed Will's face and hands, then he and Mag left happily with David. As soon as she had bolted the door, Lewsyn took her in his arms. "How are you, my love?" he asked, kissing her hungrily. "I had to see whether you were safe and well."

"I feel happier now I've seen you. Where are you living, Lew? You said that you were going back to Cardiff."

"Things didn't work out as I expected, I'm working over the mountain in Cwmbach, just outside Aberdare. It's not much of a job, but it means I can slip over to see you and be of some help." He took out of his pocket a crown, which he put in her hand. "That's for our baby, and I've saved another one towards out marriage licence," he said proudly.

She kissed him and looked at him anxiously. "How are we going to manage Lew? I'm terrified that you'll be spotted and that someone will tell the police."

"Leave the worrying to me. All I want is for you to name the day when we can be married, my love."

She sighed and he realised there were more problems than he knew about. "Our names are under discussion in Bethania Chapel, and the talk is that we are both going to be expelled. I'm afraid to see your mother in case she'll attack me."

He put a protective arm around her saying "When you come to live with me in Aberdare, we'll be far enough away from their wagging tongues."

"How can I? You can see how much the little ones depend on me."

"The main thing is that we get married and I'd like you to name the day when I come next," he said, kissing her, stroking her hair and holding her close to him.

Lewsyn left in the gathering dusk and made his way back to Ivor Lane, where his parents were surprised to see him. "Have you come all the way from Cardiff today?" his mother asked.

"No Mam, I'm not living there now, I'm over in Aberdare," he said.

"Got a job there have you?" asked his father, scrutinising him.

"Yes, labouring in Thomas Powell's Duffryn Pit. The money's not very good but Cwmbach is a quiet spot and few people know me."

"You'll stay there if you're wise, because after your last visit, the police came to question us," said Mari Jones.

"They're still looking for you and the reward is still on offer," his father affirmed.

"I sometimes wonder whether I should give myself up and take my punishment. I detest this hole and corner way of living, constantly looking over my shoulder, and fearing a knock on the door."

"Don't talk nonsense!" said his mother. "No son of mine is ever going to disgrace our family name by ending up in prison. Just keep away from Dowlais and that tip girl and you'll be safe."

"I wondered when that barb was coming. I suppose you'll be in the front row in Bethania Chapel when the deacons sit in judgement on her and decide to throw her out," he said angrily. "Well, you can tell them that we are getting married, so they needn't bother their heads about us."

Having delivered his parting shot, he left the home where he was not wanted, and made his way towards Pant, where he slept in an empty stone wagon that night. Next morning, he walked back to Aberdare and reached Phillip Row in time for his Sunday dinner. "That's my first trip accomplished," he thought with satisfaction.

For the next month, Lewsyn worked all hours and saved every penny he could earn towards the licence. The whole idea obsessed him and he even went looking around for a cottage or rooms where he and Siani could live. Accommodation was like gold in such a fast-growing area, and he slowly began to realise that Siani, in her present condition, was better off in Dowlais: "I'll have to risk my neck by going back as often as I can, because I've got to see her," he told himself.

By the time of his next visit at the end of August, Lewsyn had saved more money, half of which he gave to Siani, and the other half he put towards the licence. She was now six months pregnant and he insisted she should name the date. "I'll have enough to pay for everything by the end of September, so what about us getting married in a chapel in Aberdare?" he pleaded.

"You mean that I'll have to travel all the way over there to get married?" she said incredulously.

"Yes, I've got it worked out. Hardly anyone will know us, so we'll both be quite safe. I'll ask Moss to be the best man, and he can arrange for you and Ben to travel with him through the tunnel as I did, only in a nice compartment, and I can meet you in Abernant."

She looked unsure until he said, "We can't risk waiting much longer, Siani, say 'Yes' for all our sakes, including the baby's."

She agreed. "But you won't expect me to live in Cwmbach, will you?" she pleaded.

"Not yet, but if I can find a place for you and the youngsters later on, that would solve a lot of problems."

She nodded her head and he quickly sealed her assent with a kiss. "I'm happy now my darling, and I hope you are too," he said embracing her. "I'll come once more before the wedding to see Moss about my plan, and meanwhile, you must swear Ben to secrecy. Not a word to the little 'uns in case they blab," he warned.

On his final visit, two weeks before the wedding, which was to be on Saturday, 30th September, Ben and Moss waited for Lewsyn to arrive. He was later than usual because he had worked an extra turn to boost his wages. In fact, it was getting dusk when he arrived and he explained that he had taken a devious route to avoid being recognised. "I wear this old cloth cap pulled down over my ears, but even that isn't enough of a disguise," he said. Both Ben and Moss noticed that he was slightly on edge, so they fell in with all his plans in order to make everything easier for him and Siani.

"Have no fear, we'll be there in Abernant Station by ten o'clock and we'll go with you to the chapel," Moss said confidently.

It raised Lewsyn's spirits to hear his friend talk in this way, and by the time they had finished reminiscing about their workhouse experience, it was getting dark, so Moss drained the dregs of his tea and went on his way.

Mag and Will were already in bed, Ben and David were nodding, and Lewsyn was almost sleeping on his feet. Siani was worried about him, "Are you going to stay here tonight, Lew? There's enough room in our big bed."

"Yes, come and sleep with us, Lew," Ben said, with a yawn, "you look tired out."

"I must admit that working the early shift and then walking over here afterwards does take it out of me," he said wearily.

"Right, up you go then boys and Lew will follow soon," Siani said as she turned out the lamp.

They sought each other's arms while they sat in the dark, silent kitchen, and he smothered her with kisses. "Do you remember how it was last March?" he whispered.

"Only too well," she said, and she felt the child move inside her.

"It won't be long now, my darling, before we'll be husband and wife, and we'll share our own bed together." She sighed and murmured agreement.

Lewsyn slept soundly that night and woke up to hear Siani calling them for breakfast. They were all seated around the table enjoying toast and tea when there was an almighty thump on the door, and when Ben opened it, there stood Sergeant Wilkes. Siani screamed and looked at Lewsyn, who immediately jumped up and made for the back door. Before he could unlock it, he was grabbed by another officer who accompanied the Sergeant. "Don't move, or I'll draw my truncheon," he shouted, and the Sergeant leapt forward to handcuff Lewsyn.

"You're wanted on serious charges, Lewsyn Jones. I've heard that you've been in Dowlais before, and at last, I've got you under arrest."

"What charges?" shouted Lewsyn, struggling and glaring at the two officers.

The Sergeant took from his pocket a charge sheet and read out, "Assaulting a police officer and causing a riot."

"Rubbish," retorted Lewsyn, who again tried to free himself from the officer holding on to him.

Will and Mag started to cry and Siani stifled a scream when she saw Lewsyn being marched through the door.

"I'm coming with you," shouted Ben, "and I am," David added, but Lewsyn protested.

"No, stay with Siani, and look after her."

They watched in horror as he was bundled into the horse-drawn Black Maria nearby. Ben ran after it shouting, "Don't worry Lewsyn, we'll soon get you back home."

There was uproar in the street, with people piling out of their houses to gawp at what was going on. Fingers were pointed at Lewsyn and then at Siani, and she trembled at the thought that they were both under attack. When the Black Maria finally disappeared, she turned to the family saying, "Go inside, all of you, there are troublemakers around here. Someone must have gone to the police station last night to report Lewsyn. There's a reward on offer and some people will stop at nothing to get it."

Ben looked at Siani, whose face was like chalk. He hesitated before saying, "Shall I go up to tell his father what's happened?"

She nodded agreement and sat by the table, holding her head and sobbing. Memories came flooding back of the time when she herself had been arrested, and the horror which had followed. Gradually, the awful realisation dawned on her that if Lewsyn was sent to goal, their marriage would be delayed indefinitely. She put her head on the table and howled at the prospect before them.

Llew Jones was aghast when he heard the news, and his wife became hysterical. "It's that Siani Davies's fault again," she screamed.

"Shut up!" shouted Llew, "this is no time to start blaming anyone. You stay here and look after the children, while I go with Ben to the police station."

Not one of their household ventured out to Bethania Chapel that Sunday morning and Mari Jones felt ashamed and embittered that her son should have been carted off to goal on the Sabbath of all days.

Chapter 29

At the lodge meeting on Monday evening, Llew Jones raised the question of Lewsyn's arrest. "Don't forget, he was a member of this union and was one of those who volunteered to take the Workhouse Test, so that the rest of us could have poor relief. I've come here to ask for your help," he said sternly.

Joe Griffiths, Lodge Secretary, prevaricated. "What you say is true enough, but we can't answer for what happened after that."

Moss Williams leapt to his feet, his eyes ablaze. "I was there!" he shouted, "and I know how badly Lewsyn was treated, and what courage he showed against such a terrible system. We owe it to him to defend him now, as he defended all of you then. We must get a lawyer for him."

Moss's impassioned plea touched a chord of approval and when it was put to the meeting there was substantial agreement. "Yes, we'll stand by Lewsyn, and we'll get him freed from these charges. It will be one in the eye for the Masters," said Dai Dando bitterly.

Ben rushed home to give Siani the news, and at last a faint smile crossed her face. "I hope they'll give him bail so that he can come back here to us," she said.

"More than likely he'll have to go back to his work and give his Cwmbach address," Ben pointed out, having heard Llew Jones discussing it with Moss Williams.

"I won't be satisfied until all the charges against him are dismissed," she murmured.

Mr C. H. James, solicitor, was familiar with the circumstances surrounding Lewsyn's case, and in particular, knew how cruelly men on poor relief were treated. His own brother, who had served on the Board of Guardians, had been one of the few who had dared to challenge the legality of what had been done to the thousands of able-bodied men denied poor relief because they wouldn't accept 'black-leg' work in Dowlais. When he interviewed Lewsyn in his cell, he assured him, "I'll get you bailed, and you can take it from me that the Poor Law Guardians won't want too much made of your case because it will reflect so adversely on them. I'll need to call upon a good, strong witness who can speak with authority about what went on. Is there anyone you can think of?"

"Moss Williams is your man," Lewsyn said without any hesitation. "He was with me every step of the way while we were inside the workhouse, and he's unafraid."

* * *

The Magistrates' Court was packed when Lewsyn Jones was brought before the Stipendiary Magistrate. Siani was among those on the public benches and was accompanied by Bessie Bowen and Moss Williams. In the front row sat Llew and Mari Jones, both looking extremely anxious and ill-at-ease.

Siani stared fixedly ahead and braced herself for the ordeal that she knew Lewsyn would be put through. She noticed that he had not been allowed to wash or shave and that his clothes were crumpled and dirty. "I'm sure policemen do their utmost to make sure people on trial look terrible," she thought. She managed to catch Lewsyn's eye and gave him a weak smile while they waited.

The hearing began with the charges being put to Lewsyn by the Clerk of the Court. "How do you plead?" he asked.

"Not guilty."

A ripple of excitement went through the courtroom, and when the prosecuting solicitor called upon the police sergeant to give an account of the arrest, he placed great emphasis on the resistance that he had encountered from Lewsyn Jones. He opposed bail on the grounds that he would be likely to abscond. "He's been on the run before, and he'll do it again," he said belligerently.

Mr James immediately got to his feet to plead for bail and emphasised that this was the first time his client had ever been charged in a court of law with any offence. "He hasn't run away from anything. He's had to leave Merthyr Tydfil in order to find work because of victimisation," he said boldly.

Immediately, there was an ominous rumble throughout the courtroom and the Stipendiary Magistrate quickly intervened by saying, "We're not here to hold a post-mortem on the effects of the strike, keep to the issue of bail."

Mr James continued to emphasise that his client was a hard-working man from a good family, was of fixed abode and that his father and his friend, Moss Williams, were prepared to stand surety for bail. "What could be fairer than that?" he asked.

"I'll retire to consider the matter," said the Magistrate stiffly, and then left the court for over an hour. In the meantime, Lewsyn was taken below to the cell and kept under strict observation by two police officers.

The courtroom was abuzz with conversation, and Siani began to wonder whether she could possibly see Lewsyn, but Mr James advised against it. "Leave him be, visitors now might unsettle him," he said.

"Quite right. It's her fault that he was caught and brought here," said Mari Jones spitefully. Siani chose to ignore her and felt sorry she had suggested it.

When the Magistrate returned, an ominous silence enveloped the whole courtroom and Lewsyn stood impatiently in the dock awaiting his fate.

"I've had to think long and hard about whether or not to grant you bail. There are many disquieting features about the charges before me," said the Beak. "However, I am prepared to give it, subject to the following strict conditions: that you do not interfere with witnesses, that you live at a fixed and settled address, and that your father and your friend provide a surety of £20-00."

A gasp went around the courtroom and Lewsyn stood rigidly to attention as the Magistrate fixed the date for a hearing in two months time.

Siani's heart leapt when she heard the news, both for Lewsyn's sake and her own. Yet again, she felt the child move inside her and she hoped that Lewsyn would be able to stay with her when her time came.

"Come Siani fach, we'll go outside to wait for Lewsyn," said Bessie Bowen, who realised that there were more formalities to be completed. They waited patiently on the pavement until he came, accompanied by his parents, Moss Williams and Mr James.

"Cariad annwyl," (Dear love) "it's good to see you," he said, throwing his arms around her.

Lewsyn, Siani, Moss and Mrs Bowen retired discreetly to the Coffee Tavern, where he explained his position. "I've agreed to stay at my lodgings in Cwmbach so that I can't be accused of any interference. I'll keep my promise to my father and Moss, so there's no question of me running away, and I'll be allowed to visit Dowlais to see Mr James about my case when necessary."

Siani listened to all this and realised that their wedding plans were being dashed. Bessie Bowen saw the look of anguish on her face and with her usual bluntness asked, "What arrangements are you making for you and Siani to get married?"

"Leave that to me, Siani and I have an understanding. I've got to go back to Cwmbach, otherwise I'll be locked up again." Before parting with her, he whispered in her ear, "I'll do my best to make arrangements for us, so be ready to come to Aberdare with Moss and Ben when I send word."

Reluctantly, he tore himself away and went to catch the train back to Abernant, while she returned with the others to Dowlais, feeling very uneasy about her future.

Chapter 30

The whole of Dowlais was seething with gossip about Lewsyn Jones and Siani Davies – the one likely to end up in prison, and the other carrying his child and unmarried. Bessie Bowen found it hard to defend them in face of all the criticism that she encountered in Bethania Chapel. The normally jovial, jolly Bessie became snappy, morose and sullen in self-defence.

Llew and Mari Jones kept a low profile and only appeared in chapel once a week for the Sunday night service. Llew had aged visibly and did not take his usual place in the impressive big seat, but sat alongside Mari and his children in the congregation. At last, Mari Jones had been silenced, and Bessie had failed to get a word out of her about Lewsyn's prospects in the forthcoming trial.

The Rev. Theo Evans found himself in a delicate position. Much though he wanted to visit Siani to comfort her and hear her side of the story, he knew that if certain members saw him entering her house they would use it against him. He had fended off attempts to summon her before the diaconate to receive a reprimand and expulsion, but had secretly felt let down by her immoral behaviour. He had fought for her rehabilitation in Dowlais after the scandal of the trial, and this was the end result.

As for Lewsyn Jones, if he was the father of her child, as well as being a law-breaker, then he should be the first to be reprimanded for scandalous misconduct. But he preferred to await events and see the outcome of the trial, for he was a compassionate man who abhorred strife and persecution.

As a result of the titanic struggles in the 1875 strike, suffering was etched on the faces of the people of

Dowlais, their homes were reduced to the bare essentials for survival, and workers had become bitter and hostile towards their managers. The chapels, he believed, were the only refuge for decent, self-respecting members of the community, while the alehouses were the road to damnation for the weaker brethren and their families. In his long hours of prayer, he begged that Lewsyn and Siani should be spared from being hounded out of Bethania and that they should be protected from the long-term consequences of such drastic action.

*　*　*

Lewsyn, meanwhile, thanked God that the miners' union had backed him, for without a lawyer, and a good one at that, he would stand no chance at all of vindicating himself. He had already suffered enough through being forced to leave Merthyr Tydfil, then being locked up as soon as he dared to return, and now by having his plans to marry Siani disrupted.

He was determined that their wedding should take place in October, even if it had to be by special licence. Siani would be nearing her time of giving birth by November, and the trial would also be looming, so October was their best hope. When he went to Merthyr Tydfil to see Mr James about his case, he would explain all this to her, but first he had to be sure that the Rev. David Price of Siloa Chapel in Aberdare would marry them. He sought an interview with him and found him very understanding. He had worked as a miner himself, and was now a store manager for the Glamorgan Canal Company, so he was a man of the people.

"Yes, my boy, I'll marry you and Siani on the last Saturday in October," he assured him. "Go to the registrar's office and give full particulars so that he will be in attendance that day."

Having completed these arrangements, Lewsyn was looking forward to telling Siani all about them on his next visit to Merthyr Tydfil when he had to keep an appointment with his lawyer. Moss had promised to accompany him to boost his confidence on that occasion.

They agreed to meet on Saturday morning at the station in Merthyr Tydfil and Lewsyn listened eagerly to Moss's most recent news about the trial. "Mr James has taken sworn statements from the members of our gang in the workhouse, and every one of them maintain that you did not touch a policeman. On the contrary, you were the one knocked senseless by Sergeant Flint."

Lewsyn smiled to himself and realised that Mr James was clever. They reached his office at the appointed time where the silver-haired, sharp-witted lawyer was ready to give his client a drilling. He took him through the case step by step, making sure that Lewsyn gave precisely the answers he required. "I want no hesitation or vagueness. Our case must be utterly convincing and entirely consistent," he said sternly.

Lewsyn was shaken to the core by his brusque manner, but secretly hoped that he would paralyse the witnesses for the prosecution by his relentless cross-examination. Before leaving, he summoned up the courage to ask the question bothering him most. "What are my chances, Mr James?"

"Fifty-fifty, I would say. You know what powers lie within the Board of Guardians in this town."

Lewsyn shuddered. "If we lose, what sort of sentence can I expect?" he asked nervously.

"About six months hard labour, at least."

Lewsyn swallowed and felt his stomach turn over.

Moss was put through a similar drill in respect of his corroborative evidence, so that by the time they emerged from the office two hours later, they were both chastened and exhausted.

"I'll say one thing for him, he fights to win," said Moss.

"I hope to God he does, otherwise I'm done for," said Lewsyn. "Don't breathe a word of this to Siani."

They walked back to Dowlais and he confided in Moss about the arrangements he had made for his marriage to her. "The sooner the better we are wed for both our sakes," he said solemnly.

He put on a brave face and told Siani how impressed he was with Mr James and how everything was working in their favour. "I've been able to make arrangements for us to be married on October 28th in Siloa Chapel in Aberdare and Moss will be my best man. Are you pleased, cariad?"

Siani smiled and nodded, and he took her in his arms and kissed her. You and Ben will travel with Moss and I'll meet you at Abernant Station," he added.

*　　*　　*

He was ready and waiting when the train emerged from the tunnel under the mountain to Abernant. Siani looked pale and strained as she stepped on to the platform. Lewsyn kissed her, took her arm, and they walked in the direction of the inn where a brake awaited passengers travelling into Aberdare. "Did you have a good journey, my love?" he asked.

"The tunnel was black and terrifying so I hung on to Ben with all my might," she said quietly. "It made me feel sick."

"A breath of fresh Abernant air will soon put that right," he assured her.

They piled into the brake and chatted as it sped downhill towards the town. Moss pointed out Mr Fothergill's mansion in Abernant Park, and the soaring steeple of St. Elvan's Church. They were all impressed by what they saw of Aberdare, and admitted that it looked much cleaner than Dowlais. When they reached Commercial Place they dismounted and made their way along High Street to Siloa Chapel, where they were greeted by Rev. David Price.

"Take a seat while we wait for Mr Brythonfab Griffiths, the Registrar, to arrive," he said.

Siani was glad of a rest and looked around at the chapel with interest. Though it was not as large or as imposing as Bethania Chapel, it had a fine pulpit and organ and she sensed a welcoming atmosphere. Moss meanwhile chatted with Mr Price and was delighted to learn that he was originally from St. Clears in Carmarthenshire, not far from where he himself was born.

The registrar bustled in at two o'clock, and Mr Price called them forward to the big seat. Lewsyn noticed the folds of Siani's loose grey dress shaking as she stood beside him and he realised that she was nervous. He fingered the gold wedding ring in his pocket before handing it to Moss for safekeeping. Ben, meanwhile, held on to Siani's arm to give her support, and Lewsyn gave her an encouraging smile.

The service was conducted entirely in Welsh, the beauty of the language being enhanced by the soft Carmarthenshire accent of the Rev. David Price. His reading from the scriptures and his general demeanour could not have been more impressive if the chapel had been full to capacity. Lewsyn felt Siani tremble as he took her hand and slipped the ring on her finger, and he saw her brush away a tear as Mr Price pronounced them husband and wife. It was a quiet but dignified wedding, so he thought.

Once the formalities were over, they left Siloa Chapel arm in arm and made their way back to Commercial Place where they had a bite to eat before they retraced their way to Abernant Station. Lewsyn kissed Siani, referring to her proudly as my wife, while Moss and Ben toasted their future health and happiness with fresh cups of tea all round.

Siani, for her part, heaved a sigh of relief that the wedding had gone so smoothly, and that she had been able to make her vows firmly and sincerely. She loved Lewsyn with all her heart, and whatever the outcome of his trial would be, she knew that she would stand by him to the end.

Chapter 31

Moss planned for the trial to make an impact and strike a blow for justice and fair play. When Lewsyn and Siani arrived at the courthouse in Merthyr, they were delighted to see a large gathering of supporters outside. Many colliers had come straight off the night shift to give their backing and looked a formidable sight, black from head to foot, the whites of their eyes and their teeth constituting their only relieving features. Dai Dando, Abe Jenkins and Joe Griffiths held aloft the union banner in scarlet and gold, with the words 'Unity is Strength' emblazoned upon it.

"Good luck, Lew," shouted some of the colliers whose faces were so black, it was impossible to identify them.

Moss explained that Mr James, the lawyer, thought such a show of support would make a good impression as long as it was kept well under control. Once inside the courtroom, Lewsyn had to leave Siani in order to sit near Mr James in the front. Moss led her to the public benches in the back of the courtroom where Llew Jones and Mari were already seated. No words were exchanged, but Siani felt hostile eyes probing her body as she passed. With the birth only a fortnight away, she felt very conscious of her ungainly appearance and blushed with embarrassment as she took her seat.

Memories flooded back of her own trial, and old wounds were re-opened, but she was determined to keep her emotions in check and give Lewsyn full support. They all stood as the Stipendiary Magistrate entered and took his seat in the high chair. The formalities were disposed of, Lewsyn was put in the dock and the charges were put to him. In a loud, clear voice he pleaded "Not Guilty to causing a riot in the workhouse" and "Not Guilty to assaulting a policeman."

Joseph Lloyd, the workhouse master, was called as the first witness for the prosecution and gave a long catalogue of complaints about Lewsyn's behaviour throughout the time he was in the workhouse. "He was nothing but a trouble-maker from the outset, and had to be put in the refractory cell to bring him to his senses," said the florid, corpulent, bleary-eyed master.

"Come now, Mr Lloyd, how can you say that when the defendant had been beaten unconscious by a police officer almost before he was admitted to the House?" said Mr James, in his cross-examination.

Mr Lloyd snorted in protest. "He deserved what he got and should have been thrown out there and then," he said dismissively.

There were boos and hisses from the back of the courtroom and the clerk got up to call the protestors to order.

Mr James tried in vain to establish whether or not Joseph Lloyd actually saw or heard the defendant inciting others to violence on that fateful Sunday morning.

"How could I? I was leading the service in chapel wasn't I?" he said with a look of righteous indignation all over his face.

"By the same token, you could not possibly have seen whether or not he aimed a blow at a police officer in the yard," continued Mr James. Clearly discomfited, the master admitted that he did not.

When Myfanwy Lloyd, the fat, fussy matron entered the witness box, she was so flustered that she had difficulty in taking the oath. Her evidence was largely incoherent, and her main concern was that when she left the chapel to see what was going on in the yard, she was promptly bundled into a large, dirty-linen basket and the lid was barred. "It was a terrible thing to happen to a decent woman carrying out her duty," she whined. Then turning to Lewsyn she added, "He was the one who did it."

"How can you be so sure?" asked Mr James.

"Because of his long, red hair."

"But he had been given the standard short haircut on admission. Are you saying that he was the only one with red hair in the workhouse? Haven't you mixed him up with someone else?" he asked.

She shook her head. She had to admit that because of her incarceration in the linen basket she was unaware of what happened in the Board Room or in the yard, though she heard a lot of noise, which had drowned her cries for help. It was several hours later that one of the porters sent to remove the basket realised that there was someone in it. "I had almost fainted due to the disgusting smells inside and I almost died of fright," she said, dabbing her eyes.

Billy Toose, the orderly on duty in the back of the workhouse chapel, seemed to have a hazy recollection of the event. His concern was that someone stole his keys from his pocket. When asked how that could possibly have happened, he defended himself by saying that it must have been when his eyes were closed while praying. "One moment everything was peaceful and quiet, and the next thing these hooligans had gone through the door and locked it," he complained.

When Jack Bowen, in charge of the porter's lodge, took the stand, he described how four men had overpowered him and tied him up. "I was unable to summon help because they gagged me as well," he said. "I could hear all this hammering going on above me, and glass shattering, but I couldn't raise a finger to defend the place. It was terrifying."

"Did Lewsyn Jones tie you up? Did you see him brandishing a sledge-hammer?" asked Mr James.

He shook his head. "I was bundled underneath the counter," he said.

The prosecution failed to produce as a witness the police officer whose nose was broken during this fracas because he had retired and left the area. Instead a sworn statement was read out to the effect that his attacker had red hair and had his back to the officer when he was climbing the workhouse wall adjoining the graveyard.

Mr James seized upon this point with great vehemence. "How much credence can you attach to the evidence of an officer who did not even see the face of his assailant?" he asked in a tone bordering on exasperation.

At that point, the beetle-browed magistrate decided to adjourn the court until the afternoon so that he could have a break from all this melodrama.

"How do you think the case is going, Mr James?" Lewsyn asked as his lawyer gathered his papers together before leaving the court.

"Not badly," he said with a hint of a smile. There was the sound of loud booing from the crowd outside when the master and matron left the court. "Make sure your friends behave themselves this afternoon," he said, giving Lewsyn a stern look.

Lewsyn sought out Siani and Moss and discussed with them the morning's events. It was quite obvious to him that Siani was under strain and he was worried about her. "Do you think you should come back to court this afternoon, my love? You look pale and exhausted," he said.

"I must stay here, Lewsyn, and nothing will stop me," she said, her voice charged with emotion.

"Keep an eye on her Moss, I don't want Siani to give birth just yet," he said. Then, looking serious, he added, "If the verdict goes against me, I hope you'll look after her for me until I come out of prison."

"What's the betting that you won't go to gaol?" said Moss. "When I go into the witness box, I'll give them the full works. Dry your tears, Siani fach, we'll take Lewsyn home with us tonight."

The atmosphere in the courtroom in the afternoon was tense. More men coming off the early shift had gathered outside, unwashed, their lamps and 'jacks' hanging from their belts. "Good luck, boyo," they shouted, when they saw Lewsyn about to re-enter it.

"Behave yourselves, and wait until the verdict comes before you let off steam," Moss warned.

The public benches were packed and Siani sat alongside Bessie Bowen who had turned up to give her support in the final stages.

The first witness for the defence was Mr Moses Williams who explained that he had been with Lewsyn Jones throughout the time he was in the workhouse. "He was felled by a policeman's baton only for obeying instructions," he said. "Then he was thrown into a punishment cell where all he had for twenty-four hours was bread and water. It's a wonder he's still alive after the terrible food they doled out and all the hard work he had to do in the cruel winter weather."

There was an ominous growl of disapproval from the back of the court as Moss described the workhouse regime. Mr James directed his attention to the 27th February, they day of the so-called riot.

"Were you with him throughout the day?"

"Yes, it was a Sunday and after breakfast we went to the service in the workhouse chapel."

"Was there any talk of a riot?"

"No, the young able-bodied men, among whom were Lewsyn and myself, were so sick of being there that our one aim was to get out of the place."

"Were you with Lewsyn Jones in the outside yard?"

"Yes, for part of the time until we ran for the wall."

"Did you see him organising an attack on the Boardroom and hitting a policeman on the nose with an iron bar?"

"Certainly not. People were running in all directions trying to get out, and when we got to the wall, it was every man for himself."

"Stay there while my friend puts some questions to you," said Mr James.

The prosecuting solicitor tried his utmost to discredit Moss's evidence, but he remained rock-firm. "I know what I saw and did, and nobody is going to make me say anything different," he said. There was an audible murmur of approval when he stepped down.

Dai Dando and two others gave evidence briefly and re-affirmed that their one aim was to get away from the workhouse not to cause a riot. None of them saw Lewsyn Jones assaulting anyone and were aghast at the idea.

Finally, Lewsyn himself was put into the witness box amidst a wave of excitement. As the law stood, he was not allowed to give evidence, nor could he be cross-examined. Instead, Mr C.H. James took him through his unsworn statement.

In comparison with Moss and the others, Lewsyn looked an ill-used specimen of humanity, thin, poverty-stricken and scarred. He insisted that he had only entered the workhouse in order that heads of families, then on strike, should qualify for poor relief by doing stone-breaking. It would have been a terrible injustice to force them into the workhouse. Llew Jones buried his face in his hands as he heard his eldest son admit to this sacrifice.

Mr James went on to the remainder of the statement in which Lewsyn described the inhuman treatment he had received in the workhouse, where the food was poorer in quality and amount than that given to prisoners in gaol. He and his mates soon realised that they would have to escape from its harsh regime, otherwise they would become too weak and demoralised to make any such attempt. That was the reason they left the chapel and climbed the wall. Their stay in the workhouse had achieved its objective because the Board of Guardians had to give out relief to men on strike, albeit as a loan.

There were hisses around the courtroom at the mention of loans and Lewsyn looked directly at his father who was one of the victims. Mr James then reached the point in the statement where Lewsyn was accused of wilfully assaulting a policeman. He maintained that it must have been part of the iron railing on the top of the wall, which had fallen on him. It had been loosened over a period of time by people climbing over the wall. He further maintained that damage to the Board Room was caused by half-crazed paupers whose hunger pangs had made them light-headed. To describe it as a riot was a gross exaggeration for which he denied all responsibility.

There was a feeling of relief mingled with hope on the public benches when Lewsyn was allowed to step down at the end of his statement.

Mr James got ready for his summing up; he pulled himself up to his full height, and cleared his throat before he began addressing the magistrate. "The defendant is a hard-working, responsible, married man who has been falsely accused of crimes he did not commit. The flimsy evidence we have heard today makes it extremely unsafe to convict him. He is a man of principle who sacrificed himself for others and is now expected to carry sole responsibility for damage done to the workhouse. The word 'riot' is a complete misnomer: it was a bid for freedom by Lewsyn Jones and all the others anxious to get away from such a hated institution. Why else should there be such a massive show of support for him today from so many fellow-sufferers? He does not deserve to be made a scapegoat or to become a martyr. I ask you to acquit him of these charges which should never have been brought against him," he thundered.

There was a spontaneous outburst of cheering as Mr James sat down, and immediately the Clerk to the Court jumped to his feet and called out, "Order! Order!" The police officer on duty moved forward ready to draw his truncheon and eject troublemakers. Siani trembled at the sight of him, and Mrs Bowen shielded her instinctively from a possible fracas.

The prosecuting solicitor began rehashing his case, repeating unsupported accusations until eventually he was stopped in his tracks by the Stipendiary Magistrate who warned him that unless he had any further fresh information, he should complete his summing up. He scratched his chin, made a few random points and brought his remarks to an abrupt end. A sigh of relief ran through the public benches.

"All stand," shouted the court clerk, as the magistrate gathered his papers and went out to consider his decision.

Lewsyn waited for Mr James to speak, but all he had was a sharp reminder to keep his mouth shut until the verdict was announced.

He looked anxiously at Siani and crossed the courtroom to the public benches. Before he could get there, his mother approached him asking, "Did I hear that lawyer say that you are a <u>married</u> man?"

"Yes, Mam, Siani and I were married last month. Aren't you going to congratulate me?"

"Certainly not."

"Never mind about that, Mari, all we want is for him to walk free from court today," said Llew Jones.

Lewsyn left them to join Siani, Bessie and Ben who were now with her. "There's a big crowd outside and Moss is trying to calm them down," said Ben, who had just arrived. "The police are finding it difficult to hold them back."

Bessie Bowen tried to persuade Siani to leave by the side door in case there was violence.

"No, I'm staying where I am," she said, firmly.

Lewsyn was worried. "Go with Mrs Bowen, I don't want you to be hurt," he pleaded, but she shook her head. His nerves were ragged, and he looked around, hoping desperately that there was something Mr James could do to protect her.

"Listen," said Ben, "that's Moss's voice, he's leading them in singing William Williams' great hymn.

The sound of men's voices grew in volume,
'Guide me, O thou great Jehovah,

Pilgrim through this barren land,
I am weak, but thou art mighty,
Hold me with thy powerful hand:
Bread of heaven, Bread of heaven,
Feed me now and evermore,
Feed me now and evermore'

Tears streamed down Siani's face, and Lewsyn swallowed hard, as the rich harmony of men's voices filled the courtroom and the whole building.

* * *

After what seemed an age, the magistrate returned. "All rise," barked the court clerk. "Remain standing," he said to Lewsyn, who held on to a ledge to stop himself shaking.

"This case has deep significance and I'm conscious that it has aroused strong feeling," said the magistrate sternly, while emphasising the importance of maintaining law and order in society. Lewsyn stood with his head bowed, and Moss Williams waited impatiently by the door, anxious to relay the verdict to his mates outside. There was a pause. "Having considered all the evidence carefully, I find the charges have not been proved, so they are dismissed," the Beak announced at last.

Immediately, there was a spontaneous outburst of clapping and cheering from the public benches, and outside the chanting of 'Lewsyn Jones is innocent' could be heard.

"Clear the court," shouted the clerk. Lewsyn blew a kiss to Siani and went over the thank Mr James.

"The outcome might have been different if the prosecution had been more effective," he said with a sly smile.

Outside, Lewsyn was seized upon and carried shoulder-high through Glebeland Street and along Castle Street to the sound of 'Lewsyn Jones is innocent! Down with the workhouse!'

Siani stood waiting and wondering what the consequences would be for Lewsyn of this momentous day.

Chapter 32

Lewsyn revelled in his newly-acquired status of local hero. "What a day! I would never have dreamed of such an exciting outcome," he said, looking at Siani and Moss who faced him across the table in the kitchen at 2 Nant Row.

"You deserved it, you put your life on the line for the boys who carried you through Merthyr today. They know as well as we do that your acquittal was a slap in the face for the Board of Guardians and the ironmasters."

Siani looked serious and said little until Moss asked her what she thought. "Yes, I agree with every word you say, but the effects of the strike have been disastrous. You, Ben and Dave are paying the price by being black-listed, and though Lewsyn may be a hero for the time being, I don't suppose he'll ever have a job in Dowlais again or in Merthyr Tydfil."

Lewsyn took her hand. "Come over to Aberdare to live with me, Siani, and we'll make a fresh start," he pleaded.

She shook her head. "I've always said I can't leave the little 'uns, and besides, where would we find friends like Moss, Bessie and Blod?"

"We'll wait until the baby is born, then perhaps you'll feel more like taking a chance. Mag and Will are welcome to come with us wherever we go," he added.

Lewsyn prepared for his long walk to Cwmbach next day with an uneasy feeling that it would not be long before he would have to retrace his footsteps. "Promise me that you'll send word with Ben when the baby comes, " he said urgently before parting with her.

"I'll do my best, but you never know how things will turn out. Bessie has promised to be with me when I need her," she said, trying to reassure him.

Secretly, Siani was dreading the ordeal of giving birth and was feeling unwell. Her legs were badly swollen and she found it hard to get through her endless duties. The worry and stress associated with the trial had left her exhausted and fearful for the future. She kept Mag home from school for company, and now that she was nine years old, she relied on her to help around the house.

On the Friday after Lewsyn had returned to Cwmbach, she had to send Mag to Mrs Bowen to summon help. "Come quick, our Siani says that the baby is coming," Mag exclaimed.

Bessie Bowen dropped what she was doing and came bustling into the kitchen. "What's happening, Siani? Have the waters broken yet?"

"Yes, that's why I sent Mag for you," she said, starting to shake.

"I'll undress you and put you to bed. Hold on to me, bach, I'll look after you."

Bessie put the boiler on the fire ready for the boys when they came home and also in order to have plenty of hot water for Siani's needs. Tell the boys that they'll have to make do with bread and cheese tonight, and warn them to get bathed as quickly as possible," she said to Mag before she slipped home to get clean linen and enamel bowls ready for Siani's confinement.

She returned with Blod, who sat at the bedside with Siani while her mother restored some sort of law and order in the kitchen after the bathing ritual was over. "Build up the fire, Ben, we may have a long night ahead of us," Bessie warned.

Siani's contractions started before midnight and went on throughout the night. She was bathed in sweat and in such distress that Bessie began to realise that she and Blod would not be able to deliver the baby without help. "Go down to Dr. James's surgery and tell him that Lewsyn's wife is giving birth and is having a hard time. Ask him to come quickly," she said, then added, "and to bring his instruments."

Blod disappeared fast. Shortly after six o'clock the doctor arrived and soon concluded that the baby was suffering. "I'm going to give you a little nick, my dear, to make things easier for you." Siani was so exhausted that she was hardly aware of what was happening. Her groans filled the house to the great distress of the boys and Mag who remained upstairs.

"Now Siani fach, give one more push so the doctor can deliver your lovely baby," Bessie said soothingly. "Come, now, there's a good girl," she urged.

Amid agonising screams, she was delivered of a baby boy who had a mass of red-gold hair and a lusty pair of lungs.

"Take him out and clean him up while I see to the mother," said the doctor urgently.

Siani's life seemed to hang in the balance, as waves of weakness brought on by severe loss of blood and acute pain, swept over her. "Where's her husband?" asked Dr. James, showing concern.

"He's working over in Aberdare," Bessie said.

"You'd better send for him." He stood back and surveyed the scene. "That poor girl has been half-starved and is in a state of delirium," he said.

Bessie put her arm around Siani's shoulder and tried to spoon some hot water mixed with brandy and sugar into her mouth.

"I'll call back later when I've done my round. If she can get some sleep, perhaps she'll rally," he said anxiously.

Blod, meanwhile, sat at the fireside nursing the baby in a flannelette sheet. "He's small, but he's in good shape," said the doctor after he examined him.

* * *

Ben left to catch the nine o'clock train to Aberdare. He wasn't sure how to find Cwmbach, or Phillip Row, but he was determined that Lewsyn should know that he had a son and that Siani needed him. He eventually reached the lodgings, just as Lewsyn was stepping out of the bath after working the Saturday morning shift.

"What's happened?" he asked, his voice quivering at the sight of Ben.

"You've got a son! The doctor says he's small, but perfect, and he's got red hair like you,"

"What about Siani?"

"She's very ill, Lew, you'd better come back with me," said Ben, his voice breaking.

Questions tumbled from Lewsyn as Ben tried to explain that it was a difficult birth. Flinging his clothes on anyhow, he grabbed what money he had left and called to his landlady, "I've got a son and I'm going home to see him and my wife."

He and Ben rushed up the mountainside in the direction of Abernant Station and reached it just in time to get the three o'clock train to Merthyr. All the time, Lewsyn questioned Ben anxiously about Siani.

"I've told you all I know. I hope she'll be a bit better by now, but she's had a rough time and the baby came early," was all that Ben could say.

They reached Dowlais Station just as it was getting dark and Lewsyn raced down to Nant Row, leaving Ben trailing wearily behind. He burst into the kitchen where Blod was nursing the baby and she put him into Lewsyn's arms, saying, "Hold him, Lewsyn, and take him in to see Siani. My mother is sitting with her, trying to bring her around," she said.

Gently, he edged into the bedroom and saw Siani lying prone and helpless on the bed. Bessie stood up and tried to ease her head so that she could see Lewsyn and the baby, but there was no response. He sensed mortal danger and handed the child to Blod. "Leave us for a while so that I can try to bring her back to us," he said.

With infinite tenderness, he enfolded her in his arms, willing his strength to pass into her. He kissed her brow, her eyes, her parched lips and held her to him saying, "Stay with me, dearest Siani, I need you so much." He stroked her hair, her face and neck and whispered into her ear, "It's Lewsyn, my love, speak to me."

He elicited a faint response, and she eventually stirred as if awakening from a bad dream. "Lew? Is it you?"

"Yes, my darling."

"Hold me, don't let me go, it's so dark."

Yet again, he willed his strength to flow into her and held her in his arms where she lay weak and helpless. Bessie put her head around the door and saw Lewsyn nursing Siani, then she retreated, fearing that death was about to snatch her from him.

An hour or so later, Siani stirred and opened her eyes. Gradually, she regained consciousness, and it seemed almost as though the dense clouds, which had enshrouded her mind, had rolled away. She gave a flicker of a smile and Lewsyn soothed her pain away by stroking her hair and face gently. "I'm here now to look after you, my sweetheart, and to make you well," he murmured.

He stayed with her night and day, tending to her every need. Bessie Bowen made broth, beef tea and milky porridge, which Lewsyn spooned patiently into her mouth. Nothing mattered to him but saving Siani and ministering to their child. Dr. James, who was a regular visitor, complimented him on the devotion and care he showered upon them.

"You gave Siani the will to live. She has regained her strength through you," he said emphatically.

Lewsyn had lost count of the days and was surprised when Bessie Bowen reminded him that his son was now a week old. "What are you going to call him?" she asked.

Lewsyn and Siani looked at each other and smiled. "Siani owes her life to Dr. J.W. James and I owe my freedom to Mr. C.H. James, so we think we'll call him James after both of these great men."

"And a very good choice too," added Bessie, who knew of the sterling service the James family had rendered in Merthyr Tydfil.

The following week, Lewsyn went to the registrar's office to register his son as James Jones, born December 1st 1875.

Chapter 33

After nursing Siani for two weeks, Lewsyn became acutely aware that his money was running out. He didn't like being dependent on Ben and David, whose hard-earned wages were little enough as it was, so he decided to try to get night work in a Merthyr colliery. On Ben's advice he went to speak to Moss about it.

"If I could get a labouring job working nights, then I'd be able to stay at home to look after Siani and the baby during the day. Do you think there's any hope of my having a job in the Graig Pit?" he asked.

Moss hesitated before replying. "You can try, but remember that when we started, your trial had not taken place. You are much better known than we are and for that reason I think you'll find it more difficult to obtain work."

Lewsyn's face fell, but he persisted. "I can't leave Siani yet and with Christmas coming up we'll need money, so I **must** work."

His appearance at Graig Colliery, belonging to the Plymouth Company, caused a bit of a stir, which Lewsyn thought was a good sign. Some of the hauliers working on the surface recognised him, and called out "Shw' mae Lewsyn?" But when he appeared before the under-manager, his hopes were dashed.

"We have no vacancies of any sort," he said gruffly, and opened the door for him to leave.

"When do you think you'll need more men?" Lewsyn asked urgently.

"Depends on trade," was the vague reply, which promptly ended the interview.

A feeling of anger and desperation swept over him and gritting his teeth, he resolved to try at the Duffryn Colliery. Moss had said that Fothergill & Co. were not such hard-liners as some of the Merthyr owners, so he thought it worth another try. He talked to an overman who interviewed him in the colliery lamp-room and felt his hopes rising until he gave his name and address. "Are you the rebel whose trial we read about in 'The Merthyr Express' a few months back?" he asked.

Lewsyn's temper flared. "I'm not a rebel, I'm an honest working man, free of any taint of law-breaking," he shouted.

"You can clear off from here, I don't want any fire-brands and agitators stirring up trouble among my men," he barked.

As he trudged home in the gathering darkness of a December night, Lewsyn had to face facts. He was blacklisted not only in Dowlais, but also throughout the valley. Once Siani was stronger, she and the baby would **have** to come back with him to Cwmbach. There was no other way around it, but in the meantime, how was he to exist?"

He called on Moss Williams in his lodgings before returning home to Siani. "Wherever I go I'm not wanted, my reputation has gone before me," he complained.

"It's the bosses' network that you're up against," Moss said bitterly. "Your only hope is to go back to Cwmbach."

"But Mag is too young to look after Siani and the baby. I can't leave them yet, and there's no question of us going on the parish. I'm desperate, Moss, I'm down to my last shilling."

"Let me think about it Lewsyn, I'll call to see you soon," Moss said quietly.

That evening he paid a visit to the Secretary of the Buffaloes Friendly Society and outlined the hardship and victimisation that Lewsyn was suffering. "He was always a paid-up member before the strike, but since then his life has been turned upside down," Moss pleaded. "Is there any hope of a handout to help him and his wife over the next week or so?"

Tom Davies, the secretary, looked up his records to substantiate what Moss was saying. "His father, Llewelyn Jones, has been one of our members for the last thirty years. It's a wonder that he hasn't been to see me on his behalf."

"There's a family rift, so I don't suppose Lewsyn would ask him for help, but if you would talk to him on the quiet, I'm sure it would make all the difference."

"I'll see what I can do," said Tom.

By the end of the week, Llew Jones had signed for a loan of £10-00 to be given to his son, which he guaranteed to pay back at the rate of half-a-crown a week.

Moss was pleased to be able to tell Lewsyn that the 'Buffs' had coughed up some money to tide him over until the New Year. Lewsyn couldn't believe his luck and shook him warmly by the hand.

Slowly, Siani regained her strength and was able to nurse her baby. She began to take more notice of what was going on and questioned Lewsyn about going back to work.

"I'll go in the New Year when you're feeling better," he said, trying to shrug off her worries.

"Any hope of a job this side of the mountain?" she asked.

"No, my love, I've tried, but it seems I'm a marked man."

She began to cry. "It's all my fault that you're in this mess," she gulped.

"Nonsense, I brought it on my own head, but I had to make a stand."

Still Siani shook her head and sobbed loudly. "What is it, Siani? Tell me," he said.

Gradually, she unfolded the story of George Williams, his attempt to rape her, and the consequences of her attack on him.

"The swine!" he gasped, "I knew I should have hammered him. Promise me that you'll tell me if he ever comes near you again. I'll kill him!"

Strangely, she felt a sense of relief for having unburdened her share of responsibility for the problems that faced them.

* * *

After Christmas, Lewsyn prepared for his return to Cwmbach. He hated the thought of leaving Siani, but she was now able to see to the baby and do more for herself in the home.

"I'll try to come home every other weekend," he promised. Secretly, he was now worried whether his job was still available, and had developed a morbid fear that his reputation would have gone before him, even to Cwmbach. With great difficulty he wrenched himself away from Siani and the baby and walked over the bleak mountains to Aberdare, then down into Cwmbach.

The harsh weather in January and February made it impossible for him to go back to Dowlais as regularly as he hoped, but he never failed to send Siani a weekly allowance. He missed her and James more than he had ever imagined and began to suffer bouts of black depression.

"I'm living in a world of darkness," he told Sam Hughes, one of his fellow lodgers. "It's dark when I go to work and dark when I come back here. In between, I'm in total darkness down the pit, where the only lights are from our lamps, which remind me of corpse candles which I see flickering all around me, warning me of death," he said.

"Cheer up, it's not all gloom. Before long, you'll be able to make the journey to Dowlais every week and you'll feel a lot better," said Sam.

But Lewsyn's problems were more deep-rooted than Sam realised, because not only did he miss Siani and James, but he was also developing a morbid fear of going down into the pit. He had nightmares of being trapped and burnt alive. Even his landlady became concerned as she noticed that he was losing so much weight.

"Go out for a few pints of beer with the boys, it will do you good," she urged.

"I can't afford it. I need every penny I earn," he retorted.

To get him out of his depression, Sam persuaded him to go to Cwmbach Workmen's Hall one evening to listen to a free lecture. Reluctantly, he went, only to find that there was a large crowd present, and a buzz of excitement rippled throughout the hall. There were posters around the walls advertising passages to North America, and leaflets giving information about the assistance offered by the Aberdare and Rhondda Emigration Society to would-be emigrants.

To begin with, Lewsyn sat back sullenly until the atmosphere began to get to him and he felt some interest stir inside himself. By the time Thomas L. Thomas, the emigration agent took the stage, he was even prepared to listen to him. He heard with growing excitement about the developments in the iron and steel works of Pennsylvania, U.S.A. "It's the land of opportunity, of freedom and the brotherhood of man," the agent said, painting a glorious picture of life in a new country.

Lewsyn listened almost with disbelief, as he heard the speaker say, "They need puddlers and rail-rollers because the demand for iron and steel is never-ending now the country is being opened up."

He held his breath and thought, "I've had experience in rolling rails, that was my last job in the Dowlais Works before the 1875 strike and I love working in iron, where light and life are all one and the same thing to me."

The agent continued, outlining arrangements for would-be emigrants. "There are steamships sailing from Liverpool to New York every Thursday, and passengers travelling steerage pay only £5-5-0, children under twelve go at half-price and infants below twelve months at £1-1-0."

Lewsyn thought of his beloved son and decided it would be the best possible chance for him in the future. Then he realised that Mag and Will would have to be included, so that Siani would not be put off by the thought of leaving them behind. The project began to take shape in his mind and he began to feel elated.

"Loans can be arranged by the Aberdare and Rhondda and Emigration Society, which can be repaid by emigrants from their wages. I've got application forms for those interested, so don't miss this chance, come to the platform before you leave," the agent concluded.

Lewsyn was one of the first there, and came away with forms and pamphlets, feeling as though a ray of sunshine had penetrated the thick darkness surrounding him. He poured over them in his lodgings and read about jobs in iron, steel and coal-mining in Pittsburgh, Wilkes Barr, Carbondale and Bethlehem. The more he thought about it, the more he felt that this was his destiny.

"I'm going to tell Siani about these opportunities," he said to Sam Hughes, "I'll never get anywhere if I stay in these parts."

That weekend, despite the icy weather of mid-February, he battled his way through to Dowlais to talk to Siani about his American dream. She could tell by him that this was no passing fancy for there was a gleam in his eye, which conveyed intense interest.

Chapter 34

The Aberdare and Rhondda Emigration Society meeting became the talking point in 2 Nant Row, on the occasion of his next visit. "There's plenty of work to be had in the iron and steelworks of Pennsylvania and you can have loans to get you there," Lewsyn said enthusiastically.

David studied the leaflets brought home for him and showed interest, but Ben was more guarded. "Now that I'm courting Sarah Jane, I have to think of her, her father has promised to get me a job in Fochriw No. 2 Pit, where he's an official," he said.

Mag and Will had picked up a picture of a steamship and were curious to know where it was bound. Lewsyn took Will on his knee and explained that this ship could take them all to America.

"Is that where the coconuts come from?" he asked, his eyes wide with wonder.

"Not very far away from there," Lewsyn said, thinking of the exotic palms and deep blue seas. Turning to Siani, he asked, "You're not saying much, what do you think of the idea?"

She was singing quietly to the baby, now three months old, and had been wondering whether Lewsyn's restless spirit lay behind this sudden development. She raised her eyes and said quietly, "Maybe we can talk about it when Jim is a bit older."

In bed that night, he confided in her his deep unhappiness. "Being separated from you and the baby is bad enough, but working in Duffryn Pit is absolute hell, and I hate it. I don't know how much longer I can put up with it."

Siani began to realise that talk of emigration was more than a passing fancy, and that Lewsyn, like many others, including her mother's family, was now seeking an escape from this miserable existence. It came as a shock to her to realise that she herself was now confronted with this decision and so were Mag and Will, and even David. The whole idea unsettled her and she began to search for some letters that she remembered her mother talking about. What advice would she have given her if she were alive? Siani thought about little else but emigration in the weeks after Lewsyn returned to Aberdare.

Her search was in vain and she decided that the letters had either been lost or burnt. Later in the week, after she had done the washing and ironing, had aired the clothes and had set about folding them up to put them away, she met another problem. The chest of drawers in the kitchen was getting the worse for wear, and much to her annoyance, the bottom drawer got stuck. She tugged and pushed, until eventually it came right out and she saw the cause of the trouble. There was a faded envelope, which had got jammed in the side runner. Throwing it aside, she put the drawer back in position, piled in the sheets, blankets and towels and shut it, heaving a sigh of relief.

She picked up the envelope intending to throw it out when she noticed faint handwriting on the front of it, looked again and saw a foreign stamp. She peered inside and saw several sheets of neatly folded paper, and nervously took them out. She trembled as she held the first sheet in her hand, and for a moment she felt as though her mother was at her elbow, urging her on. She looked and read and gasped. It was a letter from America!

104 Grace Street,
Bethlehem,
Penn. U.S.A.
5ᵗʰ December 1857

Dear Lizzie & Joshua,

At last we have settled here in Bethlehem and have a home which we can call our own. Your mother and I are getting used to this new country and are pleased to live in a place where there are lots of Welsh people. We go to a Welsh Independent Chapel called Zoar to worship on Sundays and have made several friends.

I've found a job as a puddler in the ironworks. The wages are good and there is a better relationship between master and men than there was in Merthyr Tydfil. This town is growing rapidly and is blessed with clean water and good drainage, which are important, especially in the summer months when it gets very hot.

We often talk about you and wonder how little Siani's coming on. Mam, David, Rebecca and Samuel send you their love and beg you to write back. Look after yourself, Lizzie, and tell the members of Bethania Chapel that all is well with us, as we hope it is with you.

Your loving father,
Benjamin John

Tears flowed down Siani's cheeks and she read the letter yet again to recapture the warmth, love and yearning it aroused in her. How she wished she had known her grandfather, whose firm, clear handwriting had withstood the ravages of time.

She looked at two more letters, one of which described how they had bought a five-roomed house, now that the children were all working. Enclosed with the third was an account of her Aunt Rebecca's wedding, as printed in their local newspaper. She was married in July 1859 in Zoar Chapel to a former Welshman, now a mining engineer, by the name of Harry Richards. Her wedding dress was described as "ice-blue lace over deep blue taffeta, which contrasted with the bride's beautiful auburn, wavy hair." Siani pictured it and wished she could have been present at the wedding and reception in the vestry at Zoar Chapel, where there were one hundred guests. She began to feel that she knew her relatives and realised how much she had missed.

The last letter in the envelope brought the sad news of her grandfather's death from pneumonia in 1866, and included the tribute paid to him by the minister of his chapel who described him as "an upright, honourable man who was a devoted husband and a loving father." Siani cried when she read these words and tried to imagine how her mother must have felt when reading them.

She folded the creased, discoloured letters carefully and put them back into the envelope, then put them in the top right-hand drawer of the chest for safety. "I'll have to show these to Ben and Dave," she thought. "It's the first contact we've had with Mam's family and it's come at an especially important time."

The more she thought about the letters, the more she realised that her mother might also have gone to America but for her becoming pregnant and having to get married. "Perhaps I owe it to Mam to go there myself," she thought.

She waited until the youngsters were in bed and James was asleep in the Moses basket on the settle before she produced the letters. "I've got something to show you," she said to Ben and David, handing the first letter to them across the kitchen table.

David's eyebrows shot up at the sight of the address and he read it avidly. He was quick to respond, "This is great news. Where did you find it?" he asked excitedly.

Siani unfolded the story about how she remembered her mother telling her as a little girl about her grand-dad and grandma and her uncles and aunt out in America, and she thought she had mentioned having some letters from them

"I've been searching for days. I looked in the family Bible and in the chest under the bed, but could find nothing. I had given up when, by accident, I found them behind the bottom drawer in the chest. I think Mam might have hidden them there for safety."

Ben was impressed by the letter and particularly by his grandfather's writing and signature. "I wish I could write like that," he said.

They read the other letters eagerly, and once again, it was David who responded first. "They did well out in Pennsylvania and our grand-dad was highly respected. I wonder how many of them are still alive, I'd love to know."

Siani looked at the address again before saying, "There's only one way to find out, Dave, you'll have to write. You have a good hand, so why don't you compose a letter?"

"I'm all for it. What do you say Ben?"

"I'd like to know more about them, but I wouldn't want to go out there. I'm going to hang on until things get better here"

"Thinking of Sarah Jane are you?" David taunted, and looked again at the faded letter which lay on the table. "Buy a packet of writing paper and envelopes tomorrow, Siani, and think of what you want to say, then I'll write the letter tomorrow evening," said David promptly.

Seated at the table near the oil-lamp, he settled down to write. After a few false starts, he turned to Siani, saying, "Come on, you've got to help me, it's not easy to write to people you've never met."

She was half-asleep in the wooden armchair, which had originally belonged to her grandfather and was nursing little James in a Welsh flannel shawl, but she roused herself and tried to recall the family as her mother had described them. Gradually the letter took shape and David wrote with greater ease.

> *2 Nant Row,*
> *Dowlais,*
> *Merthyr Tydfil,*
> *South Wales.*
> *February 1876*

Dear Grandma, Uncle David, Aunt Rebecca &Uncle Sam,

No doubt you will be surprised to hear from us after such a long silence. Much has happened since you left Dowlais, and sad to say our Mam and Dad died three years ago. Mam had T.B. and Dad died as the result of an accident. Thanks to Siani, we have managed to keep together as a family, but it has not been easy. Our middle sister, Alys, died of T.B. a year ago when she was only fifteen. Mag is now ten years old and Will is five and they go to school in Dowlais.

Siani is married to Lewsyn Jones, son of Llew and Mari Jones, and they have a baby boy called James, three months old. Lewsyn works over in Aberdare, in the Duffryn Pit, outside the village of Cwmbach. Ben and I both work together in the Graig Colliery because we can't get work here in Dowlais.

For the past five years, there have been strikes in the iron and coal industries, but the last one in 1875 was the worst. We work hard for long hours and yet we can barely make a living. I am beginning to think that we'd be better off following your example by trying out our luck in America. Is it right that there's still plenty of work to be had in iron and coal?

Lewsyn is making enquiries at the Aberdare and Rhondda Emigration Society. Before the last strike he was rolling rails in Dowlais and loved the work. I am now fifteen years old and I hope one day to be a colliery fireman. We would value your advice far more than that of an emigration agent. Siani, especially, would like to know whether you like living in America and whether you think the baby is too young to make such a journey.

We all send our warmest regards, Siani in particular, as she heard Mam talk about you so much. We'd love to hear from you, so please write soon.

Yours sincerely,
David Davies.

He signed with a flourish and passed the letter to Siani, who read it out slowly, with Mag and Will at her side listening to every word.

"Yes, Dave, you've set it out well. We'll wait for their reply before we do anything in the matter," she said quietly, while, inwardly, she felt sure that her mother's presence would guide them in making such a momentous decision.

Chapter 35

Back at work in Cwmbach, Lewsyn put in overtime to boost his wages. Secretly, he hoped that perhaps he could save a few shillings in case something came of his American project. He felt he had to have an escape route from his present situation, otherwise the black clouds of depression might come back to overwhelm him. The Duffryn Pit where he worked was owned by the Powell Duffryn Company, which supplied rich, smokeless steam coal to the Admiralty. He often wondered as he shovelled it deep underground, whether it was also used to fuel the ships which conveyed emigrants to America. The very thought of it helped to keep up his spirits.

His work included not only cleaning the pit stalls but also shoring up the roof with wooden props. Sometimes he heard them groan as movements in the roof took place. He had learnt to move fast when such warning signals presaged falls of rock and earth. This and the fear of gas in the fiery pits at Cwmbach haunted him daily. He had rejoined The Buffaloes Friendly Society in case of an accident, and to provide some protection for Siani and James if he were killed. The 'Buffs' had been good to him when he was down and out and he could not forget them.

He knew that these palliative measures were not a complete solution to his problems. His real goal was to get out of mining and back into iron-making, and, if necessary, he was prepared to go to America to achieve it. Before his next home visit, he went to see the secretary of the Emigration Society to find out more details of what help was available. Morgan Williams was very co-operative and told him, "Provided you can get guarantors, we'll give you a loan and see that you are settled in."

"Is it restricted to immediate family or would it cover other relatives," he asked anxiously.

"That would be up to you, but remember that whatever loan you require has to be backed by two guarantors."

Lewsyn swallowed hard. "How long does it take to arrange these loans and what procedures are followed?"

"As long as you are physically fit, have the necessary skills and have no criminal record, it doesn't take long."

He went away thanking his lucky stars that he was free of convictions and that the way was clear for him to take Mag and Will with them. David would be able to earn his keep as a miner, and would not be a burden to anyone, so he had no fear about getting a loan to cover him. But he racked his brains about guarantors. The only one he could think of was Moss Williams who would trust him with his life. "I'll ask him on my next visit" he decided, "and I'll talk to Siani about it."

* * *

"Have a look at this," said Siani, when Lewsyn came on his next visit, then she handed to him her grandfather's first letter.

He scrutinised it and gasped when he saw the address. "Bethlehem, Pennsylvania! Where did you get this from?"

"Read it first, then I'll explain."

Lewsyn smiled as he read the letter and looked at her in amazement. "What a coincidence! So you have family out in America in the very part where I would like to settle. I can't get over it. Tell me how you came by this letter."

"I remembered my Mam talking about some letters she had from her family out there, so I started searching and eventually found them hidden behind the bottom drawer in our chest."

"Can I see the others?" he asked eagerly. He became totally engrossed in them and gave a deep sigh as he came to the end of the last one. "What a pity your grandfather died young! By all accounts he was a highly respected man. I wonder what has become of the family and whether they are still prospering."

With a twinkle in her eye, Siani admitted that David had written to find out. "You know how curious he is; once he saw these letters he gave me no peace until I allowed him to write on behalf of us all."

"Good boy Dafydd!" Lewsyn exclaimed, and he hugged Siani, giving her a kiss. For the first time, he thought he detected in her a glimmer of interest in his American dream. "When is he due home?" he asked, anxious to reveal his news about emigration loans.

"Any time now, he helps Mr Rowlands on a Saturday with his stall. Our Ben is out courting and is not interested in anyone or anything but Sarah Jane."

Lewsyn took James into his arms and looked at him proudly. "He's coming on well, Siani and you are looking more like your old self, I hope we'll have some good news from your family in Pennsylvania. It could make all the difference to us, my sweet," he said solemnly.

Around the supper table that night, David rattled on about the letter he had sent off and asked Lewsyn what news he had from his contacts.

"I've seen the secretary of the Emigration Society and he assured me I could qualify for a loan, on condition I can obtain two guarantors."

Siani and David both looked at Lewsyn. "Guarantors! What does that involve?" asked Siani.

"People who would back us to make sure that we repay the loan."

"What about me? Am I to be included in the loan as well?" David asked eagerly. "Will it cover me?" he repeated.

"Yes, I made sure of that and Mag and Will are to be included."

Siani looked worried. "It will amount to quite a lot. What if something went wrong out there and you couldn't get work?"

"You're looking for trouble now, Siani. Why not wait for the reply to our letter?" David said hastily.

Lewsyn leaned on the table and looked hard at Siani. "With regard to guarantors, I've been wondering whether I should ask Moss."

She paused. "I suppose you could have word with him, but tell him that nothing is settled yet," she warned.

Then David spoke up. "I could ask our Ben to be a guarantor for Mag, Will and me, after all, he is our brother."

"A good idea, you do that," Lewsyn said, pleased that another hurdle in the pursuit of his plan would soon be overcome.

* * *

He delayed his next visit to Dowlais until Easter, partly because he had a deep cut over his nose and a badly bruised foot. If he had been honest with himself, he should have stayed home from work for a week, but desperate need drove him on. A fall of rock underground had killed the labourer working near him and badly bruised Lewsyn's left arm and leg. A shard of jagged rock had hit the bridge of his nose causing it to bleed, and the coal dust that entered it had left a noticeable blue scar.

Once more, his spirits began to sink and terror took over. Sam Hughes, his fellow lodger, tried to reason with him, but to no avail. Every time Lewsyn looked in the mirror whilst shaving, he saw the scar and hated it. Sam tried to convince him that it was a lucky scar, but it seemed to Lewsyn it was the badge of bondage and he was ashamed of it. "Life is cruel, life is hard!" he told himself, and the only consolation he had, came from the loan forms which the secretary of the Emigration Society had obtained for him. He studied them until he knew all their intricacies, and with a huge sigh of relief, set out on Good Friday for his journey to Dowlais, hoping that Siani would not scrutinise him too closely.

Chapter 36

"What's happened to you Lewsyn? Have you been fighting or what?" Siani asked, on seeing his scar and his battered look.

"I had a bit of an accident, nothing much," he said, trying to pass it off lightly.

"I want the truth from you," she insisted, "how did you get that gash on your nose?"

David, who had been listening, looked closely at him and asked, "Have you been in a fall underground, Lew?"

"Yes, a bit of one, but I got off lightly," he said dismissively, "let's talk about something else."

"Show him the letter, Siani," David said, trying to ease the tension.

As he read it, Lewsyn's face gradually relaxed and became wreathed in smiles.

104 Grace Street,
Bethlehem,
Pennsylvania,
U.S.A.
30th March 1876

Dear Sian, Ben, David, Lewsyn & all,

We sure were delighted to receive your letter. As you say, the years have flown by and it seems that you've had a rough time. We were very sorry to hear of Lizzie's death and also grieved to hear about Josh and little Alys. These were cruel blows, but life was always hard in Merthyr Tydfil and I fear always will be.

*Rebecca, Sam and I are all married, and your grandmother, now sixty-two years of age, lives here with us at our family home. She has been very sad since hearing of Lizzie's death, and says that you **must** come* *over here so that she can look after you. She remembers Sian as a little baby and can picture her now as the living image of her mother.*

There's plenty of work to be had in the steelworks and mines, so you need have no fears on that score. Wages are good, as there is such a demand for railroads out here in this vast country. Labor relations so far are cordial, though it's early days yet!

Your grandma says that if you come out here, you needn't worry about finding somewhere to live. You can stay with us for the time being until you get a place of your own. There's plenty of land round-about and many of our houses are made of wood.

Tell Lewsyn that we hope he'll go ahead with his application to the Emigration Society and that we are prepared to back him at this end.

Your grandma says to remember to keep in touch and that she is longing for the day when she can see you all, especially Siani and baby James.

> *Your ever-loving Uncle David*
> *on behalf of Grandma & family.*

"Siani fach, this is what we've been waiting for," he said, hugging and kissing her. "You've got nothing to worry about now, my darling."

She sobbed as she read the letter yet again. The love and warmth it radiated made her feel as though a huge gap in her life had been bridged, and at last gave her the courage to make the break that Lewsyn wanted.

Young David was elated and kept on congratulating himself that he was the author of the letter, which had renewed the contact. "We've hit the bull's eye first time, Lew," he said triumphantly.

Putting his hand into his inside pocket, Lewsyn took out a large envelope, which he passed to David. "Have a look at these and see what you can make of them," he said.

'Aberdare & Rhondda Emigration Society Application for Loan.' "You've got them! These are the loan forms!" he exclaimed. "They'll keep us busy this weekend, what do you say, Siani?" he said, beaming.

"Looks like it," she agreed, looking over his shoulder.

Lewsyn's nightmares that weekend revealed to Siani the agony he was concealing from her. His cries of anguish and terrible night sweats frightened her. "You've got to tell me what's troubling you," she said, as she tried to calm him down.

Clinging to her in abject terror, he admitted that he had missed death by inches and had now lost his nerve. "I go to work everyday wondering whether it will be my last," he sobbed.

"It's time to give in, Lew. We've had more than our fair share of bad luck and I couldn't bear to lose you," Siani said, trying to console him, though her heart was almost breaking under the strain.

The forms were filled in that weekend and were countersigned by Moss and Ben, both of whom had no doubt that Lewsyn was taking the best course of action. In the family conference that ensued, another letter was composed and copied by David.

2 Nant Row,
Dowlais,
Merthyr Tydfil.
25th April 1876

Dear Grandma, Uncle David & all,

    Thank you for your kind letter, which has given us hope and encouragement. With the exception of Ben, who is courting busily, we have decided to join you in America.

    Lewsyn has filled in the application forms for a loan to get us there, and Moses Williams and my brother Ben are to be our guarantors. It's a great help to know that you'll back us on your side of the ocean. Once we find jobs, we'll pay back every penny we owe.

    We are looking forward to seeing you, especially Grandma, and we'll give you as little trouble as possible. We talk about nothing else but the new life ahead of us. Siani has begun to think about what small items we can take with us, so if there is anything special Grandma would like, please let us know.

    We are convinced that we are doing the right thing and can't wait for the time to come when we set sail. We'll let you know when we have further details.

    With all our love, especially to Grandma,
Siani, Lewsyn, James, David, Mag and Will,
(not forgetting Ben who is staying here).

David put down his pen with a sigh of contentment. "Our plans are working out nicely, and if Lewsyn can arrange the loan, we could be on our way before the end of the year," he said confidently.

As the most bookish member of the family, he had gone to Dowlais Library to look for information on Pennsylvania, and his enthusiasm had increased when he read that it had been founded by William Penn, and was based on Quaker ideals. "That's the place for us," he told Siani, "don't cry about leaving Dowlais." He had also acquired a mass of knowledge about anthracite and bituminous coals, iron-ore deposits and steel-making in the state of Pennsylvania.

Siani had to smile. "You'll be an authority on the subject by the time you get there," she said. She had to admit that life seemed to have become more exciting and buoyant since the decision had been taken, though she prayed every night that Lewsyn would be spared in order to reach America.

He had promised to see to the loan application forms on his return to Cwmbach and wasted no time in doing so. The Secretary of the Emigration Society scrutinised them carefully and promised to put him in touch with an agent who arranged passages to America and estimated costs. He proved to be a smooth-talking, flashily-dressed individual of whom Lewsyn was initially very wary.

"We boast we can act more quickly than almost any other agency in Wales. We are very experienced because every week we have lots of able-bodied men leaving for America. They make up their minds to sell their belongings and they're off before their neighbours realise what's happening," he said.

"Thomas L. Thomas sounds very convincing, but I'm glad we've got Siani's family behind us because I can't risk anything going wrong. I have James to think of and I'll have a huge debt around my neck," Lewsyn thought to himself.

"Where do people stay in Liverpool before setting sail to New York?" he asked. "It's a long journey from

Aberdare to Liverpool and I have a baby son as well as my young nephew and niece to consider."

"That's easily solved. I could arrange for you to have lodgings with Mr David Richards of 35 Union Street. He's thoroughly Welsh and keeps and orderly house, no drinking or swearing, and he lives only five minutes from the quayside."

Thomas L. Thomas went up in Lewsyn's estimation and he began to feel confident enough to proceed with the final arrangements. "So, as soon as I have the loan from the Emigration Society for our fares, we can be on our way."

"Absolutely. Would you like me to see about employment for you? It will be on a commission basis, but I can provide the service."

"No, I can manage that. My brother-in-law and I will want to see exactly where we'll be working after our recent experiences in Dowlais and Aberdare."

"Suit yourself, I'll give you a list of your fares for the Secretary to process your loan."

Fares:		
	Lewsyn Jones	**£5-5-0**
	Sian Jones	**£5-5-0**
	James Jones	**£1-1-0**
	David Davies	**£5-5-0**
	Margaret Davies	**£2-12-6**
	William Davies	**£2-12-6**
		£22-1-0

Lewsyn looked at the figures and thought hard. On top of all that, there would be rail fares, food, lodgings and money in their pockets on the voyage, plus expenses on arriving in New York. He winced at the thought of borrowing £50-00 but was prepared to do it.

"What are you worried about? You'll soon make up for that once you get settled," Thomas L. Thomas said breezily. "Let me know when you're ready to pay, for me to make sure of your passages."

"I'm not going to tell Siani the full cost, in case she takes fright," he thought. "I'll tell her that David and I will pay it off at the rate of a pound a week, though it will be in dollars in America. In any case, we can clear it in a year," he decided.

Back in Nant Row, Siani was concerned with sorting out their few possessions, wondering what she could take with her and what she could leave for Ben, who was seriously thinking of marrying Sarah Jane, if her father gave permission.

"I'd like to take the brass candlesticks and one or two Welsh blankets, but you can have the rest, Ben," she said.

He knew how short of money she was, so he decided, "I'll save up to put half a guinea in her hand the day she leaves. It will be something, though I can never repay Siani for all she's done for us," he thought, as his memory raced back over the years.

Chapter 37

Lewsyn bounced through the door at 2 Nant Row and rushed to kiss Siani who was doing the ironing. "The loan has come through and our tickets have been ordered. We'll be on our way to America by the end of August," he said.

Her heart missed a beat and she smiled broadly at him as she said, "Go and tell David the good news, he's chopping wood out the back. He's been counting the days, praying it would be soon."

They returned quickly with David hardly able to contain himself. He hugged Siani saying, "I'll have to write another letter to Grandma and Uncle Dave telling them when we're sailing."

Lewsyn sat in the armchair and took James in his arms. He looked through the open door across the narrow valley towards the Dowlais tips. "Nothing will give me greater pleasure than to shake the dirt of Dowlais off my feet. Life has been hard on us," he said bitterly.

Siani shuddered and offered up a silent prayer. "I've bought a cheap trunk to put our belongings in, and two strong, canvas bags to carry things for our everyday needs," she said.

"When we get out there, we'll have to buy or borrow working clothes," David warned, "but I'll take my Davy lamp with me for luck."

"I won't need one because I'm going to work in the steelworks. I don't want to be entombed in any mine," Lewsyn said firmly.

Mag and Will had come back and they now sat near David, trying to take in all this talk. It seemed to them that they were embarking on a big adventure, which would lead to a long holiday in a new home with their grandmother, and they looked forward to it.

"When are you going to tell your mother and father about our departure?" Siani asked Lewsyn nervously.

"Not until a day or so before we leave. The less they know the better because of the way they've treated you."

"Go easy now Lew, we don't want any trouble before we go," Siani said.

"That's why I'm leaving it as late as possible, knowing my mother and how she'll carry on."

"Bessie and Blod know exactly what's happening, but they've promised not to tell anyone. They've been so kind that I'm going to give them my mother's lustre jug as a keepsake. I thought about giving them the picture of Daniel in the lion's den, but I think we'll take that with us."

"Oh, yes," said David, "because that's what we'll be feeling like in America." They all laughed, but Siani thought there was a lot of truth in what he said.

"I'm going to give my miner's lamp to Moss. It's all I have, and he's been a good, loyal friend to me," Lewsyn said.

He went back to Cwmbach next day, hoping it would be about the last time he would walk over the mountain, and that he would have put in his notice and have a date for sailing by the time of his next visit.

*　　*　　*

Llew and Mari Jones were seated in the kitchen when Lewsyn called on Saturday night. He took James with him to mark the occasion and to emphasise its importance. After an initial flurry of excitement and show of interest in their grandchild, Llew and Mari got down to what they thought was the real business.

"So you've come to see us at last," she said with a catch in her voice. Is it right that you're leaving for America? I've heard all sorts of rumours."

"Yes Mam, and I've got the date of our sailing."

Llew Jones looked at him. "When will that be, my boy?"

"The 21st August. We'll leave here on Monday for Liverpool, where we'll stay for two nights before sailing to New York."

Mari drew her breath in sharply and put her hand to her throat. "Are you sure you're doing the right thing? I suppose you'll have to support the whole lot of the Davies's."

"David will provide for Will and Mag, and Siani's relatives will be waiting for us when we reach Bethlehem, where they live."

Llew looked old and frail and had difficulty in breathing. He got to his feet and hobbled to the dresser where he opened a drawer. He turned to Lewsyn and put in his hand an oval, brass tobacco box. "Here, take this, it was your grandfather's and I'd like you to have it."

Lewsyn saw that it had been polished to reveal the inscription, 'Lewis Jones, puddler'. For a moment he was unable to speak. "Thanks, Dad, this means a lot to me, I'm going to work in iron and steel," he said, "and I hope that James will too when he grows up."

"You'll let us know how you're getting on," Llew said.

"Oh yes, I'll do that, and I'll tell James all about Dowlais when he's old enough to understand. The sad fact is that he'll be leaving here without knowing either of you."

Mari began to weep. "Don't cry, Mam, it's too late now; you can mention us in your prayers in Bethania Chapel," he said.

The tension was unbearable, so he stood up, bent down to shake hands with his father and put his hand on his mother's shoulder. He left hurriedly, clasped James firmly to him and gritted his teeth.

* * *

Ben stayed home from work to see them off on the seven o'clock train. He and Lewsyn put the baggage outside 2 Nant Row, ready for departure and Siani ushered Mag and Will outside while she and David took one last look around. He was unusually silent until she said, "Cheer up, Dave, we'll soon be on our way."

"I've been thinking of all that's happened in this house and of your promise to Mam. It's my turn now to promise you that whatever the future holds for us, I'll stand by you, Siani."

She hugged him and wept as she said, "I believe Mam will be with us every step of the way." With James wrapped tightly in s shawl, Welsh fashion, she stepped out of the house, called to Will and Mag and walked quickly up the road, not daring to look back.

When they reached the railway platform, there stood Mrs Bowen, Blod, Moss and the Rev. Theo Evans. Siani smiled through her tears and heard Mr Evans say, "We've come to wish you 'God speed' my children." He blessed them all and kissed Siani and the baby saying, "You'll always be in my thoughts."

The train screeched to a halt and they climbed into their third class compartment with its hard, wooden seats.

"Don't forget to write," said Ben, choking on his words, "and remember I want to know everything."

They continued to wave, until the small group on the platform were mere specks. The train gathered speed and they gradually left behind the hideous lunar landscape, belching furnaces and scarred villages along the heads of the valleys. Lewsyn settled back in his seat. "Goodbye Dowlais, soon we'll all be Americans," he said triumphantly.

"Yes, Welsh ones," added Siani, as she watched the towering tips of Dowlais fade out of her life.